NINETY FEET TO THE SUN

NINETY FEET TO THE SUN

A Sea Novel of World War II

Eric J. Collenette

Walker and Company
New York

Oz Edition

Copyright © 1984 E.J. Collenette

First published in the United States of America in 1986 by the Walker Publishing Company, Inc.

Published simultaneously in Canada by John Wiley & Sons Canada, Limited, Rexdale, Ontario.

Library of Congress Cataloging-in-Publication Data

Collenette, Eric J.
  Ninety feet to the sun.

  1. World War, 1939–1945—Fiction. I. Title.
PR6053.04236N5   1986   823′.914   85-29607
ISBN 0-8027-0893-5

Printed in the United States of America
        ΩT 15·95/ 8 96 - 5/86
10 9 8 7 6 5 4 3 2 1

To my wife Pam
and my daughter Sue
with heartfelt thanks

I

The face that stares back at me from the glass dial of the shallow-water depth-gauge is that of a stranger. It is a submariner's face; deprived of sunlight, wind and rain in this metal cocoon where night and day are measured only by mealtimes and sea-watches. I am Ben Grant, coxswain of the submarine *Scavenger* on patrol off the coast of Norway in the early autumn of 1940, and I sit in suspense with my shipmates listening to sounds as the boat rolls easily in the long swell and I try to fight back the nausea of anxiety that grips my insides. For we are wallowing on the surface in broad daylight with engines stopped while the first lieutenant and second coxswain scramble about in the icy water to free our after hydroplanes of a fishing trawl that threatens to wrap itself round our screws.

We should be used to waiting, for it is part of the game we play and we are all seasoned men, but no one ever gets used to it — not if they have imagination to paint pictures in the mind. Long minutes tick by filled with tension and my nerves stretch as we slowly roll with the undulations of this alien ocean, listening to the wind whining in the conning-tower and the distant voices of those men up top, trying hard to refrain from tapping with a nervous finger and to keep the tension from showing on my face. For I am the coxswain; immune to fear or any emotion that would undermine the authority that goes with my status.

In the vastness of mighty oceans other communities just like ours carry on their daily duties in the stale confines of their steel pods — unlike us they creep down into the murky obscurity of the depths during daylight hours, where it is possible to relax in comparative comfort. The tense atmosphere in *Scavenger* can almost be tasted as it breathes tenuous sighs of gut-knotting anxiety through the boat. White faces strain with the effort of hiding fear and fingers fidget uneasily on valves and wheels while tongues moisten dry mouths.

'Can I 'ave some flour ter make a clacker, Swain?'

I am jolted back to reality by the sudden appearance of 'Dinger' Bell. He stands there scratching his left chest with his right hand, staring down at me across his arm.

'What the hell are you doing here? You're supposed to be at diving stations.'

'Oh!' He looks round at the upturned faces for some sign of support and finds only amusement.

'Thought we'd relaxed like, Swain. Thought it a good time ter get the dinner up ter the galley.'

There isn't much you can do with Bell; he is a fine torpedo-man but goes through life in a world of his own and conformity is not one of his strong points; the result is that he gets away with murder. It must be his turn to prepare the meal for the galley under that peculiar messing system prevalent in British submarines whereby an allowance is paid so that we can cater for ourselves and the food is prepared by the crew before being taken to the cook — all he needs to do is the actual cooking, and in the small area set aside for his purpose he could cope with little more.

'Go back to the TI and if he can spare you, prepare the meal and take it to the chef. When you've finished get back to your diving station — and Bell.'

'Yers, Swain?'

'Next time you leave your diving station without asking me I will see that you spend some time in chokey; all right?'

'Yers, Swain.'

He shufffles off and I can visualise the faces he is making at the others now that I can no longer see his features. Every boat has its 'Dinger' Bell and provided they carry out their duties properly any cox'n who clamps down on them would be an utter idiot.

My eyes shift to another youngster sitting nervously in a corner of the control-room, chewing at the end of a pencil which he uses to note down every order in the control-room log. A complete contrast to Bell, he is intelligent, imaginative and a constant worry to me. I feel and hope that he will shape up in time; his ship-mates should see to that. The only question is if he will get through the initial stages of his life in boats before breaking: it is a gamble taken by the first lieutenant and myself.

He seems to spend much of his time ashore going to see films. The influence of some of the more lurid war stories is evident in the way he acts, and it is a source of amusement to his mess-mates. Just two days ago when we were being slightly harassed by a couple of nosy enemy patrol boats he was seated in the fore-ends with his mind obviously going over a similar situation portrayed on the silver screen — a scene where the hard-bitten sergeant admits to the nervous rookey that he too gets scared when tension builds up. Kirby, the young log keeper, decided to put it all to the test. Unfortunately he chose Wally Barnes, who has no time for filmstars or melodramatics.

'Wally.'

'What?'

'What do you do when you're scared, like me?'

'Who says I'm scared?'

'Ain't you?'

'I wouldn't tell you if I was — best thing to do is take your mind off it.'

'I've tried but I can't.'

Heavy sighs from the older man, 'Look, Sprogg, you got your troubles, I've got my troubles — I don't give a sod what you do.'

'Come dahn the tubes-space wiv me — I'll soon take yer mind orf it.' The lecherous voice of A. B. Morgan brings a titter from the others.

Kirby is indignant, 'I'm serious — trouble with you is your mind is like a cess-pit.'

Morgan grins lewdly. 'I've orlways fancied yer, Sprogg — it's legal three miles out ter sea, yer know.'

Kirby doesn't answer, wishing he had not started it all and wanting only to crawl back into his shell again. Morgan is not so easily put off. 'I bet yer've got skin like a she-mouse's belly, Sprogg.'

'Yeah — a bloody 'ippopotter — mouse!' Wally's retort brings a roar of laughter from the others and Kirby can only join in after a moment of embarrassed protest. The moment dissolves and for the time being Kirby has something other than fear to occupy his mind.

I'm smiling to myself at the memory of the encounter when a yell from up top freezes my inside. It coincides with the appearance of 'Subby' as he emerges from the wardroom. His long, gangling body flounders into the control-room and everyone gives him plenty of room. He is a mobile disaster area; he can be depended upon to spill coffee on charts, place his big feet in other people's faces when getting out of his bunk and every other disrupting blunder possible in the close confines of a small submarine. Now he stands with long arms dangling at his sides gazing up the conning tower.

'I'm supposed to be on watch,' he says to no one in particular.

'You're the only officer in the boat at the moment, sir. I think you'd better wait — it sounds like something's going on up top.' I talk to him like a Dutch uncle, but he is fidgeting about like a fish out of water.

'That's why I think I should be up top and the navigator down here.'

Before I can stop him — even if I was in a position to — he clambers up the brass ladder to disappear into the conning-tower.

'Bastard!' I breathe under my breath, now all the officers are on the casing or the bridge and I am the senior man in the boat. I try to blot out a mental picture of the mad scramble that will occur if we have to dive in a hurry and curse inexperienced sub-lieutenants still wet behind the ears.

A further noise from the conning-tower hatch saves me from further contemplation as every eye sweeps in that direction and the thumping, scrambling sound of someone clambering down the ladder in a hell of a hurry draws our attention to a pair of sea-boots that emerge, half sliding, half pushing in their effort to descend. Finally the duffle-coated shape of the signalman falls into the control-room, to pick himself up and rush over to his flag locker near the chart-table and frantically haul out ensigns until he holds up the biggest, cleanest white ensign he can find before starting his journey back up again — oblivious of all the anxious eyes that are following his every move.

I wriggle out of my seat and shove my bulk in his way. I have to know what is happening up top and once he disappears again we will be left with only the sounds. I grab his shoulders with talons of steel.

'What's going on?'

For a second he struggles to wrench clear before realising how hungry we are for news.

'Two aircraft low on the horizon — we think they might be Hudsons — Skipper wants a flag draped over the side of the bridge so they can recognise us. I think they're Dorniers — hope to Christ I'm wrong.'

I let go in a hurry and push him on his way, 'Go to it, lad — don't stand there waffling on.'

He makes a face at someone behind me before launching himself onto the ladder. He almost makes it too — before the biggest, God-Almighty explosion heaves the boat over and him off the rungs, along with half the anti-condensation corking on the deckhead. I'm thrown back into my seat as the submarine rears up like a bucking bronco and the control-room fills with a cloud of debris.

There is no time to take all this in before the second upheaval comes and we are all thrown into an untidy heap of flaying arms and legs, across a deck that slopes until it is hard to say which is bulkhead and which is deck. A solid mass of ocean bursts in on us from the open hatch and the whole boat shakes like a gigantic animal.

My shoulder fetches up against the lip of the periscope well and the sharp edge bites deeply into the flesh of my upper arm. The breath is knocked out of my body and I struggle vainly to regain my feet. All is noise and chaos — it is difficult to breathe and the pain in my shoulder makes me groan. I strive to fill my lungs, heaving in long gasping breaths. The deck reels and coloured lights flash before my eyes while the world goes crazy.

Gradually my breath comes under control and my vision begins to clear, I am able to rise up on to my knees and grab the oily periscope wires to begin to haul myself upright.

Somewhere in the depths of my brain another sound is registering — a stuttering noise that comes in short bursts and grows along with the sour note of aircraft engines until it fills the control-room with an overpowering crescendo, before changing and fading quickly away.

It is a morning of sounds and the one that comes next will live in my memory forever — the naked screams of someone suffering excruciating agony.

I pick myself up and stare down at the deck beneath the hatch where great gobbets of blood fall in regular splatters. Still numbed by it all I look up the tower and into the dead eyes of someone I would know if all the face was there, not just half a mask with naked teeth snarling out of an exposed jaw.

All about me men are picking themselves up from where they have been thrown, staring questioningly in my direction. Poor ignorant duffers; as if I have any answers! My befuddled brain refuses to function and all I can do is stare back at the apparition with its dead eyes.

What to do next? 'Come on!' I urge myself; 'this is what they made you a coxswain for — buck up! — start making decisions.'

Decisions! All I can think of is to find a hole to crawl into and escape those trusting eyes.

The matter is taken out of my hands for, with a lurch that almost makes me scream, the hideous shape wrenches clear of the hatch as though of its own volition, to be replaced by another face distorted beyond belief — staring down at me with wide, horror-filled eyes. I know it is the gunlayer because of the woollen hat which was once red and white, but is now faded and bleached to a greyish mixture that blends in well with his ashen face.

'For Christ's sake, Swain! They're all dead — the whole lot of them — I'm the only one alive up here.'

'Pull yourself together,' I bark, telling myself to do the same. I have to go up there to look at the carnage and do something for that poor, half-hysterical bastard with the shocked eyes and trembling lips.

I find myself climbing the ladder, with the bloodstained rungs messing my hands. I feel something strange about this simple act, which I have performed thousands of times before, and realise what is missing; I have never climbed the tower at sea without the dragging down-draught caused by the diesels sucking in great gasps of air. Now they are silent and dormant, reminding me that the boat is still sitting on the surface, presenting a prime target for any enemy in the area.

The bridge is full of dead bodies and the gunlayer stands dejectedly to one side with his hands flapping in despair, a haunted look on his face. Old 'Guns' is a free and easy bloke with a professional pride in his three-inch gun and a simple, honest humour that warms anyone who comes into contact with him: so the shock is more pronounced when reflected in his open features.

No more than two minutes have elapsed since I picked myself off the deck of the control-room, so where is that bloody aircraft? I look expectantly into the sky, searching the edges of the scudding clouds for the first glimpse of a black shape howling in to spray us with another burst of shells.

'It's over there.'

Two vague shapes are moving away towards the grey shape of the shore. We must have caught them at the end of their patrol with enough fuel and ammunition for only the short attack — I'm still too shaken to be grateful. One thing sure, their mates will be back; probably already on their way. If we're still on the surface when they reach us it'll be curtains. So much for the friendly Hudsons.

I move to the side of the bridge and stare aft along the narrow casing towards the 'duck's-arse' where I should see two figures finishing off the work of freeing the hydroplanes from the tangle of trawl that started all this. The stern lifts and slaps down in the swell with no sign of human life.

'They were blown clear by the first bomb,' drawls the voice of doom. 'The second one must have finished them off.'

There is no doubting that: I have seen the state of fish after a depth-charge attack; there will be no point in searching round for them. Christ! that means there are no officers left on board and leaves me in charge. The whole bloody boat and its crew wait for me to sort things out. Two boilersuited figures are climbing out of the hatch, taking in the scene with pained expressions. I give them time to absorb it all for themselves. I'll have to get a signal away, tell them we are without officers and the boat is under the command of an inadequate, quaking excuse for a coxswain. I'll have to rely on 'Bunts' to compose a signal; he has far more experience than I have. Although I reckon Shakespeare couldn't think up a short message to cover this bloody situation.

'This is a right mess,' says Chief ERA Welks in a tone that implies that once again the deck brigade have balled things up. 'How come all the wardroom was up top in one go?'

'Subby thought he should come up and relieve the First Lieutenant as it was his watch. I did try to stop him but he was a bit nervous of being left in charge down below on his own.'

My tone brings a sharp look in return, but he can see that I'm in no mood for any nonsense on this occasion. His views about seamen are well known to everyone, for he makes no secret of them. We need each other now more than ever and there will be no time for stupid arguments if we are to succeed in getting this bucket back to harbour. I turn to the TI — Petty Officer Soleway — a bird-like man with fidgeting fingers and ever-darting eyes, who is never still for more than seconds at a time.

'Will you stand watch up here with Bunts while I go aft with the gunlayer to see what the situation is?'

'Right.'

'And will you go below and see that all is ready for getting under way, George? If possible I want to be ready to dive when I give the word.' I shiver in the cold wind. 'We've got a hell of a job ahead of us.'

For a moment I wait for the ERA to object to being told what to do by an acting chief petty officer, but he grunts and backs down the ladder without further comment.

'Come on, Guns.'

Together we climb down unto the casing, balancing warily against the movement as we move aft along the slippery, exposed deck. Clear of the bridge the wind plucks at our clothing and bites into our bones. I feel I can smell the frozen snows of Norway in that keen wind. It is always difficult to walk along that steel deck in a swell and today the boat is rolling quite heavily in the leaden swells that rise up on each side to make a man realise how small he is when he stands near to the level of the sea.

We are at the stern now and I warn Guns to go carefully as he crawls out unto the 'plane-guard to lean over to look under it. He recoils violently, twists over to one side and spews up his guts.

'Oh bloody hell!' he splutters. 'Oh flamin' bloody hell!'

I drag him back to peer over myself. The gorge rises in my throat as I see what is tangled in the net. Now I know what an underwater explosion can do to a human being, and I also know what a man's inside looks like when it spills out. Strangely enough it's all I need to straighten me up; a surfeit of horror must lose its ability to shock and I can feel my brain getting into gear. I can take stock of the situation enough to see that the weight of that body has pulled the trawl away from the hydroplanes and only one strand holds it from coming away completely. With one hand I am able to free it and the whole horrible mess drifts away. Pushing the heavy shape of Guns in front of me I hurry back to the bridge.

'Get below, all of you,' I order sharply. 'Let's get down out of it before their mates arrive.'

'What about these?' asks Soleway, indicating the recumbent forms strewn all over the place.

'We'll say a prayer later.'

He gives me a sharp look as he clambers down the hatch. What the heck does he expect me to do with them — keep them in cold storage until we reach home?

'Stand by to dive!' I yell down the voicepipe. 'Out clutches half ahead together, group down. Normal diving stations with Morgan taking my place on the after 'planes and Smithy on the fore 'planes. Tell me when you're ready.'

I take one last look about the empty sea and search the shoreline with binoculars for a sign of enemy aircraft. There is no strange speck in the grey sky and I thank my maker for the one small miracle we are allowed on this day of calamities. Beneath me the boat begins to gather speed.

'Steer two seven oh!'

'Two seven oh, sir-er-Swain,' repeats Scouse's voice — first time he has ever replied to orders from the bridge without using 'sir' as a rider. 'Ready to dive, Swain.'

'Right, we'll do it in slow time — no klaxon — I'm coming down now.'

'Aye aye, Swain.'

I shut the voicepipe before taking one more look round the horizon and to spare one glance for the bodies rocking in their final sleep. One deep breath and I enter the hatch to shut out the daylight — clamping both clips firmly, as though to shut out the horror we leave to the sea.

When I reach the deck the onerous weight of the responsibility I have assumed bears down on me. I stand in total isolation, surrounded by thirty-seven shipmates, all relying on me to do the right thing. The signalman shuts the lower hatch and they all wait expectantly.

I refuse to be rushed. One by one I check each compartment is ready for diving.

'We'll go to thirty-two feet and try to get a good trim on the boat. Remember it is my first attempt, so you'll have to work hard on the 'planes. Gently does it, my old son,' — this last to the diving panel ERA.

'Open one, three and five main vents.'

My voice chokes on phlegm, but it must have registered because fingers are tugging at levers and I hear the heavy sigh of sea entering ballast tanks. The needles on the gauges remain on zero, despite the sensation that comes when she changes from full buoyancy to that of a waterlogged treetrunk. She lurches with a sickening motion and still we remain surfaced with both 'planes at full dive.

'Flood all main ballast!'

The remaining vents thump open and the last tanks flood up. The long needle wavers and then begins to move round the dial. I watch the hands on the wheels and wait for them to take off the dive at about twenty-five feet, which should level us out at thirty-two.

'Shut main vents!' I want everything ready to blow if things go wrong and we have to get up fast.

The hydroplanes indicators go to 'rise' now, and Glory be! the boat is levelling off nicely — no reason it shouldn't of course — we have done this a thousand times before, and 'Jimmy's' trims were always reliable. It's just that I am surprised that something is going right for a change. Anyway, even he had to fiddle about with buoyancy tanks to compete with differing densities in the sea, and we are light by the weight of five bodies.

'Thirty-two feet,' reports the 'planesman.

'Right, let's see how she goes,' I mutter, watching the spirit levels and the hydroplane indicators to see what is needed to keep her steady on an even keel. For a moment she swims along quite well, and I am relieved to see that there are no drastic adjustments to make. No point in trying to be clever, I'm no expert and a happy medium is all I can hope for. Already Morgan is using 'rise' on his controls.

Bow-heavy then? I glance at the other man and his indicator shows 'rise' too. So the boat is heavy and I must get rid of some ballast. Just above my head is a small, oblong box, with windows and knobs; by using these I can transmit signals to a stoker sitting just inside the engine-room who can pump water from one trim tank to another to balance the boat, or discharge it overall to lighten her. Before I give the order there is a niggling thought in my head that warns that I have forgotten something — an order that always seems to follow naturally when we dive and level off.

'Is Q flooded?' I ask the ERA.

Without looking he replies, 'Yes, Swain.'

The quick diving tank is always flooded when we are on the surface on patrol; designed to take us down fast when the need arises and must be blown to bring us back to neutral buoyancy when the desired depth is reached.

'Blow Q,' I order. 'Have a look round, Bunts, while I sort things out here.'

The signalman nods at a pale-faced stoker sitting between the fore 'planesman and the helmsman, who responds by lifting a handle at his side. The forward periscope slithers up until Bunts snaps down the handles, sets his eyes at the lens and peers out at the ocean above us.

I ignore him and go on watching my trim with a horrible feeling that I am going to spend the remainder of the diving time on this trip trying to balance the boat. The thought makes me aware of another urgent problem; somehow we have to work out a system of running the boat without officers. Even the basic process of keeping the boat trimmed is a constant job and I have to organise a rota of men who are capable of doing that and a hundred others things needed to run the boat. If possible I must leave myself free to navigate and take charge of everything.

The task is more difficult than it sounds, for many of those who I feel best able to take over the officers' duties are not the most senior. There could be some ill-feeling and noses put out of joint if I make too clumsy a job of it. Diplomacy is not one of my virtues and now is no time to change my ways. There is no room for bolshie 'votes for all' type of announcements, and I have no intention of arguing our way back to harbour, with every 'expert' putting his oar in. I think I know this crew well enough to be confident that they will accept my authority — it's a nice thought — until I observe Chief ERA Welks striding into the control-room, wearing a look on his scraggy features that says he has his own ideas about that.

'The boat's heavy by the bow,' says Smithy quietly.

Automatically I send a signal to that remote stoker on the ballast pump to shift weight from forward to aft — how much I can only guess at — but then, even 'Jimmy' must have had his fingers crossed at times.

'Try that for a while,' I tell him. 'There's only an hour or so till dusk, so try and struggle on for a bit. I'll surface as soon as it is dark.'

That settled I turned to look for Welks and the next problem to overcome. He has disappeared and Bunts nods meaningfully in the direction of the wardroom. I can leave things as they are for the moment, so, with a nod at Soleway to tell him to watch over it all, I stalk off after my arch enemy.

My blood boils when I come upon him sprawling luxuriously with a generous tot of wardroom whisky sitting on the table in front of him — obviously my problems are not over yet — and I square up to do battle with this paragon of the engine-room.

II

There is no privacy in a submarine so I am unable to shut a door and have it out with Welks without a dozen pricked ears flapping within range. What happens in the next few minutes will affect my status and the way the engine-room will co-operate. My biggest ally is a long tradition in the submarine service, born of the need for men to carry out their duties with the minimum of supervision and a special kind of discipline all of their own, different from any other section of the Navy. I know I can rely on them doing what needs to be done with their own special skills, provided the senior ratings can refrain from acting like prima donnas. I squeeze into the seat opposite, sliding my legs under the wardroom table with difficulty; for the space is small.

Welks gazes at me with cold eyes, fully aware of my anger, but content to allow me to make the pace. I'd like nothing better than to plant a fist into his smirking mouth — he's about my size and this is not the first time we have come to grips. Instead I reach out and grab the whisky bottle, screwing the top on firmly.

'That's the first and last, Chief. The wardroom is out of bounds, along with its stock of liquor — understand?'

'Oh, so you're giving the orders now — is that what you think?'

'I don't intend throwing my weight about, if that's what you mean, but you can have it whichever way you want. I reckon we have about five hundred miles to go through minefields and Gawd knows what else, and as far as I know I'm the only one left in this boat that knows anything about navigation; add that to the fact that, whether you like it or not, I'm the coxswain, and I'm taking charge, with or without your help and if you don't give me what I ask for from the engine-room, you can answer to an enquiry when we get back.'

His eyes blaze and his lips tighten. He knows I'm right, but swallowing it is like being castrated. 'Just don't come the acid with me or any of my lads,' he grinds through clenched teeth. 'I don't take to being led by the nose by a bleedin' dabtoe. It's gonna take all of us to get out of this — a joint effort where no one is king-pin.'

I lean across the table, bringing my face close up to his and staring straight into his bloodshot eyes, shaking with emotion and on the verge of losing control.

'You couldn't be more wrong there, Chief. There is a king-pin on this trip — one who knows where we are and can find the way back home, through those flaming minefields. You,' and here I grab his collar to haul him up close to emphasise the point, 'you are going to run those diesels and the electricians are going to run the motors exactly as I order. Everyone is going to do exactly as he is told, because there ain't no other way. So piss off back to your engine-room and stay out of the wardroom.'

'Can I put in my two-pennyworth?'

We both turn at the sombre voice of 'Sparks' Firth who stands looking in at us with that sad, bored expression of his. I move along in my seat and nod him in. Once settled he places his hands on the table to study them for a moment while he puts his thoughts in order.

'It's not a bad idea to use the wardroom for working things out, Swain. It's next door to the control-room and all the code books are here, along with a lot of other things you're going to need.' He looks at the ERA's smirking face. 'You might be a brilliant mechanic, Chief, but you act like a bloody OD stoker at times. The skipper trusted the coxswain here to stand watch on the bridge by himself, and I know how much time and effort he has put into learning all the other things it takes to run this cigar-shaped bastard. Even if he wasn't the cox'n we would have to ask him to take over, so don't be such a bloody idiot.'

There is no vocal acceptance from Welks but his eyebrows move and he opens his hands a fraction, so we assume he agrees. The TI bobs into view to report that it is getting dark up top and it seems clear of traffic. I thank him and he jerks his body back to the control-room — knocking against every projection in the process. His announcement gives me an opening.

'As soon as it's fully dark we'll surface. I want you to put a running charge on the batteries while we puddle along with just enough way on the boat to give a chance to get down here and sort out the charts. The bridge watches will be kept by Smithy and the TI with the gun-layer doubling up with me on the morning watch — we'll try it that way for now and see how things work out — diving stations will be the same as they were when we dived last time.'

I pause for a moment — half expecting an argument from Welks, and somewhat taken aback when there isn't one. I turn to Firth. 'What about your situation, Sparks?'

He carefully studies the stain left by the whisky bottle. 'We'll carry on like normal and I'll manage the de-coding if anything comes in: I don't recommend breaking radio silence unless it's really urgent; we're not too far away from the coast, and, in any case, reception is not too brilliant.'

'Right then, if you will ask the TI to carry on as things are for now, I'll take the time to look at the chart before we start performing again. Tell him not to worry too much about the trim: if things get too unstable increase speed and see if the 'planes will cope.'

Both men slide out of their seats and trundle off aft, leaving me on my own to try to subdue a sick feeling that persists on twisting my inside. I decide that action is the only remedy and go out to look at the chart, where Subby's last dead reckoning position is marked with the time alongside shown as noon yesterday. At other times I would resent any interference from him while engaged in my favourite game; today, however, when in deadly earnest, how I would welcome the long, gangling shape hovering over me while I fiddle with dividers and parallel rulers. There must be no errors in my calculations this time; we have enough problems without slap-happy navigation. Now that I have the time to concentrate I must do so with deliberation and double checks, for there is no one to correct my mistakes today.

I wasn't exaggerating when I mentioned that submarines were my first love; though I will admit that to no one. I think it no error that a fisherman was chosen to lead the disciples, for he was the next best thing to a sea-going sailorman available at the time and in that area. If it had been possible to have chosen a real sailor then he would have needed to have been British. If the choice had been made today on the principle of the best grape from the best vine in the best vineyard, the selection would have to have been a submariner.

A famous admiral once said something like — 'It takes three years to build a ship but three hundred to build a tradition' — well it's taken far less than that to build the submarine service, but the growth has been steady and strong. It has come from the floating tin cans in which every dive was an adventure, and to surface again, a triumph. It came through the audacity of little 'C' and 'E' boats sailing into the Dardanelles to sink a bloody great battle-wagon on the enemy's doorstep and staying up there, in that narrow, dangerous Sea of Marmara, worrying the guts out of an enemy that was scared to come out of harbour.

It progressed through the ill-judged conception of steam-driven 'K' boats, which were supposed to begin a new era in submarining by operating at speed with the main fleet. So those two-funnelled bastards arrived on the scene and they were big all right — so big it took more than five minutes to dive — always providing you remembered to lower the funnels and shut off the extra holes when you did so. Lots of men died in those boats, some in collisions at sea with the fleet, when the big ships charged over them in the dark. Others when they bucketed out of control to plunge deep down below their diving depths. Still more just passed out in the superheated atmosphere of the boiler-rooms. It was a pity that those who praised their value so much didn't have to serve in them.

Common sense took over again and new classes of boats were put into service and the men came to like them and to argue about the merits of their favourite class. Perhaps the best was the new 'T' boats with their ten torpedo tubes and comfortable living spaces, designed for long patrols. The little 'U' class that were first designed just as training boats were found to be perfect for the clear waters of the Mediterranean Sea, where the smaller you are the better to hide in those transparent depths. My choice is the 'S' class — like this one — midway between the two for size, with six tubes forward and a sting in the tail too.

Living conditions are not all that brilliant and some people might be put off by the open toilet at the end of the stokers' mess table in the stern, but if you try not to go at mealtimes and if you are not self-conscious enough to be put off holding a conversation with the occupants while performing your bodily functions, the process is bearable. Most of the crew live forward, in the fore-ends, where the torpedoes are stowed, or in the small messes between the fore-ends and the wardroom. It's snug, warm and aromatic. The inmates of Dartmoor Prison would most likely riot if their living conditions deteriorated to anything like these — but hell! for us it's home.

I have plotted the position on the chart now and feel fairly confident about it. For one thing, at the speed we have been travelling, we can't be more than a couple of miles out on my estimation — even if Subby's DR is wrong.

Everything is in order when I enter the control-room to take over, if I ignore the continuous 'rise' on both hydroplanes that shows the boat to be still on the heavy side. Still, we are going up soon anyhow, no point in compensating for that now.

'Stand by to surface.' I snap my fingers in the best tradition of hardened submarine captains and the stoker working the periscope hoist raises an eyebrow in a 'get him' expression before lifting the lever. Rising with it my eyes are at the lens as the glass breaks surface. Iridescent light flickers for a moment, then clears, leaving me staring out across a mottled ocean into a pale night. Slowly, carefully I walk the 'scope round, stalking the horizon and taking in every shadow, searching the edge of every cloud.

Empty: we have the whole of the North Sea to ourselves it seems. I clip the handles up and the periscope slithers down into its well. Now is the time to have a word with the crew and I take the intercom in my hand in preparation to make a speech, and stop myself just in time; all they need is one of those blood and guts orations favoured by the cinema heroes. Instead I give the simple order: 'All compartments, stand by to surface.'

I wait for the general reshuffle to subside and have one more check to see that all is ready before taking my place at the bottom rung of the conning tower ladder.

'Blow main ballast — surface!'

The ERA's hands move over the panel like a virtuoso admitting high pressure air into the tanks. The hydroplanes go to 'rise' and immediately the needles on the depth gauges begin to swing round the dials — we're on our way up.

No time to wonder — my feet clatter up the brass rungs as Bunts peers up at me from below, watching that I do everything right — if I should slip up and open the hatch too soon he'll shut me out with the lower hatch — that's what he is there for. He's also there to watch the gauges and tell me when to open the hatch. My hand is on the first of the two clips as he shouts, 'Ten feet!'

That's enough, off with one clip then quickly off with the other. The pressure in the boat is enough to push the lid open and I get a drenching as an icy deluge pours in. I can smell the clean, cold air as I leap up over the rim onto the wet bridge where everything drips and the wind chills me with its harsh breath.

Heaving myself clear I go to the voicepipe and open the valve. 'In clutches. Slow ahead together. Tell the Chief ERA to put on a charge when he can.'

'Aye aye, Swain.'

'Start the blowers. Steer two seven oh. Lookouts on the bridge.'

The orders are repeated and we begin to pump life back into the batteries and build up pressure in the HP air system. I decide to breathe again. I remember the scene from the last time I stood here and look round for bodies — nothing — those shipmates of ours have gone forever, destined to spend eternity suspended in the swirl and currents of this cold, alien sea. I jerk myself back to reality.

'Tell the chef to get a meal going.'

'Aye aye, Swain.'

'And get someone up here to relieve me and I'll serve out the bubbly.' God knows I could do with my tot, let alone anyone else. I look out into the night, shadowy clouds drift overhead, as the diesels jump into life and splutter a moment before gathering the rhythm and settling to a steady, even throb with gouts of spray showering from the exhausts. Foam swirls up over the ballast tanks and the boat moves easily forward, the soft whisper of the sea past the hull growing into a harsher roaring sound and the wind comes cold over the forepart of the bridge. Like a ghost we move through the darkness.

'Okay, Swain. I'll take over now.'

It's Smithy standing beside me, head bent into the weather and hunched against the cold. I give him the course and tell him to yell if they see anything, pat him on the shoulder and go below.

I've hardly sat down before Sparks arrives, waving a signal pad, 'We've had a signal, Swain.' He flattens it on the table in front of my eyes. It's addressed to us and repeated to two other boats. 'Open D.46.K,' it says. 'Target reported sailed oh four hundred hours,' and gives the date for yesterday, along with further details of a number of sightings.

I look at Sparks for an explanation.

'Sealed orders, I reckon; I know where to find them, they're in the skipper's locker. Come on, let's find out what they've laid on for us.'

As we rummage into the depths of the skipper's private cupboard pairs of curious eyes follow our every move over the rims of cups filled with thick, neat rum. I have been criminally generous this time — poor sods, if only they knew how timorous their self-imposed leader is.

Sparks is familiar with confidential papers and soon roots out the relevant ones. Amongst the bundle is a buff envelope which he offers for me to open. I turn it over and over in my hands, for the prospect of opening those sealed orders seems to emphasise the awesome responsibility I have taken upon myself. This action has never been undertaken by anyone other than the commanding officer before and it is a daunting experience for me.

'It's all yours, me old mate,' says Sparks quietly, looking deep into my eyes and knowing full well what is going through my mind.

I rip the flap open roughly and pull out the contents. As I read a cold hand seems to close over my innards and a hollow, nauseous sensation dissolves my body to jelly, leaving it loose and insecure. The message is straightforward enough; we are one of a line of boats spread out into a diagonal line from the Norwegian coast, watching for a floating dock that the Germans are towing north from Trondheim fjord to God knows where. It is protected by what is described as heavy sea and air forces. The chain of submarines must stay on station for at least forty-eight hours after receiving the signal to open the envelope. It goes on to describe details of the types of escort most likely to be used, each one designed to sink my heart into my boots. My face must show my state of mind for Sparks grips my arm with his dirty hand and gives it a re-assuring shake — it'll take a lot more than that to lift the load from my mind.

I read on and the message stresses the importance of preventing the dock from reaching its destination. The mere fact that the enemy have chosen to risk such a venture in the face of all the hazards presented by the attempt proves how much they value its effect on their war effort and its threat to ours. It goes on to express confidence in the traditional resourcefulness and competence of the service to accomplish this task and to wish us luck. The words merge into meaningless jargon for me; I know only too well how the skipper would have dealt with this in the past. He would have laid it on the line for us without frills or false hopes in a quiet, confident voice; before going on to explain his ideas of the way to tackle it. Me! I am a quaking, shivering, sick incompetent, with a brain that refuses to think and a body that wants to shrink into some corner and opt out of it all. I slap the orders down unto the wardroom table and look at Sparks.

'That's it then, isn't it?' I tell him disconsolately. 'It's one thing to try and take the boat back home, but to even think about an attack is plain bloody fantasy.'

'You've seen the Skipper do it a thousand times,' he offers steadily. 'They can't tow a thing like that at any speed and you can use the whole salvo of six fish.'

I look at him in disbelief, 'You're not serious! Jerry's going to lay on the biggest exercise in anti-submarine defence you can imagine. There will be air patrols, hours, or even days ahead of the dock — God alone knows what the close escort will consist of.

Most likely this boat was chosen for this billet because of the Skipper's past reputation and experience. The powers-that-be don't know that we are without officers by the tone of that signal — how could they? I have no doubt if they did there would be a rapid change of mind and an urgent order to retire immediately. You know it takes several years of practice in attack teachers, practice at sea and dozens of genuine attacks to give a man the ability to approach a heavily escorted target with any hope of bringing it off: you are looking at a bloke who has sat on the after hydroplane seat listening with half an ear to the Skipper, Subby, Bunts and Jimmy working out attacks with the aid of the fruit machine. I can honestly say that I understood fully about one tenth of what was going on as I concentrated on keeping depth.'

Sighing heavily I gaze down at the table. 'A blind cripple with a bent barrelled rifle has more chance of hitting a target than I have, and we won't even begin to think about those escorts that'll be dodging about up top.'

'You're jumping the gun a bit, aren't you? The orders say that no one is sure where the dock is going. The odds are we won't come within a hundred miles of it. You can't leave the area because the Navy is banking on a complete line of submarines. If you take us away now, Swain, you will have a hell of a lot to answer for when we get back, and you'll have to break radio silence or chance being sunk by our own people when we turn up where we shouldn't be and. . . .'

'Don't go on,' I interrupt quickly. 'There's no way we can leave our station now — I can see that. Just don't hope for too much if that bloody dock does come our way, that's all.'

I drink back my tot in one go and relish the harsh liquid as it burns the back of my throat. Having made up my mind I take a grip on myself and go out to broadcast the news to the crew, cutting no corners and putting my cards on the table exactly as I know the Skipper would have done. I feel that I should try to end on an optimistic note, so I stress that we have certain things in our favour, though when I try to think of them my mind goes blank and I'm left with a few limp phrases about the fact that we still have everything in working order and the target is a slow, cumbersome one.

'Just think of the reception we'll get when we get back to base if we do perform a miracle and sink it — we'd be the blue-eyed boys of the service. That's all.' I can almost hear their derision as I replace the mouthpiece.

Back in the wardroom I gratefully sip a steaming cup of tea, thinking things out. Before I reach any conclusion two things happen to wreck my concentration; Welks comes blundering forward, smelling of diesel and throwing his body with an aggression that matches his facial expression.

Before he can open his mouth the helmsman yells, 'Cox'n to the bridge!' and I'm on my way to the conning-tower ladder.

As I start up the rungs with the wind roaring past my shoulders and the boat shuddering to a growing, lively sea, Welks shouts up after me, 'Before you go on with your fucking heroics you'd better know that you've got problems aft — we'll be lucky to get home — let alone carry out any attacks.'

Tell me something I don't know, I'm thinking and his final words are directed at my seaboots as they disappear into the tower. I can ignore him now because that yell from the bloke on the wheel supersedes all else. I've seen the Skipper charging through the control-room when the cry 'Captain to the bridge' rang out and can understand the concern reflected on his face at such times.

The weather has changed now and as I climb clear of the upper hatch a burst of icy spray hits me and stings my face. The boat is rolling heavily in a blustering sea, the noise of a growing gale coming in out of the darkness. Thank God for the red lighting in the control-room that allows my eyes to adjust quickly to the night.

'What is it?' I asked the hunched-backed figure clinging to the port forward corner of the bridge.

'We've spotted something on red three five — can't see for sure what it is, but it's there all right. Some clumsy bastard showed a light a few minutes ago — I got the Skipper's night glasses up for you.'

'Thanks, Smithy.' I take the glasses and stare out on the bearing indicated, sweeping them slowly across an arc where the mysterious ship should be.

'I can see her, Swain!' yells the lookout in my ear and holds his arm steady on the bearing.

I follow it and pick up the shape almost immediately — the hunched, menacing silhouette of a warship moving determinedly at an angle that is slowly closing the distance between us. I take a bearing on it because I am reluctant to dive and I want to see how near she will come. Another bearing in a few moments will show me whether she is on a collision course and, in fact, I find that she is head-reaching on us and should clear well ahead if she holds on to her course.

'Lookouts below!' I order quietly, as though someone on that distant ship might hear me.

'Diving stations!' Prepared to submerge the moment she shows a sign of altering towards us.

She is moving at speed and will not be able to use her detection gear punching into the sea like that. In any event if her anti-submarine apparatus is no more sophisticated than we have been led to believe, the odds are she won't see our low profile and we can remain undetected. I need every ounce of energy I can conserve in the batteries and I am determined to hoard it like a miser. It's a big gamble for if she does see us we'll end up chasing round trying to dodge her and using our reserves far more quickly than if we dived now and crept away slowly. Somehow I know I'm right to take the risk and stay up top.

It's a positive action on my part and the lads will be sweating down below, listening for the sound of those propellers and the emergency dive that will follow if I have misjudged the situation. Smithy is slowly searching the horizon — such as it is in the deep, solid darkness. That ship could have a mate close by and only a freak glimpse of a light had shown her to us in the first place. We are not likely to have many lucky breaks like that. Now we know where she is we can recognise the shadowy shape and the vague gleam of a bow-wave which otherwise might merge into the background.

Still the diesels grumble easily as we move smoothly across the cold, restless sea. So far so good, and my decision seems to have been the right one as our shadowy adversary fades into the night.

'Lookouts up!' I order and relax a bit. Soon I will be able to go below to try and get some sleep.

'Bridge!' The voice bleats out metallically from the voicepipe.

'Bridge!' answers Smithy.

'The Chief ERA wants to speak to the coxswain — says it is urgent.'

'I'll be down right away,' I tell him, suddenly tired and feeling a surge of anger welling up inside me. Why does Welks always loom up like the prophet of doom when things seem to be going right?

III

Going through the bulkhead into the engine-room is like stepping into Hades. On each side of the narrow, metal footplate the diesels are hammering away with a noise that fills the compartment and makes speech almost impossible. Even I realise that the engines should not be making this amount of noise at the speed we are doing. My ears tell me that the main culprit is the starboard diesel. It sounds as though the innards are shaking apart and moving round with gay abandon and the vibrations are uneven and alarming. I look into the sour features of Welks. He looks smug, as though his engine has proved what he had been insisting on all along.

He makes no comment but signals to a stoker PO who moves his hand and the starboard engine shudders violently, voicing its protest at being roused to efforts beyond its capacity. It is a very sick piece of machinery and screams its agony for all to hear before the PO mercifully allows it to subside to a more reasonable level. Welks nods me back through the bulkhead and follows me forward to the wardroom.

'All right, tell me the worst,' I say glumly, and wait for him to gloat, refusing to look into his face as he draws a deep breath before launching into a monologue.

'Those bombs shook the guts out of her; you should have asked me for my estimate of what damage had been done, like the Skipper always did. I won't go into the details of what I think is going wrong inside that starboard diesel, but I will say that she's flogging her innards out, even at this speed — and I'm only using her to put on the charge — the real work is being done by the port engine. You might as well face it — that engine is not going to last much longer, and its mate is by no means running as sweet as I would like, so we're down to one sick diesel, and I haven't much faith in that one. You dive all day tomorrow and use a lot of battery and you'll be lucky to charge up again tomorrow night — we'll be charging around on one dodgy engine in broad daylight, if you're not careful. If you take my advice you'll start for home now and use what's left of the batteries tomorrow to get us back to within range of air cover. Ignore me, and I want my recommendations to go into the log.'

It is two or three seconds before I realise he has finished. I hear him breathing heavily and know without looking that he is staring at the liquor store. The bastard thinks he has me over a barrel.

'You say you know what the Skipper would have done,' I drawl at him. 'Well I'll tell you what I think he would have done, and what I think you would have done.'

I fix him with a stare that he returns for a moment before fidgeting away and staring at the bulkhead behind me. Leaning forward I aim my words straight at him.

'Firstly, you wouldn't have spoken to him like you have to me, and if you had run to form — like we have all seen you do in the past — you would have over-stressed the situation and all your problems before going on to show what a marvellous bloke you are by offering to use your ingenuity to carry out repairs. The Skipper, being the crafty old warrior that he was, would have told you what a fine fellow you are and just how lucky we all are to have such a fantastic engineer aboard. He would have told you that the Navy is relying on us to do the job properly, or we let down all our mates in the other boats. He would have patted your shoulder like he always did at such times and said something like, "I'm sure you'll figure something out, Chief. We're all relying on you, so I'm confident you'll come up with the answer." His guts would have been crawling at the time and everybody in earshot would have been smirking at the 'prima donna' attitude of our Chief ERA and the Skipper's crafty way of handling you. Well I'm not as diplomatic as the skipper was, and I know you for the two-faced bastard you are, so I'm saying that I'm keeping the boat on station, and when we are dived tomorrow, you are going to do your utmost to get all you can out of those engines.'

With heavy sarcasm I pat his shoulder as the Skipper always did, 'I know you'll see us through, Chief — we're all relying on you to get us back home.'

His face is purple and he is glaring at me in fury. He hoists himself to his feet, shaking all over and puffing his thick lips in and out like a goldfish.

'Don't say I didn't warn you,' he snarls, sliding out past Morgan, who has watched the final scene with a stupid grin on his evil face.

'Chief!' yells the AB, and Welks turns a furious face on him.

'Well?'

'May your bollocks fester!'

The eyes bulge and a big vein pulsates in the bull-neck; for a moment he seems on the point of exploding, then he bundles off aft, past the staring faces of smiling seamen. I should feel triumphant I suppose, but I don't — in fact, that sick feeling has come back again and I could wish the last few minutes to hell. We need all the luck and co-operation we can get and this confrontation hardly increases the harmony on the boat.

Soleway and Firth come in together and sit in front of me.

'We have worked out a routine for tonight, Swain,' says Soleway, 'If I were you I'd try and get some sleep. We have also agreed that you should use one of the wardroom bunks so as to be near to the control-room.'

I allow myself to be shepherded into one of the bunks to stretch out, minus seaboots, and gaze into space while the situation swims in my brain like eels in a trap, with no way of escape, and getting bigger all the time. In the background the sea hurls a punch at the boat that sounds like a ton of gravel falling on the pressure hull. The boat lifts, shudders then falls away into a trough. Submarines are never on the surface; even when the tanks are blown and the casing, bridge and upper works are clear of the water, most of the hull is still out of sight. You get used to the noise of the seas coming from above your head — it's part of life to us.

I fix my mind on the problems of the moment because this is the first time I have been able to concentrate without interruption. Despite Welks' problems the boat is functioning well and next time we dive and get settled I'll go to patrol routine to give the off duty watch a break and allow them to go forward to their messes. The weight will be evenly distributed for a short time and I'll have a go at putting on a good trim. True I'll have to remember to adjust when we go to diving stations again and the troops come bundling aft but that's routine. In the meantime there will be the usual procession of 'Permission to go aft, Swain' or 'Permission to go forward, Swain,' as people go on their way to and from the heads or the galley.

The boat gives another lurch and a body of water crunches hard against the casing above my head. The diesels change note when the screws lift, hesitate, then resume their struggle. Welks will be cursing the weather and the world in general as he listens to the protesting starboard engine.

What about that floating dock? Will it really come our way? I have to assume that it will, and that I must do something about it when it does. I have some things in my favour — for instance, I have no other targets to worry about so I can get the TI to work out the depth settings for the torpedoes before anything turns up. I can use all six of them too and fire a spread to compensate for my inadequacies, and the target will be plodding along at walking pace.

My attempts to conjure up a list of assets to raise my hopes fail miserably when I put myself in the shoes of some anxious German admiral given the job of moving a bloody great floating dock. I would be on my knees, pleading for escorts by the score and air cover all the way. I would stay as tight to the coast as I dare and use every shore facility available. In fact I would want to know the movements of everything above or below the water larger than a porpoise. After I've done all that I would look at the charts and begin to plug up any gaps I might have missed and at the first faint sniff of anything that might be a submarine I'd pound the area to hell.

'Swain!'

I stare into a pale disc hovering inches from my head and bring into focus the muffled shape of 'Dinger' Bell, a young torpedoman with a locker full of nutty back in the depot-ship, acquired by bartering his rum and cigarette rations. His ritual before manning the boat for patrol is to allocate himself enough rations of sweets and chocolate for the duration of the trip.

'Well?' I grunt, blinkering the sleep out of my eyes.

'The TI says it's getting a bit light up top, and in any case it'll be dawn in half an hour.'

'I'll be right up.' I feel a warm glow of satisfaction for having slept half the night. As I pull on my seaboots I note the diesels still belting away, but cringe to hear a new sound, like that of someone churning bottles in a washing machine, and there is a harsh whining, like a dying were-wolf with guts ache — the Welks symphony growing to a climax.

The control-room is cold after my wardroom bunk and the helmsman is wearing a duffle-coat as he sits staring into his giro repeater. My muscles are stiff as I climb through the sucking draught and step out into the night. To my eyes it is still pitch black, but I know it must be growing lighter to the men who have spent the past two hours or so of the morning watch up here.

Recalling the movements of the boat during the night I am surprised to find the wind easy and no sign of any real swell. The TI is at the 'pig's ear' when I arrive — relieving himself into the funnel that fits into a pipe running down the side of the bridge and into the sea. When surfaced this is the main urinal for the crew. I wait for him to finish and put everything away again inside the bulky mass of clothing he has on.

'Need a pin to find the bloody thing these mornings,' he grunts. 'Get a good sleep?'

'Fine, thanks.' I repeat his performance and follow him to the front of the bridge. 'Everything okay up here?'

'We haven't seen a bloody thing all night, since those destroyers. Funny, you'd think they would be crawling all over the place, with everything they've got.'

'I've thought about that — I reckon they might be short of escorts to do forward patrols, and aircraft would be useless at night. What ships they have will be close to the convoy, and I'm willing to bet that the first 'plane will be along before the sun gets over the horizon.'

He looks at me, as though trying to weigh me up again. 'You reckon we ought to get down out of it?'

'Sooner the better.'

Lifting my binoculars clear of the metalwork I peer over the forward rim of the bridge at the long, shadowy casing stretching out into the murk. Inside that ugly, black shape a community of men are trusting their futures to me — willingly or not — the poor bastards have no choice, and even now are waiting for me to perform my next act, knowing that I am feeling my way with every step I take.

'Clear the bridge!'

Shadowy figures cluster over the hatch, scrambling down into the blustery tunnel one after another in a sort of orderly panic. The sucking noise of the downdraught comes loud to me as they half fall — half clamber down below.

'Diving stations!' I yell into the voicepipe, taking myself to task for not giving the order before sending the lookouts down — I could have had a full set of eyes up here right up to the moment I am ready to dive. I shrug it off; it's not too important on this occasion because we are not diving on the klaxon, with the crew still tumbling to their stations when the boat is already well on her way down. I'm not that brave yet and have to allow for a number of people doing jobs to which they are not accustomed.

'Closed up, diving stations!' comes a voice from the depths.

'Very good.' One final look round at the gloom which hides all manner of imaginary terrors.

'Dive — Dive — Dive!'

The vents open and great spouts of vapour leap into the air as water floods into the tanks and the boat is on her way down, even as I hustle through the hatch and pull the lid down after me. No rush of air now for the diesels have stopped and the motors have taken over with their muted monotone, pushing her nose down into a shallow dive.

'One clip on!' says the cool voice of the signalman as he watches me clamp down the handle on the upper hatch and lets everyone know that at least I haven't fumbled this simple operation.

'Two clips on!'

I can climb down more sedately now, into the quiet of the

boat which is already at twenty feet and angled down gently by the bow. It is as has been a thousand times before — except that someone else is seated at the after hydroplanes and I am watching the dials from the position usually occupied by the First Lieutenent — hardly daring to breathe as the needles go steadily past twenty-five feet.

'Thirty-two feet!' I order, and watch the fore 'planes move to 'rise', followed by the after 'planes. We begin to level off, slowing the needles to settle on the ordered depth. No criticism for the two men on the hydroplanes — they did a perfect job. It's up to me to complete the evolution, and I need to do it right — not only for myself, but for the morale of the whole crew.

'Up periscope!'

Doing a knees-bend, I straighten up with my eyes at the lens so that I can stop it before too much shows above the surface. Slowly, deliberately, I scan the horizon in a sweep that searches every degree, my feet heeling backwards as I move round with it. It's nearly light, but there's nothing to see and I resist the temptation to go round a second time. The snap of my fingers sends the periscope sliding down into its well.

'Ninety feet!'

The 'planes move and down we glide, into the safety of the ocean, in a smooth and easy descent.

'Patrol routine!' I order, and the spare hands move away as the duty watch takes over. It's up to them to sort the watches out for themselves; they managed quite well throughout the night so there is no reason for me to put my oar in, as long as I have reliable people in charge, and that's been proved already, not least by the man who hovers alongside me now — ready to take over.

'Slow ahead — group down, TI,' I tell him.

The boat comes down to a crawl and I can get to work on the trim. To my surprise I am able to set about it coolly and methodically with no hint of the apprehension I experienced on the last occasion. Using the minimum of adjustments I shift ballast from one end of the boat to the other and pump excess weight out to sea until the bubble is nice and central and the hydroplanes are controlling the boat with small, easy movements.

The atmosphere relaxes in the boat as things settle down to normal diving routine.

'Stop port!'

I am being really brave now as she comes down to her slowest speed, using only the starboard motor and moving about as fast as a one year old taking its first tottering steps. The boat behaves as sweet as a nut and a great surge of relief wells up inside me as the first hurdle of the day is cleared.

'Hands to breakfast!' I order. 'If she begins to bugger about, go to "slow ahead both", Dick. Stay on this course for half an hour then come round 180 degrees.'

The TI nods with a grin. 'Shove off and get some breakfast — I'll call you if things go haywire. In the meantime if I see so much as a vicious looking seagull I'll give you a yell.'

'Thanks, mate,' I say with deep meaning and go to the chief's mess where AB Leeming, our self-appointed acting chef, has set a plate of eggs, beans and bacon for me. This is one thing he excels at, but we won't talk about some of the more exotic dishes he attempts. The results of these gastronomic disasters defy description and are tolerated only because no one else wants to be lumbered with the cook's job — we haven't been allocated a proper cook. Pongo Leeming, we call him, because he is forever telling people about the time he is supposed to have served as a marine. Perhaps one day we will know the full story; right now it's enough to know that he enjoys working in the tiny galley and will produce a good, thick soup at the drop of a hat — it matters not that his 'clacker' would double as armour plating.

The course I gave Soleway will bring us right back to our present position in one hour from now, so I can eat in peace and sort out my charts. For the rest, it depends on what the hydrophones pick up. The bacon is delicious and I crunch away happily, thinking of nothing as we swim along in peace. Then Welks arrives and my appetite dies a sudden death.

'I should strip down the starboard engine.'

'Oh aye.'

'Christ knows what I'll find inside the flaming thing.'

I don't answer but raise one eyebrow over a forkful of egg and bacon.

'I may not have replacement parts.'

I sigh and shove my eating irons onto the plate before pushing the whole lot away from me.

'What you are saying is that you want me to decide whether you should strip that bloody engine or not.'

'You've taken the job, haven't you?' he snarls. 'If it's too big for you, give up.'

'Whatever you find in that engine won't be any worse for being found, will it?'

'Suppose not.'

'And even if there is something in there rattling about loose, it's better taken out, screwed up, or something, isn't it?'

'Could be.'

'So we will be no worse off and maybe a hell of a lot better off for knowing what it is — even if you can't repair it?'

He nods grudgingly. 'That's one way of looking at it.'

'How long then?'

'All day.'

'Do it.'

'Right.'

End of conversation.

I wish him to hell for spoiling my breakfast as he shambles off in his grey overalls and sour expression. The boat isn't big enough for the two of us and some of the crew must be lapping it up. To hell with it! Perhaps I should have someone like him on my neck all the time to help keep my feet on the ground.

'Coxswain to the control-room!'

I scramble aft through the bulkhead, past the chart-table and into the control-room to find Soleway leaning into the door of the asdic compartment where AB Formby, our best operator, concentrates on his earphones and twiddles his direction finder on a bearing.

'What's going on?'

'HE bearing green four five,' says Soleway in a voice that shushes me to silence.

I wait impatiently while Formby sorts out his noises. At last he pulls one 'phone away from his ear and looks up at me with a puzzled expression.

'Coxswain, I have a mixture I have never heard before in all my life — it's a mixture of slow, fast, reciprocating, diesel and God knows what else — listen.'

He hands me the earphones and I hear a mass of confused sound which I distinguish as propeller noises that makes no sense to my inexperienced ears. To me it sounds like a herd of wild buffalo hurtling through a cabbage patch. I hand the earphones back to the expert who clamps them back on to a pair of ears that have listened to a million 'pings' and as many propeller noises — if he can't sort it out, no one can.

'Can you guess how far away it is?'

He shrugs. 'Difficult to say, Swain. I have heard convoys before, but not like this — normally it's fairly easy to distinguish the slow pulse of merchantmen from the faster patter of the escorts, and the ratio is generally the same, with more merchantmen than escorts. What I'm hearing now is a mass of fast HE with a mixture of heavy, slow beats in the middle of it all.'

I know what those mammoth screws are, and if I was an eager-beaver young submarine captain no doubt I would be rubbing my hands with anticipation as I thrill to the sound of those tugs with their outsize screws, because it will mean that our target is approaching from the south and I am in a good position to attack. I don't deny that a thrill of excitement runs through me, but it is well-tempered with a sobering recognition of my limitations. 'What the hell! The bloody thing's there, so why not have a go?'

'Thirty-two feet!'

'Thirty-two feet,' repeats the fore-'planesman.

'Diving stations!' This order is equivalent to 'action stations' in general service.

The klaxon blares out for the first time since I took command. Bodies come tumbling into the control-room as the needles creep up to periscope depth. I remember to pump ballast from aft to forward as the weight shifts aft with the crew.

'Thirty-two feet.' A new voice comes from the fore'planes and I ask Bunts to watch the depth and the bubble while I take a look through the 'scope.

I'm still half crouched when the light shines into my eyes through a sparkle of surf, then it clears and I am looking at the sky. Swinging around to starboard I focus almost immediately onto a wisp of smoke that smudges the horizon. Moving the lens slowly to one side I recoil violently from the eyepiece as a squat, black shape shows, fanning out from the smoke – dark, menacing and purposeful – it's one of our most vicious enemies, a destroyer, big and efficient with her tail down and a big bone in her teeth. A cold bar of steel weighs down inside me and I wrench the periscope away to search further around, where another shape is moving through the water – a sister ship.

The golden rule is not to keep the periscope up for long periods when the enemy is about, but I must see the whole situation before going blind and relying on Formby's ears again. At this distance I still feel justified in using the larger one, with its magnification and wider vision – just pray that no one sees the feather spreading astern of the 'scope as it moves across the surface, or the thin black arm that is the extension of my eye and all that is between us and total blindness.

There are three more distant shapes and an unidentifiable mass at the base of the pillar of smoke. For some strange reason it reminds me of that picture by Turner, 'The Fighting Temeraire', with that scruffy little tug and rusty old buoy that turns a simple picture into a mystery.

I catch a glimpse of something else – a mote – no more than a suspicion of a dot between two banks of cloud. It might be a flaw on the lens if I didn't know that there wasn't one.

'Down 'scope!' I order urgently, snapping up the handles.

'An aircraft,' I breathe aloud. The immediate impulse is to dive deeper to hide well down in the dark ocean and in the clear blue waters of the Mediterranean there would not have been a choice. The sea up here is opaque however, with little chance of the aircraft seeing us, even at this depth. It would be overreacting and downright ill-judged to go plunging down in the circumstances.

Now is the time for cool-headed decisions. Everyone is tensed up ready now and the target is in sight. I have neither the skill nor the inclination to play silly buggers – only a long period of trial and error enabled me to obtain a good trim on the boat and I'll have enough on my plate soon without worrying about

keeping trim. If I were a praying man now would be a fine time
to bring out one of my best efforts.

'Steer one eight zero!'

'One eight zero, Swain.'

Turn the boat straight towards them for the moment, presenting a small target. Go slowly, and make as little noise as
possible, so they don't pick us up with their listening gear. We
are a stealthy, marauding fish stalking a big, fat, juicy meal —
only on this occasion the prey seems to have all the teeth.

'Stand by all tubes!' I order quietly. The indicator lights come
flickering on to show that the torpedomen are on their toes.
Almost immediately the oral confirmation comes as well to back
up a machine that is less reliable than a man.

'All tubes ready — settings fifteen feet.' That's the TI playing
his part and I can only hope he's right. Ideally the fish should
pass under the escorts and tugs to hit the dock. All I have to do is
make sure that the dock and the torpedoes arrive at the same
spot at the same time. Nothing to it, if you discount the need to
dodge escorts charging about up top with the sole intention of
blowing us to blazes.

'Ask the PO tel' to come here please, Bunts.'

'I'm already here.' Finch must have been listening at the door
of the W/T office.

'Between you and me, Sparks, we are going to work out some
sort of attack scheme. I want you on the chart table to note every
change of course and speed on this note pad — it might help me
to work out where we are when it's all over. Bunts will do his
normal job of reading off the bearings when I call the marks.'

'Right,' says Finch and moves away swiftly to take up position
while I get a nod from Bunts to show he has understood too.

On the front end of the control-room, attached to the bulkhead, is a box of tricks especially designed to take the math-
ematical problems out of working out an attack. You feed in
your own course and speed, the angle and estimated range,
course and speed of the target and the course and speed of the
torpedoes. Do it all right and the answer comes up like magic.
There's only one snag in this case — no one on board knows how
to use the bloody thing.

IV

We hold a conference in the wardroom in an effort to find the best way to solve the problem. Welks is there, along with Sparks and the TI. I have gathered them together with the idea of telling them what I have in mind; hoping that they will offer their help and co-operation. The Chief ERA is sitting in mainly because I am trying to end the growing antagonism that exists between us.

I tell them of the plan that has been formulating in my mind during the past few hours. The essential factor to make it all work is the slow speed and lack of manoeuvreability of the target. It is crawling along at something like four knots and it is a very big target, unable to take any violent evasive action. It is not as though we have to make allowances for some unencumbered zig-zagging fifteen knot ship. Given these advantages I am able to propose an unorthodox scheme that would whiten the hair of the instructors in the attack school.

The most important thing I have to establish is the range. I haven't a clue how far away the dock will be — it could be a large box far away or a small box close to — there will be no way of telling just by looking at it. To give me an idea of the distance I intend to do a running fix on it, estimating her speed at four knots or so. That will have to be good enough for me to obtain two or three bearings as we run down on her. During all this time I will stay well clear of her and move in slowly. I guess it will take all of one hour to get abreast of her.

'What about the escorts?' grunts Welks when I explain. 'Are they just going to hang about while you perform these evolutions?'

'I reckon it's aircraft we have to watch out for. The ships are staying fairly close to the dock and, for some reason, they are chasing round at a speed that makes listening on hydrophones impossible. I must say I'm bloody puzzled about that, it doesn't seem to make any sense at all.'

'It does to me,' says Sparks gruffly.

'How?'

'Well, put yourself in their place. On the face of it the whole thing's suicidal; towing a damn great target through hostile waters like that. What would you do if you had to make the trip?'

He gets no reply from us and looks from one to the other as though astounded that we haven't the brains to tumble to the same conclusion as he has.

'All right, I'll spell it out. If I were in charge of that little party I'd put hydrophones on the dock itself, where there is no interference from propellers and a guaranteed slow speed that will give the most efficient results. I would bet that there are half a dozen highly trained buds with earphones clamped to their square heads listening for the first submariner to break wind within a thousand yards of them — that's why the escorts are doing what they are — they're working to a set plan that gives the hydrophone operators clear areas to search, while they keep up a speed that can push them into an immediate attack when contact is established.'

'Bloody hell!' says the TI, echoing my thoughts exactly.

'Yes,' says I, 'and only the slow speed and distance have prevented them from hearing us up to now. If they once latch on to us we will have half the German Navy down our necks.'

'That's right,' breathes Sparks heavily. 'If you feel like praying, do it quietly.'

I move off towards the control-room. If I am going to get a fix on that thing, now is the time to make a start by taking the first bearing. I can feel their eyes on my back as I go to the forward periscope, and know what is going through their minds when they see me spurn the attack periscope in favour of the larger one, capable of magnification and far more suited for what I have in mind. They know that it shows a lot more above the surface and there is a host of enemy experts up there dedicated to sighting the first glimpse of a submarine. I'm well aware of the risk I'm taking but I have to get an accurate bearing and the small 'scope is useless for that.

Quickness is the thing. One complete swing round three sixty degrees with the periscope then focus on one definite, recognisable object in that mass of floating flotsam. While I concentrate Bunts will read off the bearings when I call out the marks, then I intend to 'double the angle on the bow' that is, take a bearing of say, ten degrees off the starboard bow, wait until the angle becomes twenty degrees and the distance we cover between the two bearings should be the same as that between us and the target.

I snap my fingers and the periscope comes slithering up out of its well.

'Hold her steady,' I urge the two men on the hydroplanes. I need all the help I can get from them by keeping the boat nice and steady during the next few minutes. It's almost as though the whole boat is holding its breath while I walk the periscope round in a circle and search the area. The weather is grey and overcast, with masses of leaden cloud rolling across the sky above a green sea, mottled with choppy, broken ranks of foam − ideal for my purpose − making it difficult for the enemy to pick out the small 'feather' of the periscope amongst the white horses.

I stop the swing and wrench the periscope back to focus on a large escorting destroyer leaning hard over as she circles to settle on a course that will take her far out ahead of the convoy; a puff of black smoke from her funnel indicates that she is increasing speed with the turn. I move the periscope away, satisfied that whatever she's chasing is well away from me.

'Stand by, Bunts.' The mass of tugs and dock is coming into view and I switch to high power. The image leaps in close to allow me to distinguish a small, box-like object on the top of the dock. I can also see why the target looks so messy; they have painted all manner of silhouettes on the big, flat sides and at this distance they look like the shadowy shapes of small ships and tugs.

'Mark!'

'Green one five,' says Bunts, and I snap my fingers at the little pale-faced stoker before stepping back as the shaft slides down into the well — we are invisible once more. One five is a nice round figure; all I have to do now is get another sight of that box when it bears green three zero. Do my sums right and I'll have the range — give or take a yard or two.

It will be a good half hour before I can carry out the second sight, so I have time to relax and leave the listening to Formby for a while. Smithy is watching the depth and seems to be getting the knack for pumping ballast fore and aft — that's fine; for it leaves me free for other worries.

The soft whine of the electric motors and the rustle of eddying water through the casing above our heads are the only sounds as we creep along slowly. The temptation to have another look at the situation is almost overwhelming but our greatest ally is our invisibility and I will not jeopardise it by showing the periscope more than necessary.

'Coxswain!'

The cry is urgent from the asdics operator and I respond with a cold feeling of fear coursing through me as I stride aft past pale faces turned in my direction from shadowy corners of the metal jungle of wheels, levers and pipes that grow out of the ship's hull like exotic flora long since dead and petrified in the stagnant atmosphere where only man would choose to live.

The TI pulls away from the asdics cabinet to allow me to lean inside over Formby's back. He is concentrating hard as he listens to the sounds coming from up top. I wait patiently for him to sort himself out — I don't really want to know what he is about to tell me — it can't be good news. He snatches the earphones away from his ears with a cry of agony and we all hear a dull thump; like someone hitting the pressure hull with a muffled sledgehammer — the sound is unmistakable.

'Depth charges,' he finally manages to say. 'I heard the escorts begin an attack, now they're plastering some poor bastard about two miles on our starboard quarter.'

Their hard luck is our good luck, I think somewhat uncharitably. Anyway the destroyers might only be attacking a school of fish or a pocket of density that sounds like a submarine to an over-anxious hydrophone operator. Whatever it is lets us off the hook for a moment. One thing is certain — I can no longer resist the urge to see what is going on up top.

The water is slow to clear the lens as the periscope breaks surface, showing how much the sea is increasing up there. Patches of grey move across the scene as snow flurries drift in from the west. The light has turned sallow and colourless as visibility begins to close in on us.

I swing the periscope steadily in a full circle — it's becoming a habit now — the shadows are more deceptive and my imagination paints all manner of vague pictures of enemy ships bearing down on us from the curtains of snow that move between me and the target.

'Fast HE bearing green one three five!' says the calm voice of Formby, and I swing to that bearing to find the sleek silhouette of an escort plunging her bows into a trough, with black smoke pouring from her funnel. Everything about her is menacing as she goes into an attack, making no effort at secrecy as she steams at full speed, with that trail of heavy, black smoke stretching out astern. Some poor bastard is in for it, if she is not chasing a shadow, and something tells me she isn't, not this time.

I catch a glimpse of her mate lying off behind her, no doubt guiding her sister in with her hydrophone gear. Just keep those efficient-looking bastards away from me, that's all. I drag the periscope back to the dock and Bunts warns me that we are almost on the second bearing now.

'Put me right on it then,' I order and he covers my hands with his great maulers and pulls the handles round so that the small box on top of the dock slides away out of vision.

'Steer small,' I murmur and the helmsman concentrates hard on the giro repeater in front of his eyes, moving the wheel easily and economically to keep the ship's head on one eight zero.

'Stand by,' says I, 'stand by to take the time when I call "mark".'

Here she comes, and I find that I am sweating now. The periscope seems to have been up for hours and must be like a bloody signpost up there, beckoning every German for miles around.

'Depth charges — distant — about green one three oh.'

That will take their minds off us, I hope fervently. Here

comes the box now, creeping steadily towards the cross-wires on the lines. My palms are slippery on the handles, clamped still by the grip of Bunts' fingers. I almost say 'stand by' again but stop myself quickly for the next word I utter must be 'mark' or someone might be confused, and it's the only chance we have to get that all-important second bearing.

'Mark!' I yell sharply as the box comes central. 'Down 'scope.'

I step back, conscious of an ache between my shoulder blades where the muscles have bunched tightly, having been held in an unnatural position for some moments.

No one interrupts me as I bend over the chart and draw my converging lines, before working out the result on a slip of paper. If my calculations are correct we have done just a little under two miles between bearings and when I get the final figure the range I settle for is three thousand, eight hundred yards, and I don't think I am far out. Glancing across at Firth standing nearby I can see in his eyes that he knows that I haven't the patience to creep on for the hour or so it will take to get to the stern of the target.

'To hell with it, Sparks!' I blurt out. 'Let's be conventional and try a beam shot.'

'Why not,' he agrees. 'That's the way we are used to doing it. Fire the whole bloody salvo, go deep, and disappear.'

'Starboard thirty!' I order, without waiting any longer, ignoring the aggrieved intake of breath when the sharp change of course causes Smithy to lose his trim and makes it necessary for him to juggle with his ballast again. He really is getting quite good at it now — looking as though he is moving the water by the egg-cupful.

'I'm going to take her in to about twelve hundred yards,' I tell nobody in particular. 'We will have to put a spurt on — group up, slow ahead together.' This brings the batteries into parallel, with the motors drawing energy from them all with insatiable voracity. All manner of detrimental things start to take effect — we are now using our batteries up much quicker, and the noise we make increases considerably. I have no choice, however, if we are to get within range and position for a shot. I pray that the Germans are still occupied elsewhere.

The whine of the motors increases and the men on the helm and hydroplanes find it easier to keep course and depth. I move to stand at the attack periscope.

'Steer two seven zero!' No fancy courses for me — I've got to keep everything as simple as possible. From due south to due west with no frills, that's me. At the speed we are doing now it will take about seventeen minutes to reach a position that will bring us within twelve hundred yards of the dock's estimated course.

'Sounds as though they have broken off the attack,' says Formby.

I resist the urge to raise the periscope for a look. Everything depends on us slipping in unnoticed now. The hydrophones will tell me if they are coming this way and there is nothing to be gained by showing a couple of feet of 'scope just to admire the scenery.

I can feel the tense atmosphere in the boat as we move in from the relative safety of the sideline towards the centre of the arena where everyone is at each other's throats. The only rule is kill or be killed, for we are a sneaky lot; submarines have no friends on the surface, and one glimpse or sound of one of these metal monsters brings out the worst in friend and foe alike, and no one waits to see if you are the enemy or not because everyone up there hates our guts and desires nothing more in this life than to plant a couple of nice fat depth charges just where they will crush the pressure hull, spilling out the innards all over the ocean.

They will look eagerly over the rails for the first sign of blood, guts and oil, shouting for joy if they manage to fill a bucket with someone's entrails to show proof that they despatched forty-one human beings to a special place designed to receive the souls of the most feared and hated of the seagoing fraternity.

'Fast HE bearing red one five — closing!'

Something in the dead tone of Formby's voice warns me that this time there is a real emergency in the sound of those threshing screws.

'Up periscope!'

My heart is pumping wildly as the lens leaps clear of the

surface and I swing round to a point just off the port bow and I freeze. I'm looking right into the sharp bows of an approaching destroyer. So straight she comes that I see neither side of her — just the pitching, spray-shrouded bows bearing down on us at a speed of a racehorse.

There is no other sight like this for chilling the blood. I'm sure I die for a moment as I stare into those bows with their anchors like the eyes of a tiger staring back at me.

Only a moment though, for out of that icy death grows a hot surge of something that has been dormant inside me for so long, while I puzzled over the problems and tactics that have brought us to this place. It drives the coldness from me and leaves a grim determination to ensure that I will not waste the hours of effort and patience we've all put into it.

I swing away from the destroyer and see the masts of the tugs and the square shape of the dock, looking like a small town standing in the middle of the ocean.

'Bearing?' I ask Bunts, without taking my eyes away from the prism.

'Red two three.'

'Put me on to red one five.'

His hands grip mine and pull the periscope round to the bearing.

'Christ!' Once again I'm staring into that destroyer's bows.

'Down periscope! Ninety feet! Flood 'Q' — shut off for depth charging!'

The hydroplanes go to hard dive and the bows dip as the water floods into the quick diving tank, dragging us down into the murky depths. Everyone is sitting or standing with bated breath, eyes staring into faceless dials, automatically carrying on their functions, but all the time listening for the first sounds of the approaching enemy.

Formby is reeling off the closing ranges now and it's only too obvious that the ship is coming straight at us. I should take evasive action I know — go to port or starboard to make him change direction — yet I feel that we would gain little at this stage by doing so. Bow-on we are a small target and I am still in a good position to attack the dock. No, I decide, we'll hold on as we are.

Here it comes; that steady pulsating swish of the screws that brings heads of sweat to your brow and tightens your fists until the knuckles are white and dries your mouth to sawdust.

Formby takes the earphones away once more — he knows what comes next — as we all do. The ear-shattering, thundering sounds that will come any moment as those canisters of destruction sink to the settings on the gauges and explode close by.

Cautiously he puts one phone to an ear as the sounds, like the pantings of some great beast with lungs the size of a house comes right over the top of us. He will hear the two small clicks of the first charge as the phial breaks and the acid eats through the dividing strip, allowing the chemicals to mix and fire the main charge. He'll have a second or so warning before all hell breaks loose. I grip tight as he whips the 'phones away sharply.

A giant hand heaves the boat to one side as the sound of the charges tears the atmosphere asunder. Cork particles are falling in a cloud all about me and the boat is see-sawing madly. Lights flicker — die — and come on again as sounds of loose gear tumbling about filters through from the fore-ends. We are shaken by four such charges and the boat reels in agony. My eyes flick towards the depth-gauges; ninety-five feet. Bloody hell! it's a miracle after all that that we are still near our proper depth and no report of serious damage is coming in.

I move over to the asdics cabinet and lean over Formby, 'Can you hear anything on red one five, or thereabouts?'

He gives me a sour look. 'All I can hear is that destroyer, like a bloody express train doing a big circle to come in behind us for another go at blasting my flaming eardrums.'

I have to risk a look — no doubt every pair of eyes on the destroyer's upper deck and bridge is searching this area for one glimpse. What kind of trouble they can expect if they let their beloved Führer down and allow the dock to be sunk is anyone's guess, but I'll bet no one up there wants to find out.

'Thirty-two feet!' I say, in a voice specially designed to show everyone how calm, cool and collected I am. It gives no indication of the way my guts have turned to jelly. 'Put the 'scope on red one five as it comes up, Bunts — up 'scope!'

One quick look is all I need, just a few seconds is all I ask. The boat is creeping along slowly towards the surface and the periscope comes right up to the stops. I see the pale daylight shimmering in the lens and then I'm looking at the target. The small, box-like cabin, or whatever it is, just left of the line.

The TI has told me that the torpedoes will take approximately one minute to cover twelve hundred yards, and at the same time the target will cover about one hundred and forty yards, so if I turn the boat slowly and fire the full salvo of six fish at intervals of five seconds as I turn I should get a spread that will fan out over the entire area that includes the floating dock – it's the best I can do in all my ignorance.

'Ninety feet!'

No need to emphasise the urgency of that order for both 'planesmen are more than ready to take the boat down, and as if to stress it even further Formby's voice is warning me that the destroyer has almost completed her turn and is heading back this way. I know, even without looking, that other units will be coming this way too.

'Port five – Fire one!' My ears pop as always when the torpedoes leave the tubes. 'Fire two!' and so on while the boat swings slowly to port. Formby reports all torpedoes running and the only thing left for me to do now is get us away from those bloody escorts who are homing in like hounds catching up with a fox, and I feel our chances of getting away are about as slim.

If that first destroyer had been just a few seconds slower in coming in I might have known if I had scored any hits on the target. Even as we creep down to ninety feet and I order the boat deeper to one hundred and fifty feet and the helm hard over to port thirty to tighten our turning circle. The sound and the screws come loud and clear to everyone as she comes racing over the top, and my stomach turns to jelly again as I tense for the nightmare to come.

The next few moments leave me numbed by the murderous ferocity of the attack. The only thing that saves us is the fact that they have gauged the depth wrong and the charges explode above us. Having said that it remains a mystery to me that the

boat doesn't cave in under the mammoth hammering deton-
ations that shake the boat and shatter our ears.

The bow dips and the needles on the depth gauges sweep past
the one hundred and fifty mark and on through one fifty-five —
fifty-seven — sixty — full rise on the 'planes to no effect and I
can almost feel the pressures coming on the hull.

The angle on the boat is now such that I have to lean well back
to balance and the 'planesmen are finding it difficult to keep from
sliding forward on their seats. There are limits on how much
angle the boat will take before she gets out of hand and nothing we
can do will bring her back again: we are rapidly coming to that
situation, and it's up to me to do something, and quickly.

'Blow number one main ballast.'

The ERA's fingers leap to the handles and high pressure air
forces into the forward tank, pushing out tons of water as I strive
to lighten the bows. We have already lost the weight of six
torpedoes and it seems impossible that the bows still hang down,
and if anything, more angle is showing on the spirit levels.
When she does respond I will have to move quickly again, for we
now have positive buoyancy and only the effects of the depth
charges are pushing us down; when she does recover she will
start up towards the surface like a cork, even though the tubes
will have automatically flooded up again to compensate. It's
like trying to control a mad porpoise.

'Fast HE approaching — Red four five.'

Formby's toneless voice reminds me of our friends upstairs,
still determined to pulverise us into a mangled mass of iron and
flesh. There is nothing anyone can do now until the boat is
under control. The needles on the smaller 'deep' gauges situ-
ated between their two big brothers, which have reached and
passed their maximum depth, are hovering on two hundred and
fifty feet. We are on our way down to depths below that for
which the submarine was designed.

A thunderous explosion shakes the boat again, and before it
recovers another, even more violent, heaves us over to starboard, rolling the boat like a barrel. The sound of objects
breaking loose up forward coincides with a yell from aft as the
lights flicker again, dim and recover.

The bubble is moving forward now — the depth charges have achieved what our own efforts could not — the bows are coming up and we are overcoming the downward plunge. Already the needles are moving anti-clockwise. Everyone's picking themselves up from the deck and recovering their wits.

A figure bursts into the control-room as I brush cork from my clothes. Welks' face is white, wide-eyed and distorted with fury. 'I hope you're bloody happy now!' he yells, spraying saliva into my vacant features. 'There's water pissing into the boat down aft and the port motor's cut out. Fucking sparks flying all over the place, and one of my stoker's bin thrown into the bilges.'

A 'phone whines on the forward bulkhead and someone snatches it to his ear; his pale face stares at me, 'The TI says the tube-space is flooding up, Swain — he has shut the bulkhead doors.'

'We are getting a bow-down angle again, Swain,' says the fore'planesman.

I look from one to the other — the staring faces with their serious, worried eyes, all waiting for me to produce the miracle needed to save a very sick submarine with her anxious crew. I look into the expressionless dials of the depth gauges for inspiration and see the needles moving clockwise again, like accusing fingers, condemning my inadequacies — the bubble moves aft as the weight of the water flooding into the tube-space begins to tell. Slowly, inevitably we are sinking.

V

If there is one commodity as precious as battery power and breathable air, it's high pressure air to blow the main ballast in a submarine. The tragic story is still told of the boat that dived with the air-whistle open and the pathetic letter written by her doomed captain, explaining that, with everything else in perfect working order in his submarine, there was no way of getting her back to the surface. He and his crew sat down to die in a boat that was without a defect in her system.

The temptation to blow main ballast to overcome the weight of the flooding tube-space is great, but I have already blown number one tanks once, and in this boat we do tend to lose a certain amount of HP air through leakage, so I hold on as the next escort comes ploughing in above our heads and the charges begin to explode again. The boat shudders and rolls, but this time the Germans have misjudged our depth, and the attack is less severe — it's about time we had a bonus of some kind — Christ knows we are in enough trouble in every other direction.

There are four main sections in an 'S' boat: starting from forward there is the tube-space, the torpedo stowage compartment, or fore-ends, where most of the crew live amongst the torpedoes, the 'mid-ships' section that stretches right aft from the fore-ends bulkhead to the engine-room and contains the control-room, wardroom and several senior hands' messes, along with the wireless office, asdics cabinet and all the nerve centre of the boat. The last compartment is the engine- and motor-room, along with the steering compartment, which includes the stokers' mess.

With one exception the flooding of any of these compartments overcomes the buoyancy of the boat, and nothing will bring her up again. The one exception is the small tube-space — or so they have always told me. The test will come when we blow all main ballast and see if we can claw our way back to daylight again; that is, always provided we don't become crushed by the increasing pressures coming on to the boat as we sink out of control, or the bulkhead between the fore-ends and the tube-space doesn't give way. Of course there is always the matter of the water that is 'pissing' in to the engine-room, as announced by Welks.

The needle is now coming up to three hundred and fifty feet — about fifty-eight fathoms. I look at the chart, staring down at the dozens of small figures giving the depths of the area. I can guess at where we are, but there seems no chance that we will hit the bottom before we crunch in these deep waters. It is all looking pretty hopeless.

'She's levelling off, Swain.'

The stubborn bubble in the spirit level is reluctantly moving forward and the boat is coming back on to an even keel. I remember that number one ballast tanks are empty — perhaps even now we are lucky enough to have compensated for the flooding tube-space — maybe I should begin to worry about holding her down if she starts to rise quickly.

One hard look at the gauges show that these hopes are 'pie in the sky' for the needles are moving towards the three-sixty mark and we are still sinking — albeit on an even keel. Once more I think about blowing main ballast, but those bloody escorts are still chasing about up there and I can't afford to get into a situation where I'm flooding up and blowing ballast willy-nilly. I have no illusions about her predicament; with the tube-space flooded there will be no nicely regulated control over the boat, even when the time comes to swim up to the surface — it will be a trimless struggle with every ounce of ballast blown and every-one holding his breath while she makes up her mind whether she is light enough to rise. To cope with that I need every ounce of air and every amp in the battery to drive her at a speed necessary to affect the attitude of the boat.

As every landsman knows, all that is needed to control a submarine is a balanced dispersal of ballast and enough positive buoyancy to bring her into line — as every submariner knows, once there is a drastic change in the weight distribution in a boat, such as a flooded tube-space, she becomes an unmanageable bucket, reluctant to respond to any efforts of her crew to control her, and determined to swivel on her keel into the sort of acrobatics more usually found in the realms of the airforce.

On the other hand, 'S' boats are popular boats, and for good reason. They are of a size that are manageable and, with an experienced crew, responsive and straightforward to handle. *Scavenger* hasn't been behaving too badly under the circumstances; despite the incompetence of her stand-in skipper, and now that the Germans seem to be having trouble locating us the depth charges are less severe in their treatment. I wouldn't say we are all brimming over with confidence, but at least we're not dashing around tearing our hair out and having hysterics — despite the fact that the needle is now resting on three hundred and sixty-eight feet.

Another pattern of charges reverberates above us and someone in the fore-ends swears blind that the escape hatch jumps so much he can see the flash of the explosion — but it is not too long since tot time so no one is really convinced. Water is coming in here and there, where rivets and seams are strained by the monstrous pressures of the depth charges. To emphasize this a trickle of icy water runs down the periscope wire and over my oily fingers.

We are used to being hurled around, thumped and deafened, so when the jarring crunch that knocks us off our feet as she hits the sea bed comes, it is accepted by everyone as just another knock in the general hammering we've been going through. She lists again, just once — seems to hover for a moment, as though on the verge of rising again, before settling more gently with a slight list to port and a bow-down angle . . . the miracle has happened.

The attacks stop and a weighty silence develops, allowing time to pick ourselves up and look about. The boat is filled with dust and haze, hanging in the air like a heavy mist. We can smell the bilges and slightly sweet-acid tang of chlorine gas — not enough to worry about at present, but a warning of what could happen if salt water gets to the batteries in any quantity.

There are mutterings and snarling curses breaking out as the crew gather themselves together and I warn against too much noise, for our persecutors are still up there, just waiting for a hefty cough or a dropped wheel-spanner to show that we are still in the area. They settle down quickly in the quietness as the dust settles and features become clear again. I decide that my best plan is to have a tour of inspection with the TI and Welks. Between us we should be able to sum up the situation and see what can be done to improve matters.

In the event four of us set out towards the fore-ends, because Sparks, with his usual quiet efficiency, brings a clipboard and pencil to make notes as we go.

The fore-ends look cold and empty when we arrive, without the usual crowd of messmates sitting either side of the wooden table which is now slung up out of the way. There is a dank, stagnant smell merging with the stench of rotting vegetables from beneath the deck-plates, where food is stowed. I can hear the water slopping about just beyond the forward bulkhead where the heavy doors are holding back the North Sea — that bulkhead never looked so fragile, with its two large and two small doors that allow the tubes to be reloaded from the stowage compartment. I thrust away the thought of what might happen if that bulkhead gave in to the pressure bearing on it and try to concentrate on the positive side of things.

There are pale, anxious faces in the fore-ends as men look at us for some glimpse of hope for an end to the hammerings and a return to normality again. They crouch in corners with their backs to the metallic cylinders of the torpedoes, each with the red of its war-head showing menacingly at the forward end. Black oilskins hang dejectedly from convenient fittings, while a bucket lies on its side near the after bulkhead. It is beginning to get cold in the boat as she sits lifeless on the seabed. A sudden loud gurgle draws all eyes to the forward bulkhead and in our imaginations we can see it straining under the pressures against it.

Wally Barnes, one of the torpedomen, whose long, horse-like features look more gloomy than most, is staring at me with great, saucer-like eyes, set in his sallow face. I know enough about Wally to realise that this is his normal expression, and his outward show of depression in all things is a source of general amusement to his shipmates. They — like me — know only too well that it is all part of a charade designed to set him up as a character amongst his contemporaries, and it succeeds, beyond his wildest expectations, in all kinds of circumstances. If things are going well and everyone is slapping each other on the back. Wally can be relied on to quell the optimism with some doleful message of doom or disaster. If, as now, things are particularly grim his mournful voice will offer some bizarre reason for the predicament and blame the whole thing on anything from the Government's desire to deprive him of his pension, to his mother-in-law's sticking pins in his waxwork image, back in his Portsmouth home where, according to him, a constant battle rages between himself, his wife and her parents. Now even he is silent, with his thoughts locked inside him like everyone else in the boat.

I look up at the fore hatch with its big strongback braced across it to give added strength to one of the weakspots in the pressure-hull. Normally I never spare it a glance when dived, or at sea, when it remains closed at all times. It is our front door in harbour, used by everyone to enter or leave the boat, load stores and torpedoes and for every other use. Now I can visualise the pressure bearing down on it from the three hundred feet of ocean, and I bless the blokes who put it together.

One after another a pattern of depth charges explode far above us — not too close though; it seems the Germans are using a certain amount of guesswork now. If we sit here quietly we might get away with it. We have been dived for some five hours now, and I haven't gone mad on the batteries or HP air, so we can afford to sit it out for a while yet; always provided the enemy doesn't get too efficient.

We move aft to the bulkhead and wait for this attack to finish before someone opens the door to allow us through — shutting themselves off again from the rest of their mates.

From here aft the boat looks more habitable, the row of senior hands' messes are well lit and comfortable, with an array of human flotsam to colour and soften the harshness of the steel hull and fittings. Men seem to be more engrossed with their duties than had been the case in the fore-ends and allow us to move by on our way to complete our tour of inspection. As we come through the next bulk-head and face to face with Welks, who has moved on ahead, the cold chill of our predicament reasserts itself.

He stands in the narrow passage betweeen the diesels, with one hand resting on the starboard engine, hiding the rest of the compartment with the bulk of his body. It's warm in here, compared with the other compartments, and I can glimpse the glittering array of switches and dials in the motor section and, as always, I marvel at the contrast between the harsh, metallic, oily atmosphere of the engine-room with the metal walkway, and the bright, clean, gleaming section of the motors. I haven't long to marvel for Welks' face is contorted with fury as he confronts me in his domain.

'What do you expect us to do about this lot then?' he demands, in a high-pitched voice that resounds through the compartment.

'You're the engineer — not me,' I say quietly; thinking he is still harping on about the sick engine.

'It's a miracle man you want for this, mate, not an engineer.' He bangs the engine with a closed fist. 'This diesel is blasted off its mountings — if you use your eyes you can see it's not even in line anymore — look over here.'

He pushes past me to where a young stoker is still crouched over the ballast pump, waiting patiently for signals from the control-room to pump water from one trim tank to another. None too gently Welks shoves him aside, ignoring the wide, protesting eyes of the scruffy little minion as he grabs a pipe to keep himself from being thrown into the bilges. The ERA jabs a hefty finger in the direction of the dark spaces beneath the port engine. Staring down into the murk I can see the black, oily scum swimming on the surface of water which is slopping well up the sides.

Welks plunges a dip-stick down into the liquid which is so thick with oil and scum that it hardly disturbs the surface. He hauls it back again and looks at the tide mark.

'Three inches!' he announces triumphantly, as though the

extra water in the boat is due to his own ingenuity. 'Three inches in the time it took for us to do your tour of inspection. Christ knows where it's coming in – probably through sprung rivet holes, or even a leaking gland. One thing for sure, that's a hell of a lot of water in a few minutes – and a hell of a lot of extra weight.' The last remark was made with special emphasis, in case I am too dim to know that water means weight, and weight is our enemy, now that we are already overloaded.

'Well, we can't start pumps and things now,' I say quietly. 'Those escorts are just waiting for us to start making noises.'

'Let me tell you something,' says Welks, with heavy, warning emphasis, 'it takes energy to run pumps, and the more water we allow in the longer it's going to take to pump out – always supposing we can pump out faster than it comes in. If you let it get too deep down there we'll never get off the bottom.'

'What I like about you is your bloody optimism and the way you put heart into your mates,' says Soleway as Welks pulls his heavy body upright again. 'All we have had from you since this lot started is a dirge of disaster. Just once I'd like to hear you say what you would do to get us out of this mess.'

'Well it's too fucking late now, isn't it?' spits the ERA. 'We 'ad no business getting involved with the attack in the first place.'

'Swain!'

The voice from the control-room door relieves the situation and I look forward to see Sparks beckoning. Gratefully I move away from Welks, 'What is it?'

Sparks moves back and nods towards Formby, who pulls his earphones away to look up at me. 'There's all sorts of sounds going on up there, Swain. The destroyer that dropped those last charges just kept on going after her run and her screws merged with a whole mess of noise coming from where I reckon the target to be. My guess is that they've broken off the attack, and are dealing with problems of their own. I have even heard breaking up noises.'

'Blimey! Do you think we might have hit the dock?'

He shrugs, 'Might have – my guess is that it is more likely we've hit one of the tugs, judging by the kind of noises I'm hearing. One thing for sure, they are churning round in one hell of a panic up there. My imagination might be working overtime but if we sunk a tug — one of those big bastards — and she didn't have time to let her go her towing hawser when she rolled over, or whatever, they could be in a right old mess, with that thing dangling from the dock.'

'I doubt even a towing hawser would hold that kind of weight for long.'

'If they were on the bottom like us it would. It's possible that there was enough hawser to act as a mooring,' says Soleway. 'I saw a frigate sink a tiny little tug in Malta once by heaving her right over on her beam-ends — it was a long time before they were able to saw through the hawser.'

'It'll be dark soon up top, Swain.' Formby's eyes are alight with eager anticipation. He's anxious, as we all are, to know what is going on up there; there comes a time when even the risk of exposing ourselves is preferable to sitting on the bottom, with water seeping steadily into the engine-room bilges, adding weight to the boat minute by minute in a boat that seems to be dying like some old man with no one to help him move his limbs and pour life into his cramped muscles again.

The clock shows sixteen hundred hours; in this latitude and at this time of the year it's almost dark up top now.

'When I do blow main ballast with all the extra weight in the tube-space and bilges I'll have to pump out all our compensating tanks as well — leaving nothing to control the attitude of the boat. If we go up, it'll be in one almighty rush; I dare not try to stop her once we start. We could pop up like a cork under the guns of a dirty great German destroyer,' I warn them grimly. 'Christ knows what sort of angle she'll have on her; we could — and most likely will — surface stern first and stick our arse out for all the world to see.'

'Better than sittin' here,' says Welks sullenly.

'Congratulations!' snarls Soleway, 'That's the first positive thing you've managed to say since we came to sea.'

'Have one more listen round then, George,' I tell Formby, 'Try to get a picture in your mind of what's happening; use that bloody imagination again, it's all we've got.'

He trains the set round and listens before beginning a running commentary, to paint a picture for me. 'All the sound is concentrated in one big area almost due west and it's a cacophony of propeller noises — fast and slow — merged with all sorts of hammerings and gurglings. Sounds like Sally's whore-house on payday.'

He moves round slowly, stopping now and then to listen intently before murmuring that it's all clear and coming back to the original bearing again. 'That's it, Swain. Everyone's gone to the party.'

'I bloody hope so!' I pray fervently. 'Let's try and get this sod up on the surface. I want everyone who isn't required forward to get aft to the stokers' mess. Blow Q tank if it isn't blown already, God help me I've long since forgotten. Pump out all the trim tanks — everyone find something to hang on to, or a corner to wedge themselves into, then hold on tight. As soon as she lifts I want "Full ahead, group up" on the motors — to hell with the expense — and full rise on both 'planes.'

Life pours back into the boat as the crew move into their places, and in a few moments all is in order and everybody is waiting for me to perform once more. I stand by the periscopes and choke back the gorge that rises to my throat. One by one the reports come in to tell me that except for main ballast every drop of water has been pumped out of her. I check the hydroplanes are at full rise and try to think of anything I might have forgotten — anything that the skipper or 'Jimmy' would have thought of automatically. Nothing, I tell myself optimistically, or if there is it's too bloody late now — poor bastards, if the crew only knew how their destiny was being gambled away by an inadequate sod like me; if I thought they wouldn't notice I'd cross my flaming fingers, because I'm trusting to luck and providence to produce the half dozen miracles I desperately need.

'Blow ones!'

A sharp look from the ERA shows that he had been expecting me to order him to blow everything at one go. Brief hesitation only though, as his hands carry out the necessary movements with the dexterity of many years' practice.

'Blow three!'

He gets the message now, and realises that I'm being cagey.

The HP air hisses into one of the amidships tanks and the boat doesn't even quiver.

'Blow two and four main ballast.'

I watch the needles closely and will them to move, or give me a sign, but they remain firmly in position, as though set solid for all time. Now I do cross my fingers. 'Blow all main ballast!'

Every ear in the submarine is concentrating on the hissing noise as the last dregs of water are blown out of her. There is no other sound in the boat as we all hold our breath in that tense atmosphere. An almost imperceptible movement stirs beneath my feet — a tremor, hardly felt at first. Slowly she begins to roll upright and then the stern lifts.

'Everyone aft — Quick!' I yell. 'Come on! Bloody well move! there's nothing more we can do now — when I give the word — full power on both motors.'

Bodies are scrambling by as the needles on the depth gauge move slowly and the deck slants. I find myself straining back on the periscope wires — trying to haul the bows up. For one moment my brain paints a picture of the whole crew crouched aft in a bloody great heap, praying for the boat to level off — and there it is too — the bubble moving forward as she see-saws quietly. I watch tensed up as it moves to the centre and creeps forward.

I spring to the telegraph and ring through 'Full ahead — group up.' Our fastest underwater speed, with the batteries pouring out energy in unison.

'Helmsman and 'planesmen to the control-room!' I yell, and the needles begin to rotate steadily anti-clockwise as they resume their stations.

We are swimming up towards the surface now and there is nothing I can do to stop her as she rises like a whale who has left it almost too late to grab a much needed lungful of air. The angle is steady too — even with the 'planes at full rise — with only a slight bow up attitude. 'Come on, you little beauty!' I urge under my breath.

'Ninety feet!' The fore'planesman warns as he shuts off the deep water gauge and we are back on the two big ones with their needles fairly racing round the dials.

She's on her own now — no hope of levelling off at periscope depth for a cautious look around — it's up top or nothing, and already I'm opening the lower conning tower hatch. One last glance at the gauges before I start up the ladder with fifteen feet to go and I feel the first roll as the boat gets the movement of the waves. The sound of the ocean outside grows as we shudder and roll again and I don't need the signalman's shout to tell me we are surfaced. With an urgency that makes my fingers fumble with the clips I open the upper hatch — In a few seconds I'll know whether we will go on living for at least a few moments more.

VI

The bridge is bleak and cold, with ice already forming on the metal-work. A howling wind comes in from the night to bite into the exposed parts of my face with agonising force, moaning through the periscope standards with demonic wailings to chill the soul and deaden the heart. The night is black and heavy with the sound of boisterous seas raging all about us and huge bodies of solid water burst over the low casing and come smashing aft against the gun, sending needles of frozen spray over me as I bend to the voicepipe and order the lookouts up with safety belts.

We are wallowing broadside unto the wild sea, rolling as only a water-logged submarine can, with slow, sickening motions, punctuated every now and again by a heavy, staggering lurch when the body of a big swell hits us. To try to pierce that solid blackness is a vain occupation and one can only listen to the mournful sound of the storm like the wailings of a thousand ghouls.

A voice from below brings my thoughts back to the moment and I brace up to get a grip on things again. The first priority is to pour life back into the batteries and build up the air pressure, so I call for a charge and to start the blowers. It is going to be a miserable, uncomfortable time for everyone while we wallow along at slow speed, for Welks has made it quite plain that we are not to be allowed enough power to butt our way into that sea. He is reluctant to promise a full charge on the batteries in the circumstances, let alone driving the boat as I would like. There is a straight choice open to me, according to the ERA: I can put a charge on the batteries or use power to push the boat along at some sort of speed — which is another way of saying that I have no choice at all — for without power we die. Those with squeezy stomachs will have to put up with it.

The diesels cough and stutter into life and despite the discomfort of the pitching, rolling motion the sound is good. The engine will suck good, clean air down into the boat and freshen the atmosphere. I hear the steady grumble hesitate for a moment before growing to an unnatural crescendo as the stern lifts to bring the screws close to the surface then slams down hard again to choke off the exhausts for a second or two. Welks must be voicing some choice expletives down there as his engine is pushed to its limits.

The voice that suddenly yells within inches of my left ear causes me to jump so much that I don't get the message first time. The lookouts must have come up the tower before the diesel started so that I didn't hear them climb through the sucking down-draught. I ask for a repeat of the report.

'Objects bearing red one oh!' shouts the gruff voice again and I can barely make out the hunched shape of a muffled figure at my side with binoculars focussed out across the port rail. I follow his gaze and find a mass of blackness even more solid than the night, a group of shapes without definition but quite obviously our old friends, the dock and its entourage.

The whole scene is suddenly illuminated by the stark glare of a brilliant flash of an explosion bursting into the night sky long before the deep rumble of sound reaches us. A bar of white light thrusts out towards the north, sweeping across the wild waste of black water, probing for the perpetrator of this new outrage. There is a mortal struggle going on over there in the midst of all that confusion and somewhere in the wild wilderness another submarine lurks to deal out more death and destruction to those frustrated Germans.

The whole scene is a Dante's inferno of flame and smoke, making it impossible to sort out what is going on in that violent, disrupted mess. A dark, low silhouette of an escort passes between us and the illuminations, steaming at full speed along the track of that search-light; hell bent on revenge by the look of her.

Optimistically I decide that one end of the dock is lower than the other; hopefully it has been hit by us or that mystery boat to the north — it's hard to tell for certain. Another burst of flame shoots up into the sky, lighting up the whole scene with an intense glare and showing clearly the shape of a ship in trouble close to the dock with other vessels standing by as though they are rescuing survivors or hauling her clear from the convoy. Formby might have been right when he suggested we might have sunk a tug.

One thing is sure — they are static in the water and unable to move, let alone take avoiding action at the moment, and here we are with flooded tubes and full torpedo racks. I curse our luck, for even I could hit a sitting target like this and I can only look on helplessly.

The glare dies away to a dull glow with just a sprinkle of sparking pin-pricks; presumably they are getting to grips with the fires, reducing the flames so that the night closes in again, dark and menacing; only for a moment though, for once more that bar of white light sears the night. What idiot would expose a light at such a time? I wonder. What extreme circumstances would cause them to disregard elementary precautions to such an extent?

One thing is clear to me, I must take full advantage of their mis-fortunes and get the boat away from the area under cover of the darkness while their attention is divided between the shambles of the convoy and that unseen enemy stalking them from the north. Totally ignored, and in a perfect position for a torpedo attack, I can only give the orders that turn us away from the scene to slink away into the darkness. A guilty feeling tells me that I should do something to divert some of the spite that is being directed at our unknown ally — I can only hope that she is in a better condition to cope than we are.

A true leader would have a clear, precise plan, well formu-lated in his brain, which goes to show how inadequate I am to the task, for all I have is a vague notion of crawling away to hide. I must make a decision though, and soon, for daylight will come in a few hours and we should be on our way to some definite place. The most obvious course is to head directly for home, and I know I will get no argument from any of the crew if I settle for that, but they are firmly convinced that I know exactly where we are, and they couldn't be more wrong. Before working out a course for anywhere I have to know the starting point and we have spent the last few hours chasing about in all directions, at different speeds, in a mixture of winds and currents making a nonsense of any deadreckoning positions I have worked out on the chart.

I could try to sneak out towards the north and make a generous allowance to clear the top of that string of islands before turning in the direction of Britain and waiting for some landmark to appear that will allow me to take a bearing. It would be a hit and miss affair but, with a little luck, could be the quickest way home.

Alternatively I could creep in towards the Norwegian coast and try for a 'fix' before we start; a far more professional method, but with the added risk of pushing even further into the area where the Germans can locate us with shore-based listening gear: I don't fancy that at all — not with a dodgy diesel and a flooded tube-space.

On the face of it the former alternative is the best, but a small, warning bell is tinkling away in the back of my brain. The boat is bucketing along at snail-pace, with the diesel stuttering pathetically. The sea is increasing, with the prospect of a hefty gale building up — quick to come and quick to go — is my theory regarding gales, and this one has been taking its time, so it doesn't take a Hull trawlerman to tell me that things are looking dead nasty. If I want further proof of what's in store all I have to do is look at the barometer dropping in sympathy.

Much as I hate to admit it, our future depends more and more on that sick diesel and Welks. I must sink my aversions and talk nicely to him in the hope that he will have a change of heart and warm to my advances — the whole idea sickens me, even more than running away from that sitting target.

I decide to tackle him after being relieved by the gunlayer and Bunts with another brace of lookouts. I try to put together some friendly approaches as I make my way down through the tower, lurching from side to side as the boat rolls and getting doused with icy water as a big wave comes inboard; it does nothing to improve my state of mind when I reach the relative warmth of the control-room.

Welks is seated on his big, fat backside when I find him in the chief's mess with his great maulers wrapped round a mug of cocoa. Whatever trials everyone else is having, and however hard his minions may be working in the engine-room, it seems this man is determined to take things as easily as possible. I choke back my anger as I ponder over what sort of man can leave things to others in such a situation, and regret that I have to deal with this — the most senior chief in the boat — when I know the real work is being done by the stoker POs and the other ERA.

'We have a problem,' I tell him, as I ease into the seat beside him. My tone is as friendly as I can make it, and I'm determined to choose my words carefully, so that he will feel he is being brought into the situation as a colleague and not as just another essential part of the machinery.

'You mean, you have a problem,' he snarls, shattering all my good intentions. 'Don't start trying to place the responsibility in my corner.'

'All right,' I breathe heavily. 'I have a problem — if that's the way you want it. Whatever we decide the one sure thing is that we are not going to get anywhere unless we can sort out some definite plan, and to do that I have to know exactly what I can expect from your blasted engines. We have got about five hundred miles to go for home and it doesn't take much working out to realise that at this speed we will take all of five days; that is if we have battery power to run the motors during the days and we can keep going at something like this speed on the surface at night.'

There is no sign that he is even listening to me, let alone taking it all in to that thick skull. 'Add to that the fact that I am going to work out some sort of trim when we are dived with the tube space flooded and water seeping into the engine-room.'

He has stared at the table right through my speech and looking at the top of his head I know he has realised every admission of the problems I face. He wants me to crawl, the bastard; to tell him how right he has been from the start and how I need him to get me out of the mess he predicted in the first place.

'That engine ain't gonna last twenty-four hours; let alone five days,' he mutters. 'We could take the tail clutch out and charge the batteries right up, then use the motors to get us to the nearest harbour, set the scuttling charges, and give ourselves up. At least that way some of us will live.'

I sigh heavily and sit back hard against the partition feeling despondent about it all. I'm too bloody tired to go on arguing with this non-cooperative bastard. The boat lurches and another wave hits us like a ton of rubble to remind me that up top things are getting nasty. A black feeling of utter despair consumes me and I wish the submarine service to hell, along with the responsibility that can't be shaken off. These northern waters are an unfriendly part of the world, as any trawlerman will tell you. It's a colourless waste of grey ocean where even fish are black and slimy, compared with their exotic counterparts in warmer climes, where the sea is warm and blue.

My mood changes as quickly as it came and in its place a hot rage builds up, blazing inside me with all the intensity of the resentment I feel for the thankless sod who moves about the boat like a prophet of doom. Nothing would give me more pleasure than to take that bullet-head and smash it against the bulkhead, spilling out some of that hate along with his brains.

Almost without thought I find myself grinding out words that come easily with the outrage I feel. 'With or without you, I'm going to get this boat and her crew home in one piece — no one's indispensable on this tub — including you, so you can get up off that fat arse of yours and give me a complete run-down on the state of those engines. After that you are going to give me your full cooperation or I'll stuff you down one of the periscope wells for the rest of the trip.'

I stand up over him, 'Get up, you lazy bastard,' I yell out for all to hear, 'Move your idle self and show me what's wrong down aft, and explain it in terms that I can understand or I'll bend you in two.'

I'm shaking all over with the intensity of my rage, very close to losing control. His mouth opens as though to raise an objection, only to close again quickly when he sees the look in my eyes. Reluctantly he drags his body out into the passageway and together we move aft, by men who avert their eyes as we go past, for these men are used to hiding their feelings and controlling their emotions; to see two senior ratings breaking these unwritten rules as we have done is an embarrassment.

The movement of the boat causes us to stagger against projections as we progress aft and I spare a thought for those on the bridge where it must be cold, wet and miserable. Blinded by spray and numbed by the cold their fingers must freeze to the binoculars as they peer endlessly into the darkness while their bodies ache with the strain of balancing against the violent movements of the boat, despite the heavy web belts shackled to the metalwork to prevent them from being swept overboard.

Someone has rigged the 'bird-bath' under the conning-tower hatch; a canvas contraption, designed to keep out the bulk of water that would otherwise swamp the control-room. If things get much worse I will have to consider shutting the upper hatch altogether and resort to the big induction valves − not a popular move for those who would be isolated on the bridge.

Welks takes me right aft, past the engines and motors to where the submarine shrinks to a small diameter and houses the minute stokers' mess and steering gear. He leans over the table.

'We've found out where much of the water is coming in. Through the thrust block − you know what that is?'

I look at him sharply. 'Yes, I know what a thrust block is − it's what stops the propeller from coming inboard under its own power.'

'Yeah, well they should keep the water out too, but right now the port one isn't doing so. It's all right when the screw isn't turning, but as soon as we put in the clutch the sea comes pissing in. On the surface we can cope because the pumps can handle it, but not dived; the pressure's too great.'

'What about the starboard engine?'

He looks at me as though I'm some sort of idiot. 'I think we can forget that one for the remainder of the trip; I explained it all to you as best I could. That engine is off its mountings and right out of line. That means the clutch won't engage and any vibration will push it even further out of line; you can forget it.'

'Is there no way it could be pushed back and secured?' I am

willing to put up with his overbearing attitude if it means getting some answers.

'In harbour, with special equipment, we might do the job without calling in the dockyard, but I wouldn't like to try it.'

My confidence is draining rapidly; on the face of it there doesn't seem much hope of getting this poor crippled boat back home. Perhaps it is time to think about getting the lads out of an impossible situation and we can all sit out the rest of the war in concentration camps. I'm about to admit defeat and return to the control-room to tell everybody the sad truth when an untidy trio of overalled men squeeze through the bulkhead to join us, bringing with them the oily, warm stench of the engine-room.

A more ill-matched group I cannot imagine, and normally they merge unobtrusively in the background, being men who are always totally immersed in their own peculiar skills when at sea. ERA Burgess is Welks' second-in-command and a lanky, unassuming bloke who hovers over his diving panel for hours without anyone noticing he's there. The only comment ever made about him is to marvel at the tolerant manner in which he accepts all the abominable habits of his senior. Anything for a quiet life seems to be his motto.

Electrical Artificer Fellows is ignored by most of his shipmates for another reason — he exists in an aura of cultural superiority that relegates the rest of us to the status of moronic nonentities, unable to understand, let alone share his love of classical music and the arts. He suffers alone amongst a horde of Philistines.

The less said about the third member of the group the better. Usually bleary-eyed with alchoholic poisoning, he spends every spare moment ashore, and every spare penny of his hard-earned cash on women and booze. He has been demoted and reinstated so many times he can sew on his badges of rank blindfolded. He'll go to bed with anything of either sex wherever and whenever possible. His personal habits are a bone of contention with his messmates and he seems to exist beneath a permanent layer of oil and grease. Only his complete competence in his duties and his vast experience makes him tolerable. Stoker PO Finney is a man to avoid if you don't wish your finer feelings to be affronted.

'We bin lookin' at the starboard diesel, and we reckon we've a chance of putting it back where it belongs, with a bit of luck,' he says, looking past my left shoulder at something in the distance with his bloodshot eyes twitching alarmingly and his thick lips slobbering over every word. He's a human slop bucket, I think to myself, nothing functions right on him, he can't focus his eyes, his hands shake like hell and his insides seem to be in a permanent state of turmoil, giving vent to frequent explosions of pent up foulness from both ends of his body, to the general disgust and discomfort of his messmates.

Welks twists his mouth in a sneer. 'Oh yes, and how do you propose to do that, might I ask?'

The blurry eyes waver about in the general direction of the ERA's left ear, 'If we rig a chain hoist across the boat and use a couple of heavy bars it's possible; mind, you would have ter get the boat in to some sort of shelter.'

'Bloody hell!' explodes Welks, having wedged himself into a corner to stare out incredulously at the three men, 'what hair-brained bastard dreamed that one up?'

'We all did,' says Fellows slowly, in that refined voice of his which seems to get everyone's backs up, looking at the ERA as though at some insignificant piece of garbage left there by untidy strangers. 'It didn't take a lot of dreaming either, because both Burgess and I have taken part in an operation of a similar nature in an 'H' boat. The engine was lined up perfectly well, and as far as I know, is still working satisfactorally to this day.'

'Did all this take place in the North Sea in a force nine gale?' asks Welks with heavy sarcasm.

'No, It fucking didn't,' snarls Finney, 'but I reckon whatever you do now will mean trying to get into some sheltered water and I know enough about Norway to know that it's got a coast-line that looks as though it's been chewed out by a Sister Street pensioner. There must be somewhere to hide while we do repairs.'

'What do you say, Burgess?' I ask the ERA, who has been hovering unspoken during the discussion. For some reason I feel the whole project might well rest on his sloping shoulders.

He looks at each of us in turn with that nervous, embarrassed way he has, which normally guarantees an end to any part he might play in any debate. There is nothing he would like more than to allow others to lead him by the nose and take no responsibility himself.

'Hard luck!' I think to myself, 'for once, me old fruit, you are going to come out of that shell of yours and put some of that skill and experience of yours into practice.'

It's pathetic to watch him summon up the will to make an effort, but eventually he does.

'Er — yes — well — I reckon it can be done okay — with luck, that is.' He looks again at each of us, hoping that's all he'll be asked to contribute, shuffling from foot to foot and biting his lower lip. 'No chance,' thinks I; 'the ball is in your court now.'

'We would have to rig up some guides — perhaps even weld them to the deck — so that when the engine does start to move it will go right into position; there's a hell of a lot of dead weight there, to manhandle in a small area.' He looks at the deckhead for inspiration, 'We'll hack out the broken bolts easily enough once it's clear, I reckon. It'll be a big job, but it's possible.'

That's a marathon speech for him, I don't recall ever hearing him put more than two or three words together before — even after his tot. He looks exhausted, as though the whole effort was too much for him, and I wonder what kind of background he comes from, and how he comes to be here.

Welks has no such contemplations on his mind. 'You're bloody daft, the lot of you! I'll have nothing to do with the whole stupid scheme.' He waves his hands in front of Burgess' face. 'What do you think the Germans are gonna be doin' all this time, eh? eh? Just bloody sit there and let you get on with it?'

'That part of it is up to me,' I tell him. 'I'll have to find the right place and get us in there; after that it's your pigeon.'

'God help us all!' breathes Welks and pushes past me to trudge off forward, turning his back on the whole lot of us and our wild schemes and seeking out some little sanctuary of his own where he can remain aloof from the fools that have taken over his world.

In a small, staggered group we follow him, and I have almost reached the control-room when a shout comes from the helmsman.

'Coxswain to the bridge!' Strident and urgent, it starts me running to the ladder, grabbing a duffle-coat as I go.

Emerging on to the bridge is like stepping into an ice-box with the addition of a forty miles an hour wind blasting hell out of my face. There is ice underfoot and the bridge rails are coated with rime. The wildness of it all takes my breath away, everywhere is noise — a cruel, mad sound, as though all the beasts of hell are up in the periscope standards, determined to undermine every last vestige of optimism left in me.

The cold is intense; penetrating the bones and sinews so that it is difficult to keep from crying with the agony of it all. Solid masses of sea burst over the front of the bridge exploding showers of spray like steel filings and I gasp at the sheer strength of the storm. At the front of the bridge hunched figures are striving to find shelter behind the lip of the rail and keep lookout at the same time. There is a flange running round the outside designed to cause an updraught and give some protection but no design on earth can take away the tortuous bite of that Arctic cold. This is no place for men; it is the realm of Norse trolls and hobgoblins that exist only in the frozen depths of a maniacal mind living somewhere in the hidden mountains where there is no reality, only a wild, frozen Hades, inhabited by beings best kept from the sight of man.

'What's up?' I ask a hairy mass near the voicepipe.

'What do you reckon that is?' The gunlayer points vaguely to starboard.

Forcing myself to stare out into the wind I try to penetrate the darkness. I can make out streaks of white cloud stretching up into the sky — I stare harder — cloud be damned! That's snow, long ridges of snow and ice, lying on ledges cut by the wind in the solid face of a black cliff towering above us with a fringe of troubled foam at its base.

'Bloody hell!' I blurt out, 'where did that come from?'

'Right out of nowhere, as far as we are concerned,' says Bunts in my other ear, 'but it's not as close as it looks — I reckon it's an island.'

My first instinct is to get the boat away from here as quickly as possible, and I am about to give the necessary order when a vision of three ardent faces seeps through to my mind and an idea begins to form.

'If that is an island, there must be a lee side to it,' I say, half to myself. 'Let's find out — starboard thirty!'

The gunlayer repeats my order down the voicepipe and *Scavenger* swings away from the wind, bringing slight relief as the pressure eases. Every move has to be watched carefully. With only one screw turning at slow speed she has to be coaxed firmly but gently; one slip and we'll be in real trouble, for if I once allow the stern to come into the eye of the wind there is the very real danger of being pooped — a nasty little phenomenon whereby the sea gets under the stern and lifts it so that we are in a bow-down angle, with not a hope of pulling out of a dive that will take us down for good and all. It can happen to a boat in perfect trim, let alone one with the bows flooded.

In my anxiety I begin talking to myself as I stoop over the gaping mouth of the voicepipe. 'Keep the sea on the port quarter and don't give her one inch to play with. If there is another side to that mass we'll find some sheltered water.'

There is a non-committal grunt from one of my companions, but I am much too busy to concern myself with their doubts and trepidations. I certainly don't mention the fact that I haven't a clue where we are, and that we are just as likely to find half the German navy round the corner, looking for the same shelter as us.

We all peer ahead, watching the heavy mass moving past our swinging bow and looking as though it stretches to infinity in every direction. Gradually we are getting in closer, and it is possible to see waves heaving great gouts of white spray high up the face of the cliff. Any minute now I expect to hear the grinding crash of the bottom being ripped out of the boat by some outcrop of rock. If it happens I'll slip quietly overside and resign myself to drowning easily out of sight of the forty odd pairs of accusing eyes that will haunt me for the remainder of my life if I stay alive.

VII

Colours change as a sullen, mist-laden day emerges from the night. The land gains definition but remains black and grey; lifting to jagged battlements etched in stark relief against the slate-coloured sky. A poet might see a mysterious charm there, but we only see a menacing bastion of harsh rock with no sign of any sort of haven for us to find shelter. I examine every shadowy line on that snow-ridged cliff and not every protrusion on the jagged top edge, where I half expect to see German blockhouses and rangefinders staring back at me, but all I do see is wheeling flocks of seabirds mewing and screeching their protestations at our intrusion into their world; it is as though we are the first humans to disturb their spartan sanctuary.

The land has cut off the wind now and we are moving quietly through a placid sea that is like a sheet of glass. The long folds of our wake fan out to wash over the black rocks that line the edge of the cliff and I have made things even more peaceful by shifting to the motors. The rumble of our diesel can be heard for miles in this sheltered place and I feel I need the added manoeuvreability of the two motors as we creep in closer to the shore.

''Swain!' Bunts is pointing a mitten towards the port bow and I lift my binoculars to peer in that direction. There is a clean line running vertical up the side of the cliff and a clearly defined notch in the rim at the top. As we creep nearer the line opens to a vee-shaped cleft widening with every yard. It is as though a giant once wielded a monstrous axe and brought it down to cleave a massive wound.

Hardly daring to hope too much I watch the gap open up until it shows the entrance to a small fjord that curves out of sight to the right and promises an anchorage large enough to accommodate us if only we can get into it. There is not a man-made marker anywhere in sight, which can be good or bad; depending which way I look at it. Good because it means the place is most likely uninhabited — bad because it could be unnavigable and all that should be there is a bloody great 'No Entry' sign.

'Port twenty!'

The bow swings in towards the small gap. Angry seagulls soar in a cloud of noise and chaos and the towering cliffs rise ever higher as we approach with the bow pointed straight at the cleft and the wake spreading out on either side to lap over outcropping rocks. The echoing cries shriek at us as Morgan and a couple of seamen climb down to the fore-casing and go right forward to peer ahead for the first sign of danger.

Ahead a gorge is opening out into a cove with shingle beaches and tufts of harsh scrub clinging desperately to every cranny big enough to support it. We slip in quietly, like a sea-monster, through the gap and into a perfect anchorage; unspoiled by time or man — a place that has waited for us from the beginning of time.

I'm watching each eddy and every swirl of water round every rock as we move in. At other times, in situations like this I would be on the wheel, tensed up ready to react to the first order from the bridge — today it's me giving the orders and the gunlayer doing the steering. I must concentrate as we slide into the gap with high cliffs lifting into the sky on each side to dwarf the submarine and shut out the world.

The fjord bends round and narrows into the start of a deep valley that curves out of sight but gives promise of a softer landscape with a line of pines lifting their spires above the sloping edge of rock leading up from what looks like a small river. There is still plenty of water under the keel and I aim the boat for the mouth of that small estuary — it could be the perfect berth, if we can get right in to it and nestle beneath the trees.

Fate is kind to us for once and we snuggle easily into the soft bank with our moorings fast round the bases of tall pines. With everything shut down and the birds settled back on their ledges a silence descends on the place and we are left staring at a beautiful valley with a fast flowing river coursing down to swirl out into the glassy floor of the fjord.

Soleway stands at my side with Bunts behind us, staring at every stone and shadow with binoculars. To say we are nervous is the understatement of the year for we are deep in enemy territory and this fjord could turn out to be the perfect trap.

'First thing we have to do is climb that flaming cliff,' says Bunts, 'it's the only way to find out if we are the only ones in this neck of the woods. It's no good starting that bloody diesel if there's a nice little town just up the creek — the noise'll be heard for miles.'

I'm not paying much attention, being more concerned with making sure we are moored correctly and snugged well in under the trees. For the moment, it seems we are secure and isolated from our enemies, who are ignorant of our existence if my assumption is right and they are convinced that there was but one submarine in the area, which has been well and truly dealt with — my condolences to those poor bastards but I'm only too glad to take advantage of their misfortune and creep out of the limelight for a while.

One by one the heads of departments come to report the damage and offer their suggestions for putting things right. Given a few hours of uninterrupted peace the fore-ends can be pumped out and made watertight once more, the stern gland can be worked on, though with no guarantee of complete success and the diesel can be moved back on to its mountings. In all this one thing is abundantly clear; I am completely superfluous — no one needs a navigator or someone going round giving orders to people who are only too able to carry out the necessary tasks without supervision: in fact I'm bloody redundant.

Having swallowed this humiliating fact with some reluctance I can concentrate on the signalman's suggestion and contemplate the advantages of climbing the cliff to find out what sort of hole we have got ourselves into. The prospect of clambering up those frozen walls doesn't fill me with eager anticipation — I wouldn't be in submarines if I was inclined towards mountaineering — but I decide there is much to be gained by knowing what lies beyond the confines of our little haven, and who knows, I might even be able to find out exactly where we are.

Four is enough for this little party and I choose Soleway,

Bunts and 'Pongo' Leeming to accompany me. Bunts is an obvious choice for he can signal back to one of the telegraphists with a lamp and keep in touch — I don't want to use 'walky talky' radio or suchlike for fear of it being detected. Pongo comes because if only a tenth of what he has told us about his time in the marines is true he will be the expert when we tackle the climb. The one I feel guilt about taking along is Soleway, for my reasons are purely selfish and, deep down, I know his place should be in the tube-space with his men. I am determined to take him though, because I need a mature man with me who is completely reliable and will back me to the hilt, yet not allow me to do anything stupid. I console myself with the knowledge that his department is competent to carry out their duties without supervision, for he is everything a submarine non-commissioned officer should be.

We waste a certain amount of time when we search the valley along the riverside, only to find that it has a natural barrier in the shape of a waterfall that is very spectacular but beyond our capacity to surmount. Retreating to the starting post we prepare to do it the hard way and trudge towards the base of the cold, hard cliff looking like a poor man's version of an Everest expedition, wrapped up as we are in all manner of seafaring gear, far more suited to standing for hours on the bridge than the energetic pursuits that lie before us.

Pongo has loaded us up with all manner of improvised climbing gear which seems on the face of it to be more of an encumbrance than an aid, but we have to have faith in our 'expert' and we follow like sheep as he launches himself enthusiastically on to the lower slopes. We carry objects from the Coxswain's store that have never seen the light of day before. I raise a tentative objection when a pair of old stanchions are produced which had been intended for a hand-rail one time when threatened with a visit from high-ranking officers who had found better things to do. My objections are adamantly over-ruled and I am assured that when firmly wedged into a rocky cleft they will greatly assist our efforts; I'm doubtful but allow him to convince me and to accept the added burden of an accumulation of weighty gear in deference to the superior knowledge of one so experienced in these matters.

'I'll go first,' announces Pongo, obviously determined to take command, "ang abaht behind me and I'll take the 'eavin' line up wiv me ter sling it dahn so you can 'ook on the rope. When I've got it secured all you will 'ave ter do is swing up after me.' There is a glow of confidence about him that makes me feel more optimistic about scaling that grey, ominous, forbidding cliff.

Within two minutes that optimism has evaporated and the confident Pongo has deteriorated into a scrambling, panic-stricken amateur, stuck halfway up the first part of the climb that should have placed him safely on a nice flat shelf from which he can throw down his heaving line to us.

We are all staring up at his spreadeagled shape and trying to dodge a shower of soft shale and rubble that falls about our ears as it is dislodged by his wildly scrambling boots. His highpitched cries of fear rival the strident screeches of enraged seabirds as they hurl themselves up in clouds of protesting animosity, outraged by the disturbance caused by this maniac who has invaded their colony in such a brash manner.

He seems to hang by his fingernails as his frantic struggles cease so that he is spreadeagled and frozen against the rock, not daring to breathe in case the soft shingle he is relying on crumbles away completely and allows his body to fall back over the over-hanging bluff just beneath him and deposits it a hundred feet below on the jagged stone floor.

'Swain!' His voice is a ludicrous hoarse whisper, as though he fears the very sound of it will dislodge him.

'I can't move, Swain. Fer Christ sake 'elp me, mates.'

'Hold on — I'll try to get up to you,' I call back, with much more confidence than I feel. The most difficult climb I have ever attempted before is an easy cliff near my home, and at the time I was overtaken by a group of boy scouts who seemed to be strolling up while I sweated and struggled every inch of the way. Never mind; heroic bastard that I am, I start off after him.

I don't get ten feet before there is another yell from above and I look up to see Pongo transformed into a mad, scrambling, maniacal monkey, arms and feet going ten to the dozen as they fight and tear their way upward through an avalanche of falling rubble. It must be the most unprofessional climb in all history as, panic-stricken, he claws his way towards the top in a dead straight line, taking no account of deviations or even the most cursory examination of what lies in his path. Blind panic takes him to the top of the cliff, going out of sight of our incredulous eyes so we are left with only the sounds of his progress and can only listen to the wheezings and gruntings until they too fade out of range and peace reigns once more. It seems even the birds are struck speechless by what they have witnessed.

I can visualise him lying somewhere up there, recovering from his ordeal and can feel compassion for the state he must be in as he sobs his way back to normality.

These visions are soon dispelled by the reappearance of the unimaginative bastard waving his long arms about and grinning all over his stupid face.

'It's okay, Swain,' he yells exultantly. 'No problem at all — knew I could do it — I'll sling you dahn the 'eavin' line — awl bloody hell! — I ain't got the rope — must 'ave left it somewhere dahn there — hang on, I'll go dahn fer it.'

'NO!!' we all yell in unison.

'No,' I call with more control, 'just tell me what you can see from the top.'

'Right, Swain!' His voice echoes across the valley, rebounding from the rocky clefts to reverberate into the thin air, and we cringe. Every German within a mile must hear him. I curse my gullibility when I realise how I have been taken in by him and his lies.

Now he has disappeared from view again and I can visualise him wandering about up there without any attempt at concealment — silhouetted against the sky and peering stupidly in all directions.

'I'm going up,' I announce firmly. 'I wouldn't trust any report from that moron anyway and I must know what the situation is.'

Soleway nods agreement and suggests a route that leads away from Pongo's more direct line and zig-zags to and fro in a series of easy tacks, offering an easier climb for us novices.

The rock is frozen with snow lying in every crevice and seam. Our boots slide on icebound rocks as we move cautiously from ledge to ledge. A seasoned climber would groan at our progress and the long periods of deliberation between each move we make, but we are not out to be record breakers and the wheezes and gruntings coming from my two companions warn that there are limits to our capabilities. Our unexercised muscles put us roughly in the category of geriatrics attempting an assault course.

We don't talk at all as we devote all our energies to the climb. Despite the cold air I find I am sweating beneath the layers of duffle-coat, oilskin, sweaters etc. Looking up seems to show no progress at all and I haven't the nerve to look down after the first fifty feet or so. I'm leading them up a fairly easy sloping ledge now which seems promising at first but disappears round a corner a little further on.

In silence — except for the sounds of our exertions — we climb towards the corner. On reaching it I peer round into a nightmarish cleft with sides of shiny black rock rising in two vertical walls, without any sign of foothold or handhold. The ledge I stand on leads into the cleft for a short way then peters out. Beyond that progress is impossible. On the other side of the cleft, opposite where I'm standing, the ledge continues, leading further up the side of the cliff in that same gentle slope. The only snag is that the gap separating it from us is about four feet across and there seems nothing to hold on to if we can jump the gap. I glance down and freeze; there is a sheer drop to a boulder-strewn valley far below.

'We'll have to jump across,' states Soleway with surprising conviction.

'Oh aye!' blurts the doubtful voice of Bunts. 'What are you gonna hang to when you do get across?'

'If we don't we'll have to go right back and start all over again,' says Soleway. 'It's only four foot wide; if it was on the deck you'd think nothing of it. Come on — I'll go first.'

I flatten against the rock to allow him to squeeze past me. He goes straight up the ledge until he stands on the lip with his toes stretched out over the edge carefully gauging the distance before swaying back and jumping across easily to land on the snow-lined ledge, flat and spread-eagled against the cliff. For a

long moment there is silence, then, to our amazement he begins
to laugh — still flattened against the wall — body shaking with
emotion.

'What the hell are you laughing at?' I yell incredulously.

His arms are slowly coming down and he is scraping the snow
clear with his feet. His laughter is choked back as he turns to
look at me. 'It's such a stupid situation when you think of it.
That daft bastard running round up there and us hanging on
li — uh! oh, Christ!'

His voice freezes in horror as the ledge begins to crumble
beneath him. For a moment he looks into my eyes with an
expression of wild terror before the ledge breaks away. The last
sound he makes in this world wails out across the valley like the
demented scream of an animal as his body falls away; a solid
black object twisting and rebounding from the walls until the
scream is cut off sharply and we are left with a silence that
clutches at my inside in a grip that squeezes my guts to water.

'Oh gentle suffering Jesus!' breathes Bunts through clenched
teeth.

Frozen in the attitudes Soleway left us in we remain silent for
long moments while the soft sounds of the fjord seep into our
numbed minds. The cold clamps down on our bodies with a
vice-like grip that aches like hell and a surge of overwhelming
tiredness takes away every last ounce of will as I look down to
where the TI's body lies in a sodden, dejected heap. The echo
of his laughter comes back to mock me as I curse the folly of it
all and the madness of our predicament. Everything that has
happened to us is due to my ignorance and stubborn persistence. What right have I to lead these men into this kind of hell
and what fantastic plan did I have to get them all out of it? The
plain answer is devastatingly simple — no plan at all — just a
series of new ideas that manifest with each succeeding event
with no real basic plan to give them form or substance. Perhaps the best thing I can do is find the nearest habitation and
surrender the boat and her crew to those who will give them a
chance to survive this damn war, albeit in a prisoner of war
camp.

A sudden avalanche of rubble and turf comes hailing from

above, shaking me out of my despondency and back into reality once more with a jolt.

'Swain!'

I look up to see Pongo's round, beaming face peering down at me from about thirty feet above our heads. If he is aware of the tragedy he shows no sign of it — in fact he looks like a dog with two tails as he fidgets up there all eager to report something to me.

'What is it, Pongo?' I ask, resignedly.

'If yer can get up 'ere, there's an easy way ter the top.'

'Have you had a good look round?'

'Yers.'

I wait for him to expand on this but realise that where Pongo is concerned every piece of information has to be prised out methodically or all you get is a disjointed monologue of jargon, useless to anyone.

'What did you see?'

'Nothing, Swain. There's nothin' nowhere 'cept trees and snow.'

'Is there any sign of a road, or even a path?' I don't want to climb any further, and if I can get any sort of clear picture from him I might be spared the effort. Deep down though I know I can't trust this raving incompetent to do any more than the basic rudiments of his normal duties. In that respect he is the odd man out in submarines where a high standard is maintained even in wartime. I wait a moment or two for him to consider my question.

'There's nuffin — nuffin at all up 'ere.'

'No footsteps in the snow,' I urge.

'There wouldn't be, it's all frozen solid. No, Swain, there ain't nuffin up 'ere.'

I don't flaming well believe him — not for one moment. I'll not be happy until I get a look myself, some inner voice tells me that the effort needed to reach the top and satisfy myself will be well rewarded, and in any case, one of my best mates is lying in a tangled mess far away from his home and loved ones because I took his advice and came up here; to give up now would be letting him down by my reckoning.

'Get back along the ledge a bit, Bunts. I think I can see a way up to Pongo and he seems to be charging round up there easy enough.'

We move carefully along the ledge, even more cautious now, after the recent reminder of what happens to a man when he steps out into thin air. As we go I can see that we must have missed quite a number of reasonably accessible climbs up from the ledge as we concentrated on moving along the narrow path to the complete disregard for any other way.

In no time we are alongside Pongo and walking up a gently sloping pathway that might have been man-made it is so wide and smooth. Far below *Scavenger* looks like a toy nestled in alongside the trees with tiny figures moving about her casing and bridge. She looks small and vulnerable from up here — not the least like the lethal weapon we know her to be.

We go round a bend and lose sight of her and climb up over the top to stand on a hump dusted with snow and dotted with clumps of harsh vegetation and scraggy rocks.

The full force of the wind comes buffeting at us with strength enough to take breath away, making it impossible to face into it. It shrieks and moans through crevasses and outcropping rocks like a malignant spirit. This is a place of utter desolation, wind-swept and cruel. The cold knifes into our bodies with bone-chilling intensity. It is a land that God has forgotten and even the birds stay below the sheltering rim of this wilderness, beyond the reach of this demonic wind.

Forcing my eyes open against the blast I can see that visibility up here is good, despite shadowy veils of snow moving ghostlike across the seascape, giving promise of a more solid buildup of continuous snow to follow. I can see that *Scavenger* is not moored in a fjord as I imagined but in a narrow strait between two chunks of land that might or might not be islands; it's hard to tell from here. The strait almost comes together further up and might even close to form a bridge beyond the curve of the valley.

We stand on the highest point of the hump and the land slopes away to the north on a long spine with sloping flanks so that it is like standing on the head of the Sphinx and looking down the length of the body. I can see something else too that makes me curse Pongo for having no eyes in his head. A distinct line of telegraph poles marches starkly across the terrain, over the saddle of the Sphinx's body, showing clear evidence of habitation.

Looking out to sea I notice the vast expanse of grey, slate-coloured water where the broken surf doesn't churn it into boiling foam, showing only too well the outcropping rocks and reefs that mottle the surface in the area on the opposite side of the island. If we had chosen that side we would be well and truly wrecked on those evil teeth of that unfriendly shore. There is nothing to show me where we are from here, but having come this far I am determined to do all I can to find out, and the only way possible seems to be to follow that row of poles until they lead me to some recognisable habitation. It is a crazy scheme, and one that will more than likely end up with me in the hands of the enemy. However, I can think of no real alternative.

I have a vague notion that if I can find some friendly locals they will be able to put me right and, if things are not too much in the hands of the enemy, give us some assistance to get under way again; after all, these are the sons of Vikings, and our allies to boot. By far the biggest snag is that I have to leave Bunts here in contact with the boat and take Pongo with me as my sole companion; a daunting enough proposition in any circumstances, and in this instance, almost enough to make me give up the idea entirely.

I guess the line of poles to be about a mile away, and there is probably a mile or so to trudge when we reach it. I could have wished for a different travelling companion, but there is no time for messing about, so I am stuck with him. I will just have to keep a very tight rein on his exuberance. I don't delude myself into thinking that he will be anything less than a walking time-bomb. One glance at the stupid grin he is wearing on his round face is enough to warn me that I will need one eye for the enemy and one, even more watchful, for him.

Without a lot of conviction we set out, leaving Bunts standing against a grey sky and looking anxiously after us; a lonely, desolate figure and my last contact with the submarine. Even to walk with Pongo is an experience that tests me to the full. He is always ten yards in front, galloping from one rock to another with no attempt at concealment. He keeps looking back at his plodding, over-cautious partner with exasperated impatience. When we reach a small, sheltered ravine where speech is possible I call him to me and explain in simple terms our position and the need for extreme caution. In spite of the blank eyes that stare at me I persevere and press it to him with an intensity designed to impress the most moronic yokel that ever chewed straw. If anything the eyes grow more blank and the grin widens. I marvel that he ever got into submarines in the first place. Finally I nod him on with a philosophical shrug of my shoulders; after all, his stupidity is as nought compared with the ill-conceived adventure I have led him into: so who am I to criticise?

Once again out into the wild, wintry day we go, leaning forward into the wind until we reach the telegraph poles and find only an overgrown railway track which doesn't seem to have been used for some time. It is Pongo who finds another narrow-gauged track running alongside its bigger neighbour, this time with the silver sheen that indicates frequent usage. It's the kind of track you find in quarries with small trucks running about on their own, loaded with stone and motivated by gravity as they run downhill towards remote destinations.

These rails run straight for a long distance and make little effort to avoid the undulations of the ground, so I assume that some kind of motive power is used to push the vehicles along. I try to remember what I have learned about the economy of Norway and what would travel on such a track as this. Iron ore is one thing that comes to mind and it is possible that the rails are used to convey the ore from remote inland sources to harbours on the coast — in which case there will be a harbour at one end of this line — but which end? I bend and place an ear to the cold steel in a manner learned when train spotting as a young lad. Right away I hear the sound of something approaching.

I drag Pongo into a hiding place and even his natural exuberance is quelled by curiosity as we wait to find out what travels along this track.

There isn't long to wait before something does come into view far down the line, so distant it is impossible to make out any detail on the small black object that seems to grow no larger for a long time. Eventually, however, I can distinguish enough to realise that we are watching the approach of a small train of square trucks, towed by an unmanned diesel engine.

My interest in the train has taken my mind away from Pongo for a moment until I hear the sound of his boots scraping on rock and look up in time to see him scrambling up from the gully to obtain a better view, mindless of the risk he is taking in doing so.

'Pongo!' I yell into the wind, as his buttocks heave and the loose ground sprays from his scrambling feet. God! was ever anyone cursed with such an idiot as this one? Surely his head and shoulders must be seen by someone as he raises them above ground to stand out stark against the sky line?

A glance at the train shows it to be moving at a slow, steady rate — about as fast as a man can walk. Mercifully it appears to be completely unmanned and I can see that it consists of about twenty iron trucks piled high with rock.

My gorge rises as Pongo comes out of his gully completely to stumble back towards me, face beaming all over and eyes ablaze with excitement.

'Swain! Swain!' he is yelling as he comes. 'We could hitch a ride on that train and see what is at the other end of the line.'

Blind fury grips me. All the pent up fury I have kept bottled up inside me for so long — the agony of Soleway's death, the frustrations of Welks and his non-cooperation, along with the doubts I have of my own shortcomings, comes boiling up to the surface to burst in an explosion of rage that vents itself on Pongo's stupid shoulders.

I grab him as soon as he is within arm's length, heaving him hard up against me with a strength born of madness, holding him there, my eyes blazing into his and shaking him with a violent force that rattles his teeth and brings a look of abject fear into his worried eyes. I hate him and his bloated, silly face, and right then I could kill him with my bare hands quite easily, enjoying every second of it. I hurl him away from me so that his back hits the hard rock behind him and repeat the process, thumping his shoulders against the rock again and again.

'You stupid, fucking bastard!' I spit at him, bringing the back of my fist hammering across his mouth so that blood spurts out from a split lip. I know he is saying something – pleading with me – bewildered by the madness of my attack, but I am incensed and wish only to hurt him and relieve my pent up emotions.

Some kind of sanity returns at last and I relax my grip on him, allowing him to scramble clear and to retire to a safe distance to lick his wounds and stare back sullenly at me, like a whipped dog. I cannot trust myself to speak for a while and he sits there, watching me with big, anxious eyes and trembling mouth, a trickle of blood running slowly down his chin.

When I find the will to look up at him I find him ogling me with wild, staring eyes, full of trepidation and shock. He sees no remorse in my face though, if the immediate heat of my anger is over, the hate is still there and I'm as determined to show him I mean business as ever. I lean towards him and level my gaze so that he cringes back from me in anticipation of a further onslaught. I don't disappoint him, only the attack is with words this time, but they are aimed at him with every bit of the intensity used in the physical assault.

'You do nothing – nothing at all – unless I tell you. You keep your great, stupid mouth shut and your useless body well down where I can see it. One more move without my order and I'll shoot you – do you understand?'

I take his silence for acceptance and go on, 'Through your bloody fairy stories and blind incompetence we have lost a man worth ten of you. I swallowed your flaming romances about being a marine and I've suffered your idiocy long enough. I'm lumbered with you now, and I've got to go on with or without you, so from now on, you don't breathe without I tell you – is that clear?'

Giving him no time to reply I repeat, 'Is that clear?'

'Yers, Swain – sorry – Swain.' The words tumble out of his babbling mouth and I fall back against the rock, exhausted and deflated. What the hell sort of mess is all this? What do I do now? At this point in time the future seems totally blank and the only real thing is that small train rumbling ever closer along that lonely track, until it comes abreast of us and rattles on away from us again. Soon that too will disappear on its journey to God knows where.

I drag myself to my feet abruptly, 'Come on!' I yell at Pongo — 'We've go to find out where that thing is going.'

Dragging my reluctant body out of our hiding place I start after the train with no certain intention formed in my mind. I know only one thing; if I don't do something definite now I'll give in to the urge to give it all up and go quietly back to the boat. It's a comfortable thought — to give in, but not this time — not this bloody time.

VIII

With Pongo dumbly following behind I scramble after the trucks and heave my body on to the last one. I ignore his awkward attempts to do the same and move forward over the piles of rock until I reach the small diesel engine. It is a utility unit, designed purely to contain the engine, with no frills; like the bonnet of a large truck with a huge exhaust pouring out black smoke from the top. I find a foothold on the base and relish the warmth that comes from the vents on either side of the casing. I see Pongo easing into position on the other side and prepare to ride the remainder of the journey in silence.

We can no longer see Bunts and a guilty feeling tells me that I am at fault for leaving the boat like this and taking myself off into the unknown without leaving any distinct orders.

The railway undulates across a terrain that lives up to my idea of what the surface of a dead planet must look like. The wind howls across it with unabated fury, driving showers of snow before it to fill up the creeks and clefts between black rocks with rimy snow. Everything freezes and the few clumps of vegetation shake stiffly in brittle defiance in its struggle to exist.

We are both staring ahead for the first sign of life and ready to abandon our transport at the first glimpse of anything moving. Nothing does, and eventually we approach some huddled, wooden buildings. The train moves over some kind of trip mechanism which releases the engine and allows it to continue along a spur that leads off to the right, while the trucks rattle on, down a long, curving slope.

Things are getting a little too urban for me and I decide it is time we abandoned ship. I catch Pongo's eye and we drop off into the deep snow to wait for the diesel to run over some more points which cuts the engine and allows it to coast out of sight toward some sort of terminal, beyond the huts. Moving into the lee of a wooden fence surrounding a store of all manner of machinery we turn our attention to the trucks as they run quietly down towards a big gantry that seems to be built out over the cliff.

The trucks ease down and come to a halt a few yards short of their destination. There is the metallic sound of couplings being manipulated and the first truck leaves its companions behind to rumble into the framework of the gantry. Once there it is raised on a hoist and tipped into a larger container before being set back on its wheels again to run down another slope in the general direction of the terminal, where the diesel lies waiting for the return trip.

One thing is certain, automation is one thing, and works well up to a point, but the operation we have seen requires more than nuts and bolts to keep it working, so I can assume that there are men tucked away out of sight close by. My guess is that they come from the base of that hoist, where there must be some kind of habitation.

Caution is the thing now and I motion Pongo down into the snow, pleased at his immediate reaction as he grovels down into it like a mole going underground. After the warmth of the diesel the cold takes over and knifes into my bones with even more intensity; there is no future in just lying here slowly freezing to death.

'Stay there!' I tell Pongo, and one look at my face leave no doubt in his mind about the consequences of disobedience.

I move forward under the protection of a veil of snow that comes drifting across the scene. Vague shadows of black buildings show ghostlike through the gloom, and just as I am convinced that nothing exists in this dead world except us I see the yellow glow of a light, like the baleful gleam of a dying moon. I creep towards it, past piles of snow-covered timber and discarded chunks of machinery. The wind whines soulfully through the huts and framework of the gantry and I find nothing inviting about that dull glow from the frosted window of a large hut, with smoke rising from a metal chimney.

The harsh clankings and bangings of the trucks merge with

the sounds of the storm as I come up the track to the hut and freeze against the wall beneath the window. I wait for a moment to control my breathing before beginning to straighten up to peer through the window.

'*Halt!*'

The harsh bellow drives into my body like a knife, accompanied by the metalic click of a rifle bolt, which clinches things. I rise and turn to stare at three heavily clad figures aiming black muzzles at my chest. The coal-scuttle helmets tell me that all my nightmares have come true and I'm face to face with the opposition.

More orders bark at me and their meaning is made clear by the motions of the rifle barrels in the direction of the door close by. I shuffle along, not the least like the upright, steadfast British sailor I'd always imagined myself to be in such circumstances, but more like a shambling jellyfish whose spirit of adventure has been limited to a few wild runs ashore.

Inside the hut the air is clammy and hot. Two more German soldiers come to life as I enter and bring my dishevelled figure into the light. My appearance must convince them more than any speech of Hitler's that victory for them is just a matter of time.

Someone grunts another order and I find myself sitting in a hard chair being ogled by five curious enemy pongos, obviously wondering where the hell I've dropped in from. Their eyes widen even more when one drags open my duffle-coat to expose the red badges and insignia of my uniform. A shocked voice gasps out something in German which I'm sure would offend my delicate ears if I understood the language. One word I do distinguish is 'Britisher' and I see that light has dawned somewhat vaguely on one of them.

'English?' demands an unshaven wretch, nudging me with his rifle to impress on me the fact that he knows my nationality.

I nod reluctantly, as though admitting to a vile disease.

'English mariner!' A toothy grin of triumph splits his features from ear to ear — obviously the brains of the outfit.

Again I nod, if only to keep him from further nudgings with his rifle.

They go into a rapid discussion, accompanied by occasional glances in my direction. Strangely enough my confidence is returning as I realise that here is just a group of ordinary pongos doing a lousy job a long way from home and faced with a predicament they don't really know how to cope with — join the club — I invite soundlessly. For one thing they are all mature blokes — the sort who are roped into the service to help the eager-beaver regulars by doing all the less glamorous jobs.

The argument develops until someone suddenly remembers that there isn't only one seaman in the British navy and where one is there might be others. Two of the more gullible ones are persuaded by their oppos to go out into the weather to search round, their enthusiasm is not exactly unbounding, but they go out, muttering and cursing to themselves, leaving the rest of us nice and cosy together. I've no doubt that they will be back shortly with Pongo even more convinced of their superiority.

With the door shut the rest of us begin to peel off our outer garments by mutual consent. A pot-bellied stove is busting a gut to produce heat from an overloaded firebox. One thing these lads are determined on is comfort and warmth — you could bake bread in the hut with the door closed.

We all look a little more human without the heavy gear and they are wearing the sort of uniforms I have only seen on films in which the wearers are being massacred by the dozen by people like Clark Gable and Errol Flynn. They settle quietly into chairs and stare at me with intense curiosity. Only a war would make men look at each other with such interest and I feel like I've come from outer space.

Two or three promptings from his companions urge the man who last spoke to try his English once more.

'You come from ship?' Not very original but, let's face it, he's doing better in my language than I could in his.

We are now getting into the area where people like Clark Gable and Errol Flynn tighten their lips and refuse to say anything in spite of all the vile tortures the enemy can devise and I suppose I should square my jaw and defy this lot. However, I think it's reasonable to assume that they know full well that sailors come out of ships so I nod once more, on the principle that if I go along with them willingly on things that don't really matter, they will ease up on me when I tell lies or clam up completely.

There is a fair amount of rapid discussion again before a further attempt by the reluctant interpreter.

'Where ship?'

I decide the time has come to make things harder for him and shrug my shoulders like an idiot.

His big forefinger jabs at my chest to emphasise each word, 'You — ship — where?'

Judging by the way he jabs he expects my ship to be somewhere under my left shoulder. I shake my head and stare down with great interest at his boots.

There is a more ominous tone in the mutterings that follow this little duel of words. When I look up the eyes that stare back are less bewildered and a lot more unfriendly. I suppose it will be a feather in their caps if they can squeeze even a small amount of information out of me and it isn't every day that such an opportunity comes into their dull lives, after months of boredom and hard slog in this God-forsaken climate with nothing but snowstorms to relieve the monotony.

A hard note is creeping into the voice of my interrogator. He looks to his mates for support and approval for this new aggressive approach. This is the first time he has ever been in the limelight, and he is determined to make the most of it. That bit of pidgin English he learned at school has set him one rung above his mates and he will milk the situation dry. Unfortunately his next effort is incomprehensible, so I decide to give the stock reply.

'My name is Ben Grant, my rank, Acting Chief Petty Officer, number P.J.X.—' and so on. I say all this in cold, even tones and any feeling we had for each other is gone.

His eyes cloud over in consternation and he looks a little uncomfortable as he struggles with the mass of information I have just divulged. He shifts nervously from foot to foot and gathers his faculties for another go. The result is even more confusing and I stare back blankly.

'Parley vous Frances?' pipes up one of his more doubting

comrades and earns a tirade of violent protest for his effort from someone else, causing him to retire sullenly into himself.

'Speak slow,' insists the linguist, showing them all how it should be done, and readjusting his rumpled feathers.

'Ben — Grant.' It's my turn to jab a thumb into my breast.

They all look at each other and nod appreciation for this bit of success.

'Chief — Petty — Officer,' I persist, jabbing even harder at the red badges on my lapels, and my audience almost clap their appreciation for my performance.

I'm beginning to warm to it all now and decide I can keep it up all day when the long drawn out version of my serial number is interrupted by a roar from the biggest member of the group who wears a couple of stripes on his arm. He has sat through all the proceedings in silence up to now, glaring at me from beneath heavy eyebrows. Now his patience is exhausted and a fist the size of a melon crashes down on the table and his brutish, pugnacious face is thrust within inches of my own, so that I get a close-up of a devastated nose that gives evidence of the more violent aspect of this man's life. Two pig-like eyes flash hate and venom into mine and the war seems suddenly a lot nearer.

'Speak, English bastard!' he roars at me, exhausting his entire bi-lingual vocabulary in one go and spraying me with half a pint of saliva.

I freeze, feeling a momentary surge of pity for Pongo who had faced up to roughly the same situation a little while ago. There is no messing about with this bloke, and I get the feeling that he has earned his stripes more by aggression than brain power. The ham-fist comes up and clutches my lapels and a few extra pounds of my clothing in the process, along with some skin. The hut seems to have shrunk all of a sudden to a size just big enough to frame the huge face so close to my own.

Just when it seems he is about to do me an injury he thrusts me aside and turns on the linguist with as much venom as he has shown me. The unfortunate underling flinches under an onslaught of commands that reduces him to limp shades of his former self. Once more he girds up his loins for another go at me.

'You − tell − all − now,' he tells me, looking for approval from his burly mate, and receiving none goes on. 'What is ship name?'

This is the moment I have been frightened of. I know just how gentle I would be if I found a German snooping about in Portsmouth dockyard, in the middle of the afternoon, with no idea where he has come from or how numerous his mates are. I shake my head and prepare for the sky to drop in on me.

It comes in the form of an explosion right in front of my left eye, a sensation of turning a back somersault and a blinding pain in my head. Lights are dancing about and bells jingling in my ears. When it all comes back into focus I'm staring up at the towering shapes of the three men standing over me, staring down from a great height, while I wallow on the deck blinking and gasping with agony. That fist is like a sledge-hammer and I have no desire to get up for more of the same.

They are in no mood for procrastination and I'm gripped hard on my shoulders and wrenched up to my feet. The hut has become very unstable now and the light is dancing crazily above my head.

'Speak!' demands the heavy voice of the corporal, obviously hoping that I won't, so that he can give me more punishment. I surprise myself by shaking my stupid head and tensing up for the next earthquake.

The fist slams into my guts like a piston − driving right through to my spine and shattering my bruised entrails. I double up, gasping − or trying to gasp for air − all I get is an agonising, sucking, retching inside me as colours undulate in vivid patterns at the back of my eyeballs. I struggle to open a channel through my tortured inside and closed throat. Bile gorges up into my mouth and I can do nothing but make noises as I go down on my knees.

Again the fist comes crashing in. This time smashing into my jaw, jerking my head round and hurling me backwards to crash my skull against the hard timber of the hut wall. I don't feel the boot hit my balls, I only know the excruciating agony that follows the blow and hear my own scream that bursts from my open mouth. My knees automatically jack-knife to my chest and

I'm rolling on the floor, moaning, with hands clutching at my genitals; my body afire with every kind of tortuous pain that can bend a man's mind.

What follows in the next few moments is entirely lost to me, and it is a long time before I begin to take things in again, vaguely wondering why further hammerings have not taken place. When I do regain some of my faculties I find the corporal being held back by his associates, obviously concerned that he might kill me before they can extract any further information. The struggle is about even as the two of them try to hold him and pacify him.

Eventually they succeed to a degree that allows them to stop sitting on him and resort to just holding him prone. A few more words — probably warning him of the consequences of killing me — placate him even more and he becomes more manageable. Once again they can devote their attention to me. What they find is the broken wreck of a man, gasping in agony and trying to ease his nether regions back into place. They haul me back to a chair again, with a little more tenderness this time and stand clear while I moan and splatter foamy blood all over their uniforms. My crutch is a disaster area with knifing flashes of excruciating agony shooting through me and my mouth is a swollen mess.

Gradually my brain begins to function again to the extent that I am able to take in my surroundings again. The hut is shaking to the force of the wind that buffets the framework continuously. I can even hear the snow pecking at the window and the roaring of the flame in the stove, so things can't be too bad — marvellous thing the body, any car that had received the battering I have would be on the scrapheap now. The only other sounds I hear are those I am making myself. My breathing is still difficult and I wheeze with every intake and find it impossible to quell the occasional groan of agony as searing surges of pain grip my innards.

I'm just beginning to gain real control when things split apart again. The door bursts open to admit the two men who had gone out previously to look for my mates — if any. There is a rapid interchange with frequent glances in my direction before the interrogator return to the fray.

'A friend you haf — in der snow his foots we see.'

I struggle with this one for a moment, because my brain doesn't really want to work any more today, having enough pain to cope with for the time being. Obviously they have found two sets of footprints in the snow. It amazes me that they haven't found Pongo — or have they? Maybe they're just keeping us apart so that they can play one against the other. After all, that is probably what I would do under the same circumstances. I doubt it though, for both these blokes have come back and I reckon there are no more Germans about, so that would leave Pongo unguarded. How could they have missed him?

I am being yelled at impatiently now. Obviously they are getting short of patience again. The big corporal is making ominous noises too. Obviously convincing the others that his methods, crude as they are will have the most effect, and it looks as though they are becoming convinced. He rises like a great leviathan from his chair, moving across to loom over me like the side of a mountain. 'Roll on death' I think to myself as he grunts at me and hauls back to launch another attack. I close my eyes and pray.

The blow is never delivered, for at that moment the door bursts open and the place is suddenly swarming with strangers and the shattering blast of gunfire. Someone flattens me to the deck with the same sort of gentleness displayed by the big corporal. Above my head bodies are moving about and I can hear other people screaming and groaning. Voices are yelling in all kinds of languages. The world has gone mad, but I don't really care, for I am flat on the deck and, except for a weight lying across my legs I'm left alone. Even my groin is beginning to ease as two hands grab me under the armpits and hoist me into my chair again.

As far as I can see there are four newcomers in the hut and the place would have been overcrowded were it not for the fact that the previous occupants are all strewn about the floor in attitudes human bodies were never designed to adopt. There is the stench of spent cartridges and the soft moanings of someone still alive somewhere.

'Well now, and where the hell did you come from?' asks a

strong English voice and I look up into the heavy-browed features of a man who would have needed no make-up to have played Long John Silver on the stage.

Bewildered I look at his companions and find they are typical Norwegians with blond hair and tough-looking faces, made even more aggressive by the fact that they are all armed and unshaven.

'You are English, aren't you?' asks the dark one again.

'Yeah, yeah,' I reply hurriedly, having seen what they do to aliens.

'What the hell are you doing up here, all on your own then?'

'Hang on a moment,' I splutter through swollen lips, 'Let me gather my thoughts. Who are you, anyway?'

The man turns with a piratical grin to his mates and raps out orders in their language, sending one outside to stand guard and allowing the others to sit. He adds something else that amuses them no end.

'You're a suspicious bastard,' he says with a grin and points to the untidy piles at his feet. 'I would have thought that this lot would have convinced you that we are not exactly pro-Nazi.'

I look at the bodies. The place is beginning to look like a slaughterhouse now with blood oozing all over the floor.

'We are not going to introduce ourselves, if that is what you want. The fewer people who know our names the better — we will have to go on living here long after you are gone. Suffice to say that we are all Norwegian — despite the way I look and talk — my father was an agent for the company who own the workings you can see about here and I've spent most of my life in England, where me mum comes from — these other lads are thoroughbreds with an aversion to strange Germans walking in and taking over their hard earned enterprises. We are all definitely on your side, me lad, so you might as well tell us how you got here.'

'I'm coxswain of the submarine *Scavenger*, and she is moored under some trees on the other side of the island. Our officers have been killed and the boat is in a bit of a mess. We are trying to repair her enough to get us back home again. While the crew are doing what they can to put things right I decided to take a look at the countryside and try to establish exactly where we are.'

'On your own?'

I look up in surprise, suddenly realising that Pongo isn't with them. 'You haven't seen my mate then?'

'Didn't know you had one.'

'I left him hiding in a ditch before I got myself caught.'

'Well, we had better find him quickly, because we can't hang about here. Those jokers are supposed to travel back down below on the lift about now. When they don't turn up there will be hell to pay.'

I come fully alive then, full of apprehension when I think how vulnerable we are. 'The whole bloody island will be alive with Germans then?'

'Not before morning it won't. Those boys won't venture up here when the light fades.' A look of concern crosses his face, 'Tomorrow will see them crawling all over the place though. Sure as eggs they will see that submarine of yours. This 'island', as you keep calling it, is really a continuation of the mainland. If you had come along the cliff instead of the railway, you would have seen that there is a place where the gorge closes to meet half way along the valley. A road goes right across to the other side. In fact, if I get the picture right your submarine is nestling just under a smaller headland, beyond which is a large anchorage where the Germans carry out all kinds of tests with their ships: plus of course, the jetty where the ore is shipped from. By what I can gather, you came up from the south, and if you had gone on for a further four or five miles you would have opened up the anchorage and found yourselves in full view of a lot of German ships.'

'Bloody hell!'

'Bloody hell is right, but your luck is still a bit on the dodgy side. They have a habit of coming into the creek where your ship is moored every now and again. I'd say you're gonna need every bit of that luck to get out again.' He eased his long body into a chair. 'If they had not been so busy getting ready for the floating dock you would have found the place swarming.'

'What floating dock?'

'The one that's due here any day now.' He shrugs it off lightly, obviously holding little interest for things nautical.

'Not now there isn't,' I state smugly, preparing to bask in their admiration. 'We have sunk it.'

Their reaction is beyond my expectations, for he half rises to convey my last remarks to his mates, who exchange looks that show that they are not particularly impressed; in fact they seem downright amused at what I have told them.

'You did what?'

A terrible doubt grows within me as I explain that it is my belief that between us and that other mysterious submarine we have sunk the dock. I tell him of the breaking up noises we heard and the firework display, but I can see that my words are falling on stony ground. I add, somewhat lamely, that in my opinion the target was either sinking or damaged beyond repair when we left the scene.

'Come,' says he, in a tone that hardly suggests congratulations, 'I have something to show you.'

I follow dumbly, with a querying look towards his smiling companions. There's still a lot of daylight and he leads me to a tower alongside the lift gear. We climb an iron ladder with rungs that would take the skin off my hands if it were not for the heavy mittens I pinched from one of the bodies back in the hut. The wind tugs at my clothing, and if I can bring myself to look down I can see a maze of roadways and works, with a truck or two moving about, like dinky toys.

My guide yells back at me, 'Don't worry, they are used to seeing people climbing up to the top of this tower. At this distance they'll take you for part of the normal staff.'

When we reach the cabin at the top it is like walking into the innards of a giant's watch, with large and small cogs giving out all manner of clangings and knockings. He leads me to a row of windows that overlook the workings and, through the deep 'V' of the valley to our left, I can see the broad expanse of the sea. I can see something else too. A sight that dissolves my innards to water again and adds to my despondency; sitting there, in full view, is the great, ugly, square shape of the floating dock, with the small cabin on top to convince me that this is not the twin brother of the one we have been chasing all over the place. It looks unscathed, without even that slight list my optimism had conjured up.

'Takes some sinking, doesn't it?' says the sympathetic voice of my companion, in a vain attempt to relieve my feelings.

'Bloody hell!' I blurt out. That phrase seems to be the limit of my vocabulary these days. Total failure stares me right in the face. In the short time I have been in command of the boat I have really excelled myself; having brought the boat here to this creek next door to an enemy anchorage, and which is occasionally visited by them, with the fore-ends flooded, one engine useless and the other on the sick list and with no means of defending ourselves; while the object of the exercise floats by contemptuously on the horizon.

'Well I'm damned!'

The exclamation breaks into my despair and I look up to see what new disaster has caused this outburst by Long John. I half expect to be told that *Scavenger* is being escorted into harbour by the Germans, but I see he is looking inshore, through the windows on the other side of the hut.

I walk over and follow his gaze, and there is Pongo, still stretched prone in his hollow where I left him so long ago with my dire threats ringing in his thick ears.

'Is that your mate?' he asks incredulously.

'That's him,' I admit, in the voice a man uses when he has to admit to owning a dog that has just done something on the best carpet.

'What is he doing?'

'Waiting.'

Long John looks in all directions. 'For what?'

I gulp and look away into the distance. 'For me.'

I can feel his eyes on me but choose to avert my own gaze as he explodes, 'But you've been gone a long time and it is freezing down there.'

I cough and shuffle in embarrassment. 'I − er − I ordered him to stay put.'

His eyes travel to and fro between the figure far below and my set features. I can feel his wonder at a service that can instil such powers of command into its non-commissioned officers.

'Crikey! and I always thought the Germans had the monopoly when it came to iron discipline. How long would he remain like that if you had not come back?'

My awkward shuffling increases. I have a vision of Pongo lying there until he freezes to a solid mass in the eons of time, waiting in vain for my return and desperately anxious about receiving further punishment if he so much as breathes too heavily.

'Shall we go down?' I ask, leaving him gaping at my back as I move to the door.

When we do reach Pongo he is too frozen to show any reactions when the Norwegians try to rub life back into his frozen limbs. His chattering teeth are the only sign of life as they lift him to a sitting position. I have never seen a man so iced up in my life; his eyebrows are stiff and white over dull, fishlike eyes that stare back at us piteously. His lips are blue and lifeless above a stubbled chin, while his nose shows the first signs of frostbite.

Gradually they straighten him up on his feet until he is more or less standing. They rub his shivering body and eventually get him moving in a shuffling, stiff walk and we are rewarded with a big, broad grin spreading across his face like dawn breaking. The Norwegians pat him on the back as he begins to thaw out and increase his stride when we move out in a small procession. The looks they cast in my direction leave me in no doubt of the way they feel about one who misuses his authority with such blatant disregard for his fellow man.

Long John leads us away from the gantry and along the cliff top in the direction of the boat. It's getting twilight now as we descend along a path that takes us below the rim of the cliff, cutting off the wind and opening up a view of the valley. It is a zig-zagging track, wending down to the floor of the fjord in a series of gentle slopes.

The umbilical cord that joins this promontory to the mainland shows plainly to our left — a narrow causeway with a road running along its spine to wind away into a long climb to disappear into a forest of pines further inland. Only the curve of the valley hides *Scavanger* from the travellers on that road.

IX

We trudge along, sometimes on grass, sometimes on shingle, along the track that levels out and follows the base of the cliff. A thousand streams come tumbling down in a series of cascading waterfalls from the heights of invisible mountains somewhere deep inland. The shadows are deep here and the sound of nature in all its hard, coldness is trapped between the black cliffs, and bears down on me with an oppressive power that seems to dwarf our little group with its awful magnitude, for nature in this place seems bigger than anywhere else in the world.

The hard expressions on the faces of the Norwegians set even more firmly when we recover the body of Soleway. There is just enough light to show us the way back to the submarine where we are met by a silent, brooding crew who stand looking down at us with cold expressions. They have grown old in the last few days and death has become part of their lives, but the limp form of one of the most popular and respected members of their company reaches into them to drain their resilience.

Tired and bruised I climb wearily over the sloping plank, along the casing and down through the fore-hatch. Even in my numbed state my brain registers the fact that the tube-space doors are open, showing that somehow they have managed to pump out the sea and make the compartment watertight. A torpedo dominates the stowage compartment as it hangs from the loading rails in readiness to be pushed into number three tube. Soleway's men have not been lax in his absence and in this area at least we are once again a fighting unit.

The rumble of the diesel had travelled with us along the valley and it is no surprise to find that they have managed to put on a standing charge with the one good diesel. The noise had been evident to us for quite some time and it doesn't take a genius to work out that if we could hear it so far away everyone within the same sort of range must hear it too. I decide to be philosophical about it and hope that we are away from here before the curious enemy troops arrive on the scene.

That thought brings back the present situation with all its perilous connotations. The enemy must be fully alerted now to the fact that there is a submarine in the area and dawn should find them swarming round like flies. My priority is to get the boat out to sea and dived before they arrive.

The newcomers settle into the wardroom with difficulty, for they are not used to easing their huge frames into an area quite so small and I can detect their natural aversion to the claustrophobic confines of this oily, smelly world, so different from their own clean atmosphere with its wide spaces and endless horizons. Even the hefty tots of rum I give them seem only to make them more fidgety.

The effect on me could not be more contrasting, for I relish the warmth of the boat as it seeps into my bones and eases the aches in my limbs. An almost overpowering urge to sleep overcomes me and I suddenly realise just how desperately tired I am. People come to the wardroom one by one to report the progress they have made during my absence and I am obliged to look interested and make suitably intelligent replies. Even Welks has made vast improvements to the state of the engine-room, having pumped the bilges dry and worked on the one good diesel to make it more reliable. The efforts to get the other one back on its mountings have failed, however, much to his satisfaction, and we are left with the port one, which is capable of putting on a charge, but incapable of being used to drive the boat due to the intake of water through that stern gland whenever the screws are turned.

All in all I am reassured by the progress that has been made, but I have no illusions about the difficulties that lie before us. On the plus side of things, however, my little escapade shows some results now that I am able to establish our whereabouts with the Norwegians. In consultation with Long John I plot our position on the chart with complete confidence for the first time. I am much too tired to make any real calculations regarding the future movements of the boat, but I can rest with the knowledge that wherever we end up, at least I know that starting place.

Sleep is what we all need and I call a brief conference of the chiefs to give them the bare details of our situation before going to my bunk, leaving the crew to look after our friends. I am almost climbing into it when Welks arrives to demand my attention in the engine-room. Pulling myself together I allow him to lead me aft to where the diesel is churning away steadily with a reassuring sound and stokers are lounging about in the attitudes they always adopt when things are going along smoothly. I can see someone testing the density of the batteries as though we are alongside the depot-ship and my confidence begins to grow.

I get a thumbs up sign from ERA Burgess as he comes out of the shadows cleaning his hands on a piece of rag. I nod back and pull back through the bulkhead door to the relative quiet of the control-room. It would be pointless to try and hold a conversation beside that noisy diesel. The icy wind is roaring down the tower so we stand forward on the wardroom side where the draught is less severe.

'Looks good,' I venture warily as I look at each of them in turn.

'Enjoy it while you can,' drawls Welks sardonically. 'We are down to one screw which can only be driven by the starboard motor. To keep that motor going we have to charge the battery with the port diesel when we are on the surface. Because we cannot use the engine to drive the boat along and put on a charge, we will have to wallow with no way on at all while we do it. We will be lucky to get four knots out of her, so I reckon any thoughts of taking her all the way back home is fantasy.'

The bottom falls out of my world and one glance at the steady features of Burgess shows that on this occasion the Chief ERA has not lied. The feeling of euphoria that had built up when I saw how well the torpedomen had carried out their repairs dissolves into black despair. In truth the problems seem insurmountable and there is little hope for us now. I don't feel I have the skill or the right to take the boat out to sea again; to subject the crew to a further bout of hazardous ordeal. With shoulders slumped I go back to the chief's mess to sit staring at the scrubbed table in utter dejection.

A small group joins me after a few moments, a motley band of men, consisting of *Scavenger*'s crew and the Norwegians. They sit and stare at me as though I am some strange animal that needs feeding and no one knows what the diet is. I can almost feel the darkness closing in round the outside of the boat and despite the muggy atmosphere a shiver moves through me like a shadow crossing my grave. With several pairs of eyes looking into mine I feel very much alone. Firth is the one who finally breaks the silence with his down to earth voice.

'We have been chatting while you were with Welks down aft. Whatever you decide to do is okay with us, Ben. Seems a shame to see that dock go floating by after all we've done though and we thought you should know how we all feel about things. These blokes,' and here he nods towards the Norwegians, 'have been watching for that dock for weeks and trying to figure out some way of stopping the Germans from getting it into position. We have now got a full salvo of torpedoes in the forward tubes and reckon it will take Jerry until morning to tow the dock to a point just south of here. It would be a sitting target when daylight comes and we would be in a perfect position to attack the moment we get through the gap. In these circumstances it doesn't seem right to do nothing about it. It's your decision though and we will go along with anything you decide — just wanted to make certain you knew how we felt.'

'That's right, Swain,' says Smithy, totally transformed from his usual reserved self. 'Fire the whole bloody lot at it and slip off quietly before they know what's hit 'em.'

To be honest it isn't really sinking in and I sit there with a bemused expression on my face that prompts Long John to add his weight to the discussion. I see their mouths moving and I hear the sound of the voices, but my mind refuses to take any more and I want nothing more than to be left to sleep. The Norwegian is aware of my state of mind but insists on pressing home his point. He leans forward and speaks slowly and deliberately; as though he is talking to an infant. He is making sure that I get every word he is saying and that I realise the implication behind his proposal.

'The British want that dock destroyed, Ben. If you knew how much effort they have put into the operation you would know how much they want it. The chances are that we have already lost one submarine and several aircraft in the attempt already, and it is still there creeping along. Your boat is the last barrier before it reaches the safety of the anchorage and the Germans can go about slapping each other on the back and saying how they have put one over on the British again. All those blokes will have died for nothing and the U-boats will be able to come in for refits whenever they want without having to go thousands of miles to the pens at Brest. They can repair damaged ships before they make the return trip to Germany with ore, and there are numerous other functions that make it a prime target. You are our last hope, Ben.'

He has got through to me and I lean hard against the bulkhead, sighing heavily. 'You know what you are asking, don't you?'

They all fidget uncomfortably as I stare into each face in turn. It's one thing to talk, it's quite another to put those words into action. Somehow I have got to make them see how impossible their proposals are. I force my tired brain to find the words that will leave no doubt in their minds and enable them to accept the fact that the Germans have won in this instance. After that perhaps they will leave me in peace and I can get some sleep.

'Let us just suppose I can get the boat out of here without being detected − bearing in mind that our little expedition to the gantry must have alerted every German in Norway − we have only one motor to give us an underwater speed of something like four knots flat out. They will be after us like hounds chasing a wounded fox in the morning; one sniff is all they need. Given that by some miracle we achieve that much, we still have hundreds of miles to go before we reach home waters and the protection of our own aircraft, and if I am not going to use those batteries up too quickly our speed will be cut down to about two knots − now, come with me and I will show you something.'

They shuffle out after me to stand in a group at the chart table, on which is spread a nightmarish picture of Norway's jagged coastline, hundreds of islands and what seems to be thousands of lighthouses and buoys, all blacked out. We have to travel in darkness through that mess at two knots and I explain in one syllable terms what lies before us. I show them the twenty-odd miles we have to travel north to clear the lighthouse that marks the top of the menacing string of islands before we are able to swing south on to a course that will eventually take us home.

'That small diversion alone will take something like ten hours to accomplish − deduct the time it will take to carry out an attack on the dock, even supposing we get clean away afterwards, and anyone can see that we will be hard-pressed to make that first leg in daylight. If we don't we will have to surface to charge in daylight with no means of propulsion. In fact the whole bloody operation can be summed up by one word − suicide.'

I see that there is still doubt in those faces and so I stress a further point to convince them that there is no way we can win if we try an attack. 'One other thing I haven't mentioned yet is the depth of water in this area. We have already used the one miracle we are allowed when we bottomed on what must have been the only shallow bank for miles − two or three miles in any direction and we would have gone on down to a depth that would have crushed us like a rotten egg. The whole area is like that; high mountains and deep valleys under the ocean as well as inshore. There will be no sitting quietly on the bottom for us when the enemy come tearing in with their depth-charges to wait for them to go away. We will have to twist and squirm our way out of any sort of mess we find ourselves in, and on one motor it's impossible − believe me − it is impossible.'

I fling the dividers onto the table and retire quietly to the chief's mess. Having got that lot off my chest I feel relieved and enjoy a certain sadistic pleasure in having shared the weight of hopelessness that presses on my shoulders like a cloak of doom. That'll flatten their eagerness and deflate their fighting spirit − now, perhaps they'll allow me to rest, and tomorrow we'll quietly slip out of here and creep off as quietly as we can while they are engaged in getting their precious dock into harbour.

Not so — in a moment or so, following a muttered discussion over the chart table, they all come trooping back to me. This time there are several hangers-on with them and they all gather at the doorway and peer in at me like a dozen Olivers all summoning up courage to ask for more. God, it's like being on show at the zoo!

'We would like to have a go,' says Firth bluntly. 'Your plan seems to have a chance of succeeding and we want to give it a try. If it doesn't come off, no one will blame you — we're all in the same mind, Ben; we want to have a go — not just crawl away with our tails between our legs.'

I look at them all in disbelief — can they really be this stupid? Do they really think I am putting forward a plan to go after that dock? I lift my arms in despair, for looking at their faces I can see that they do.

'What bloody plan?' I blurt out at last, fuming at their refusal to realise that I am joining to Welks' brigade and admitting defeat. 'What bloody stupid plan? You haven't heard a word I said, have you?' I'm almost crying with exasperation now, 'Christ: have I got to spell it out for you?'

'You've done that already, Swain,' says Smithy. 'I want to get home to my missus and kids like everyone else and I know what we are up against, but I don't fancy sittin' the war out in some internment camp, so that leaves only two options open to us by my reckoning; either we creep away and show our backs to the Germans or we have a go at sinking that big square bastard, and making a name for ourselves — I know what I want to do.'

'Believe me, if we try this stupid scheme you'll very likely never see your family again.' I change my tone to one of persuasion. 'Look, you've seen my pathetic efforts to control the boat, and I'm not being falsely coy about all this; I'd even say that I have done very well, under the circumstances, but bloody hell! there are limits, and there comes a moment when you have to decide when to give up in the face of impossible odds — and that time has come — right now, me buckos — take my word for it.'

They go quiet now and just at this point Welks knocks off the charge and the diesel stutters away to silence, leaving only the soft sound of water lapping on the ballast tanks. The world seems to stand still for a few seconds.

Kirby, a young AB who generally sits in the control-room with a pencil and pad noting every change of speed and course, along with every order, pokes his pale face through the mass and blinks at me with wide innocent eyes. 'We all know what we are up against, Swain.'

Eighteen years old and he knows what we are up against. I look to Firth for support and could kill him when he just shrugs his shoulders as if to say, 'There you are — even the sprogs are with us.'

'Think of those boats in World War One, Swain. Up the Dardanelles; they didn't think it impossible,' says Smithy.

'They didn't have to cope with modern detection gear,' I roar at him. 'They didn't even have depth charges. Christ; the only thing the enemy could do then was try and lasso their periscopes or ram them.'

Firth looks abashed. 'Yeah, yeah, we know, Swain; it's a stupid comparison to make. It's just it don't seem right to give up after all the work the lads have put in to pump out the tube-space and reload the tubes. They sweated blood, Ben. While you were away they worked like bloody slaves to get things right.'

Blackmail, that's what it is, moral bloody blackmail! I peer into their faces, dirty and pale in the yellow light of the harsh bulb. A choking feeling lifts into my throat; who can deny these scruffy, dedicated blokes when they plead like this? Something akin to love wells up inside me as I look into their eyes and see the honest anxious eagerness written there. To live amongst men like these is a privilege — to fulfil the aims of all their hard work and training would be an accomplishment far beyond the empty gestures of patriotism politicians are given to raving about. Right now these blokes have no thoughts of medals or painted slogans on the side of the bridge — all they ask is the chance to put into practice what they have been trained for. To offer them the opportunity to do so is an obligation not to be refused. To share in such a triumph if it comes off would be worth all the frustrations I have gone through — to die with them if we fail will be to share a steel coffin with a magnificent band of men.

Long John knows better than to interrupt at this point. He can see enough to realise that there is something deeper here than just carrying out decisions made by people sitting in far away offices surrounded by wall maps with coloured flags stuck all over the place. This is the close-to war where men with grimy hands and dirty faces sweat in the metallic belly of a sick submarine in the deep, cold waters of a harsh ocean. Close as he is to the battle he can only observe these events as an outsider.

'We'll have to work out everything carefully,' I find myself saying, 'there will be no second chance if we miss first time. We'll have to get under way before first light and get out of here before the enemy comes nosing around. We'll have no time to spare, so the attack will have to be worked out in advance, as much as possible, on the assumption that the dock is where we expect it to be. I'll have to fire the full salvo and move off straight away, without checking for results. The chances are we will never know whether we have succeeded or not.'

'Oh yes you will,' says Long John firmly. 'We'll be watching from the cliff top and I can assure you we will see it all. Somehow we will get the results to your people.'

'All right, let's get down to working things out,' I say. 'We are going to have a busy old time tomorrow. Smithy, go and tell the Chief ERA to come and join us − I'm gonna enjoy telling him all about the plans which are going to destroy any dreams he has of spending the rest of the war in some prisoner-of-war camp.' What's more, the odds are, he is going to work harder than he has ever done before, and in conditions that will hardly be ideal. Oh yes, I'm going to enjoy watching his face when I tell him − it's compensation for the sick feeling in my belly and the trepidation that makes me bite my lower lip.

X

When they have all gone my tired body should have fallen into a deep, relaxing slumber the moment my head touches the pillow, but things don't happen that way at all. My brain has been kicked back into life by the prospect of what faces me tomorrow. I am still wide awake long after the Norwegians have left us to pursue their unenviable task of climbing back to the top of that cliff in the dark to be positioned by dawn to signal any change in the course of the target.

My mind is going over detail after detail. Without doubt the most anxious time will be first light, when we try to slip out of here unobserved. I try to picture the layout of the fjord, with all the natural hazards I can recall observing when we came in. A great deal depends on me in the morning and preknowledge of the situation is going to save me a lot of grief. If I foul things up I face the awesome prospect of taking all the combined skills of the crew and throwing them down the drain.

If my calculations are right the dock will be standing out clear against the dawn sky when we clear the entrance to the fjord and dive for the attack. In theory it should be a sitting duck as it enters the narrow confines of the channel that leads in on the final approach to the anchorage, allowing them no room for manoeuvre as they creep up dead slow on the last leg of their long journey. I try to visualise the shape of the target and anticipate how they will undertake the last few miles of what must have been an ordeal no-one would like to repeat. What state of mind will they be in as they see their destination crawling ever closer? Will they relax a bit and breath easier, or will they tense up even more with the knowledge that there could be a submarine lurking close by even at this stage of the operation?

I know the answer only too well. There will not be any relaxation until that dock is safely moored inside her torpedo nets, and well protected by camouflage. Still further reason for my attack to be quick and decisive; before their counterparts ashore can radio our position. In theory I can hardly miss if everything runs out as we expect, but theory goes right up the spout at such times, as I know only too well. Torpedoes can run astray and things can go to pot when everything is happening fast. All through the night I wrestle with the problems that beset me and I am like a wet rag when the diesel starts up again to complete the final topping-up of the charge.

Painfully I ease my bruised body out of the bunk and sit for a moment, trying to assemble my thoughts. It is a luxury to find the deck steady underfoot as I go aft in search of a cup of coffee from the galley. The diesel steadies to an even rumble and a blast of cold air restores my faculties as I pass the opening conning-tower hatch. My mouth is full of slime and I have to blink to focus my bleary eyes in the baleful light.

I change my mind about the coffee; having a more urgent need to use the 'pigs-ear'. I climb the tower with the icy Norwegian air shocking me back to reality like a cold bath. There is time to look about the fjord as I use the funnel, piercing the gloom to take in the pale patches of frozen snow that seem to hang in mid-air against the black cliff.

It is by no means totally dark, and shadows loom up from all directions. Above my head the steeples of tall pines thrust high into the sky and the wind rustles ghostlike through the stiff needles. Humped shapes of rocky outcrops grow out of the water like the heads of basking hippos, brooding in anticipation of ripping the bottom out of the boat when we move away from our berth. The smooth water looks solid and polished in the vague light and the exhausts hurl continuous clouds of spray across the stern as the charge comes to an end. The boat trembles with the vibration and I am worried about the noise we are making, but shrug off my fears with the knowledge that there is no alternative and perhaps the wind is strong enough to carry the sound out to sea.

Someone comes clambering up the tower and I move to the

front of the bridge before a procession of sailors arrives, all bent on making use of the 'pigs ear'. Only the silent service would expect its sailors to begin a new day by dangling their genitals in the cold morning air.

I study the scene carefully, getting my eyes adjusted to the deep gloom. I can see nearly all the creek, though not in full detail, and trust to my memory and imagination to do the rest. There seems adequate room to turn the boat round on one screw so that the bows will be pointed in the direction of the exit when the evolution is completed. It is a piece of luck that the one working propeller is on the starboard side.

My thoughts are interrupted by the diesel choking to a stop, the fjord turns into a soft, whispering gallery of mysterious sound and my frozen clothing creaks at the seams as I move to the voicepipe to yell down to anyone within range. A voice answers and I order the men to stations for getting under way. Within minutes the boat comes to life with the ladders ringing to the noise of men climbing up to the bridge. Dark shapes haul themselves over the side of the bridge and stride out on to the forward casing, their voices hard in the thin air to merge with the scrape of mooring wires.

Welks arrives on the bridge and stands brooding at my side until I can find time to hear what he has to say.

'The batteries are charged up,' he announces grudgingly. 'We're ready to get under way.'

'Thanks.' I glance at my watch and reckon another hour to sunrise, 'Now's as good a time as any.'

He grunts and shuffles off without another word; in his wake Bunts and a couple of lookouts have arrived and the bridge is getting crowded. Time I began to get her moving. I receive the signal from Morgan that all is singled up; ready for letting go. Time for one last, measuring look at the width of the fjord before bending to the voicepipe to order 'Stand by' on the telegraphs.

'Let go!' I shout to the men on the casing and hear the splash of hawsers hitting the water.

'All gone forward!' yells Morgan, echoed by someone on the after casing and we are free of the land once more.

'Slow astern starboard!' I order, and lean over the side of the bridge, to watch as the screw begins to drag our stern aft. A swirl spreads forward as the screw bites and, as always, it's the shore that seems to glide past us, rather than the other way round.

'Port twenty!' The rudder should help to get our stern away from the shore in time to clear that hefty chunk of earth and rock sticking out to menace our propellers. I might have misjudged the distance, hoping that I would have room to clear it comfortably, but even now I can see that she is reluctant to come clear of the bank, despite the rudder and screw.

I begin to pray quietly to myself, for if she doesn't respond soon I will have to go ahead on that same screw and try to push her out bow first. It will mean swinging the stern in tight to the bank with the risk of damaging the screw. A kind of cold panic seems to grip my inside as she makes no move to clear the shore, and we scrape aft against the vegetation.

'Stop starboard!' I order as the chunk of rock comes too close for comfort. 'Slow ahead starboard!'

The boat stops, hesitates, then the screw begins to push us ahead and I can see that my fear of the stern swinging in to the shore was unfounded, for she is still determined to remain close alongside — if anything even tighter than before.

'Christ!' I curse between clenched teeth, for I have not reckoned on anything like this. We are wasting time and battery power playing silly buggers while the first streaks of dawn begin to outline the rim of the surrounding hills.

'Stop starboard!'

What the hell is holding her in like this? I look for signs of anything that might be the reason for this, for there seems no logic in it at all. Hanging over the side of the bridge I stare down at the ballast tanks to find the answer in the form of a clump of leaves and twigs moving slowly past the black hull. The force that pushes them along the side of the boat is the same one that is holding us so firmly inshore, and it is coming from the mouth of the river — a surging flow of water funnelling in a steady stream from the curve of the far bank and straight into us — pressing us against the bank. I recall the waterfalls that we saw

on our journey inland and the tumbling gouts of white water
that sluiced over the smooth rocks. No silly little submarine
propeller is going to push us out against that lot.

'Christ!' I blurt out again, bashing a frustrated fist on the
front of the bridge. I look around for some inspiration in the
wilderness about me and find myself looking at a large, black
rock; showing clearly in the stillness of the water, beyond the
reach of the current, and about thirty yards away from our
berth. All I need to do is get the bow angled out about twenty
degrees from the bank so that the current will come on to the
other side and push us the rest of the way.

'If only we could get a warp on to that rock, we could winch
the bow out,' I murmur, half to myself.

'If only,' says Bunts bitterly. 'All you need is a motor-cutter
and a pair of buoy jumpers.'

'Nevertheless that is the only way we will ever get the bow
away from the bank — the screw will never do it. It's getting
lighter already: soon it will be fully daylight and if we're not
away from here within the next few minutes, we might as well
chuck our hands in and call it a day.'

'Only a spit from here — that bloody rock,' says Bunts. 'We
could almost lasso it.'

'It might as well be on the other side of the moon.'

'I reckon I could swim acrorst,' says an all too familiar voice
from the gloom.

I wince as Pongo pushes his way past the signalman. 'Once I
get through that stream, I could swim the rest of the way easy,
with an 'eavin' line rahnd me waist, then I could haul a rope
acrorst ter that rock.'

'Flaming heck!' says Bunts, when he sees that I'm too dis-
traught to make any comment of my own, 'even if you managed
to reach that rock without freezing to death, and did haul the
hawser over, how would you get back on board?'

'You could 'eave me back wiv the 'awser when I casts it orf.'

I look at the heavy jowled features with the low forehead and
wide eyes to say firmly, 'You'll freeze your balls off before you
get half-way across; but you can give it a go if you like — we
can't be any worse off than we are now.'

'I'd like ter give it a go, Swain.' He looks away disconsolately, 'I let yer dahn before, I know I did; but this time — no kiddin' — I'll get that rope acrorst.'

'One thing,' I tell him,' don't try to come back on the hawser — we will have to leave it there. Just wait on the rock until we are clear of the current and in smooth water, then we will pick you up, somehow — understand?'

He looks dubious, so I enlarge a little, 'Look, Pongo, when I move the boat away from the bank I will have to keep that screw going until we are well clear of the river-mouth or we will wind up back where we started from; so you must not try to use the hawser or both you and the hawser will end up in the propellers, and that will put the muckers on everything — understand?'

The blank features stare back at me, but I tell myself that there is a glint of comprehension in his face, and anyway, I have no choice, so I resign myself to accepting the situation.

'Aw, I'll be okay, Swain,' he beams all over his fat face, 'you don't have ter worry abaht me.'

I raise my eyes to heaven for support, it is like sending a child into battle, 'Go on then: and good luck, lad.'

Over he goes, lowering his great, awkward bulk down to the casing to scramble eagerly forwards, shuffling his feet sideways along the narrow ledge of metal that leads round the base of the bridge. I can see him explaining the plan to a wide-eyed Morgan and the rest of the seamen on the fore-casing. A couple of furtive looks in my direction shows their opinion of me — a cold-blooded bastard, taking advantage of an idiot.

'Hang on!' There is still one thing I can do, and I send a seaman below for an oilskin and a length of cod-line.

'Morgan!' I call down to the casing, 'tell him to strip to his underwear and wrap his clothing in this oilskin. You can send them across to him on a heaving-line. There is enough room on that rock for him to get dressed and it'll save him from freezing to death in wet gear.'

It is my one concession to his comfort, and I ensure that the seaman has had the foresight to produce woollen underwear and submarine sweaters in the parcel. Even so I don't envy

Pongo his ordeal in the icy wind as he tries to cling to his slippery perch and heave over a heavy mooring rope on his own.

There is little time to wrestle with my conscience, however, for already he is clambering down on to the swell of the ballast-tank and bracing himself to leap as far out across the full surge of that flood as he can. At least he knows enough to realise that to succeed he must reach slack water quickly before his strength fails.

I find myself holding my breath as he hurls himself into the water and begins to battle with the current. His strokes are wild and unorthodox, great windmilling thrashings which consume energy at an alarming rate, but seem to drag his body out of the flood in remarkably quick time. I relax a bit as I watch him splashing away like a mad thing, the rock getting nearer with each second. Within a minute or two he is climbing out onto the rock and waving back to us like a demented goblin.

A heaving-line snakes out from the fore-casing and, thanks to Morgan's skill, falls across Pongo's shoulders. A black bundle crosses the water and soon he is dressed in an assortment of warm clothing — so far so good.

'Stand by starboard!' I order into the voicepipe, and watch the antics of Pongo as he prepares to heave across the heavy rope that Morgan's men have secured to the heaving-line. It's one of the manilla hawsers that serve as breast ropes in normal times, and if he gets it over all right he should have no difficulty placing the very large eye over the rock. I tense with every haul he makes on the line, even bending and straightening my body as he does. Gradually the rope snakes across the water until he heaves the dripping eye over a bollard-like projection near the top. He straightens and waves happily, grinning all over his face.

The men on the casing don't need any orders from me to set them hauling in on the small capstan and I watch anxiously as the bows begin to move away from the shore; at last we are fighting our way against the current. If only the Germans hold off for a little while longer, for the light is getting stronger now and Pongo's features are plain to see, even at this distance.

I watch carefully, gauging the angle as she pivots until the bows point at a forty-five degree tangent across the fjord. The rope is stretched taut, sending sprays of water into the air. I bend to the voicepipe, forgetting all about Pongo and concentrating only on the right moment to add the thrust of the starboard propeller to the pull of the hawser. Suddenly the rope slackens and stays that way; the bows are moving without the aid of the rope now and I have to act quickly or lose control of the situation.

'Half ahead starboard!' I yell, gripping the voicepipe anxiously; it's all or nothing now. 'Port thirty!'

Round she comes in a tight arc, with the stern ironing out a glossy curve as it skids sideways away from the turn. Already we are moving out of the influence of the current and the rudder is biting as we gather speed.

'Heh! Hang on, Pongo, hang on!'

The shout wrenches me away from the voicepipe to find Morgan cupping his hands to his mouth and yelling across the water to where Pongo is obviously struggling to cast off the hawser — just what I told him not to do — even now one of Morgan's seamen is preparing to cast off the rope from this end.

He hesitates and straightens to look towards the agitated men on our casing, just as the rope tautens up sharply to finish the job he began, jerking off the rock and starting to slide away from him. Automatically, without thinking, he grabs at it, as though he is trying to rectify his error. We all watch speechless as he clutches the eye and is dragged from the rock.

I dare not stop the motor now, for if I do we will surely finish up on the rocks. I can only join the rest of the casing party and watch as he is hauled across the surface, struggling and splashing, too stupid to let go of the rope and getting ever nearer to that churning screw.

Morgan leaps into action and heaves in on that hawser in a vain effort to bring Pongo forward of the stern. Inevitably the rope drags him towards the swirling water under the 'planeguard and the slicing, ripping blades of the propeller. He disappears for a moment and is then thrust out astern like a bundle of dirty laundry, to roll over and over in our wake.

Turning away from the scene I direct my attention to navigating the boat. There is nothing any of us can do for him now, except write a letter to his relatives; so I peer across the compass to line the boat with the exit of the fjord. Pongo of all people; and I thought nothing ever happened to drunks and idiots.

Down on the casing Morgan's men are stowing away their gear in brooding silence, while others on the bridge are withdrawing to remote corners, everyone keeping his thoughts to himself. We are well on our way now, all thanks to that great, awkward oaf, who had even managed to die by his own stupidity. The knowledge that if he had only done as I had ordered he would probably still be alive is no comfort at all, for I have had plenty of opportunity to learn his ways and capabilities. It was almost inevitable that he would botch up the job: no good trying to shift the blame, for I knew full well the risk I was asking him to take.

I shrug the thought from me and concentrate on conning the boat towards the exit, vaguely aware that somewhere high above our starboard bow a light is flickering, and the sharp click of Bunts' aldis is replying.

'The dock is still on course, Swain,' he reports.

The cold bites into me as we swing out in a wide turn towards the narrow gate. Beyond I can see the roughened surface of grey water, pale in the growing light, with rolling, black clouds moving ponderously across the vee shaped exit. I coax her through easily enough and the bow lifts to the first swell as we emerge once again into open water. We are leaving behind the high cliffs, looming like huge, crouching animals each side of the channel, and buffeting out into a choppy sea. I relish the free, unhindered wind as it comes over the bridge-rail into my face.

The dark shapes of Morgan's men come climbing over the side and he follows behind to report the casing secure and ready for sea. They have lashed down the gear beneath the casing and checked all the lashings before coming up – a procedure carried out every time we leave port, and very important if we are not to have wires trailing aft to foul the propellers. They will have had to stow away the breast rope now that Pongo's foolishness has allowed us to retrieve it.

'Clear the bridge!' I order as the last of the casing party goes below.

In a moment I have the empty bridge to myself and I take a careful look round the horizon. There is a new feeling inside me now, a cold anger at the sight of the dock sitting ugly and solid in the water as we leave the shelter of the shore and bring it into view. I know I will not rest until I have sent it to the bottom. Just allow me one chance is all I ask, and I'll ram a full salvo of torpedoes right down their throats. They've killed my shipmates and bruised my body and pride, but now it is their turn, and I am going to take full measure out of their hides.

I jerk myself back to the present. 'Dive! Dive! Dive!' I shout into the gaping mouth of the voicepipe before shutting it off and striding aft to the tower. Before my head is below the rim the vents open with a roar of escaping air and we are on our way below. I clamp out the grey morning with the upper hatch and descend slowly to the control-room where the sour tang of the oily interior warms my nostrils and the crouching figures of men are hunched over their instruments with serious expressions and concentrating fully on what they are about. I am left in isolation to stand by the periscope, forming a picture of the enemy's layout in my mind. I check every detail carefully while there is still time, trusting the crew to perform their parts on their own, without any interference from me. 'Now — take hold of yourself and take charge of the attack. Look at the gauges as the needles sweep round and order periscope depth.'

'Thirty-two feet,' repeats the fore'planesman, and the needle settles easily on the ordered depth. We have sunk out of the sight of men, like some gruesome serpent, to slink along with our obscene cargo and murderous intentions.

'Up periscope!'

I make a complete turn with the lens, swinging past the dock and its escorts while I scan the whole area for a sign of other menacing vessels. There is none and I focus on the target again, this time lining up on that small cabin on the top. She is moving agonisingly slowly, with two big tugs out in front, straining their engines to hurry her along. Just astern a destroyer moves out to port on a tack that will take her right out on our port beam if she continues. Another escort is weaving a zig-zag on our side of the convoy, and he is the one I shall need to keep an eye on when we move in. I snap up the handles and the 'scope slides down into its well.

'Stand by, all tubes — slow ahead starboard!'

There is no need to alter course for she is moving nicely into position for us. It'll be a sitting target once we get lined up for a shot, and I can hardly miss at this range.

I go across to Formby and lean in over his arched back. 'Let me know if you hear anything on our port quarter,' I tell him. 'I don't want anything to come creeping up on us from that anchorage. They must be well alerted now and I can't imagine that they will not send something out from there to have a go at us.'

Returning to the periscope I snap my fingers and set my eye to the lens as it comes up, telling Bunts to put it on a bearing for me, so that I am looking right at the dock when the top breaks surface. There is hardly any deflection to allow for and already the edge of the target is coming into view and moving towards the cross-wires. There won't be a second chance this time and it is all happening fast. It is just like shooting at a slowly moving haystack — just fire all the torpedoes in one go and there seems no way we can miss. The panic will start afterwards, when Jerry comes racing in with his tail up, thirsting for vengeance.

'Stand by, all tubes!'

The order is repeated quietly and we are primed ready for the attack. My hands sweat as I watch the dock creep towards the cross-wires and I wait for the exact moment to fire. 'Here's for Soleway and Pongo, and for all the others who have died in the past few days,' I tell myself as the moment approaches. I'm aware that there is a foot or so of periscope sticking out of the water, but break all the rules and keep it there until the dock is centred in the lens. My fingers open and close on the handles and I lick my dry lips as the time comes.

'Fire all tubes!'

Repeater lights flicker on the panel and all the fish are on their way as the periscope slithers down and we are blind again. Formby is the only man in the boat who can tell us what is happening up there now, and he reports that all the torpedoes are running. It is all a matter of time before the sound of the explosions will confirm that we have earned our bread. In the meantime I'm working out a way to get us away from here as quickly as possible.

'One hundred and fifty feet!'

Let's get down out of it. With no reserves of speed to put a spurt on I have to rely on discretion rather than wiliness to get us out of danger.

'Starboard thirty — stand by for depth charging!'

I'm taking her straight for the last known position of the weaving destroyer; gambling on him being taken by surprise and still belting along at a speed that will not allow him to use his hydrophones. If I guessed right, I am doing the one thing he will not expect: running right at his throat — If I'm wrong — God help us!

The needles on the gauges show that we are deep enough to clear his keel when he comes over the top of us.

'Fast HE coming in from starboard,' reports Formby.

Here he comes, just as I anticipated and hoped he would, screws pounding away for all to hear on the next leg of his zig-zag. Now comes the next part of my gamble. If it works and we score at least one hit, he will wake up with a start and take a few moments to absorb the situation and figure out what has disturbed the peace of the morning. His own speed will carry him over us and by the time he has recovered his wits we will be slipping astern, towards the open sea, at the pace of an old age pensioner galloping to the post office on pension day.

No need for Formby and his hydrophones now as the destroyer comes right over the top and her propellers monopolise the atmosphere with their threshing pulsations.

There is a sound like someone dumping gravel on the pressure-hull and Formby whips the earphones away with a cry of agony. We all hear the sound, but hardly dare to admit to its meaning. Formby reports two explosions when he recovers from the shock to his delicate ears from the amplified sound. Two hits at least, whether on the target or the escorts is uncertain, but I must assume that it is the target, for the settings should have taken them clear of the escort and tugs. Even as we hope, a further explosion comes and we have hit with three out of six. It must mean success and there is a subdued cheer from somewhere up forward.

'What can you hear now?' I ask Formby, and he gives me a rueful look before gingerly replacing his earphones and training his antennae round to listen.

'That destroyer is still heading away on the same bearing, going astern of us.' He trains carefully, face set in concentration. 'Breaking up noises on red two five.' Further round yet, hands moving slowly. 'Fast HE − distant − on red nine five.'

That will be the other escort, manoeuvring far out on the other side of the dock. They seem to be well occupied elsewhere at the moment. Confusion must reign, for they would not expect a submarine to be daft enough to attack from our position; hemmed in by the shore and close to an anchorage which might conceal a host of German anti-submarine vessels. In fact they don't really allow for daft bastards like me.

'I must have a look!' I exclaim, and receive nods of approval from those about me. If ever we needed a boost to morale it is now, and I reckon the risk will be well compensated for if the periscope shows we have been successful.

'Where are the destroyers now?' I ask Formby.

'Still moving away and merging with the sounds of the target.'

'Thirty-two feet!'

The 'planes move and we are on our way to periscope depth. There is no doubting the eagerness of the 'planesmen for they turn to full 'rise' almost before my words are out. They are all as stupid as me.

At thirty-seven feet the periscope is raised and I am glued to the eyepiece. As the lens clears I am focused right on to the dock and see a sight that is beyond my wildest expectations. A pall of black smoke is lifting into the sky and the dock is slumped over on to one side as the busy little tugs fluster about it. Even as I watch the angle increases and flames are leaping up to embellish the smoke with orange light.

'Look, Bunts!' I hand the periscope over to him and he gazes into the lens with his mouth working like a cow chewing the cud.

When he straightens up there is a gleam in his eye that tells it all.

'We've done it, lads,' he says breathlessly. 'The bloody dock is a shambles and it's going down quickly.'

'No doubt at all this time,' I stress as I snap my fingers and the periscope descends once again. 'We have sunk it good and proper.'

This time a cheer does ring through the boat. It wouldn't have worried the police at Wembley on cup final day, but for us it is loud enough, for there are those who have earned it who will never hear it.

I must risk one last look, if only to establish where those escorts have got to. Up comes the 'scope and I peer out across the mottled surface. The dock is well down at one end now, losing its shape as the water swallows one end. I am hardly able to drag my eyes away from the glorious sight. The cold light of reason prevails, however, and I focus on the escorts. The distant one is hidden by the drifting smoke and I swing to the nearest one to find him plodding away, as though he is heading for home. Now − slowly, deliberately − I walk the periscope round in a full circle, holding my breath as I do.

Lady Luck seems to have smiled on us at last, for nothing is to be seen in all that vast area except the shoreline and the mess we have created beneath that heavy pall of smoke. Every minute we gain as we creep away is precious. The open sea stretches like a vast desert where we can hide in its opaque depths and leave all this trauma behind. I snap my fingers and we are blind again. A feeling of elation surges through me for a moment before I recall the problems that still lie before us.

XI

We settle on course to take us past the lighthouse marking the topmost point of that archipelago of islands and rocks that stands between us and the broad expanse of the North Sea and home. It's the long way round, and if I were a competent navigator I would most likely risk threading my way through the southern passage and shorten our journey by a hundred miles or so. I'm hoping the Germans think along the same lines and predict a break-out to the south, leaving us to pursue our quiet way northwards without any nasty little episodes to mar the trip.

Scouse Walker produces a feed of cheese and pickles which we eat with our tots. He seems to have accepted Pongo's role in the galley, though there will be no cooking this trip. We settle into three watches for the moment, and even Welks has stopped dripping for the time being. If I could shake off the sour memory of Soleway and Pongo things wouldn't be too bad at all as I leave the control-room and seek the comfort of a wardroom bunk.

If the Norwegians manage to fulfil their promise of getting a signal off to the Admiralty we should be receiving a message when we surface tonight. It'll be great to be in contact again and know that someone will be doing their utmost to provide help for our trip home. The prospect of air cover and possibly a surface escort warms me through, but I refrain from speaking my thoughts aloud for fear that they will not materialise. A hell of a lot can happen between here and home — things that I don't even want to think about.

I stretch luxuriously on the bunk and place my hands behind my head. My eyes grow heavy and the gentle surge of the water outside the hull lulls me into a shallow sleep.

'Coxswain to the control-room!'

The shout drives into my head like a rusty nail. For a moment I fight against it, as though it is a bad dream, but it comes again, even more urgently this time. Numbed by the unfairness of it all I scramble from the bunk, reeling with tiredness as I stagger aft to the control-room, bleary-eyed and furious.

'What's wrong now!' I snarl at them, as though blaming them for the new event that has wrenched me back to life.

'Fast HE approaching on two different bearings from north-wards. It sounds like two ships together on green three oh and one on red one five — coming in fast.' Formby's voice makes no allowance for my state of mind and he seems determined to hit me below the belt with each word.

'What do you think?' I ask morosely.

'No doubt about it this time, Swain. Destroyers — all of 'em. The sound is exactly the same as those of our friends back there — I'd stake my life on it.'

'Side echoes?' I ask hopefully, regretting my suggestion immediately when I see the pitying look on Formby's face — how can I presume to doubt his skills?

'Well, there's no need to sound so bloody cheerful about it,' I add by way of an apology. Surprise surprise, someone even laughs at my weak joke. Maybe those ships are independent of the others to the south and have no idea we are in the vicinity: it's a hope anyway.

'Up periscope!' One look is all I need to dispel that hope, for as far as those boys are concerned we are the only fish in the ocean and they are coming in to get us. Even as I watch they are fanning out to cover a wide area, I expect their mates are cover-ing the south passage, while these three sort themselves out for a long, persistent search for us. The two ships on our starboard side are ranging out to come in abreast of each other while the one to port slows to a speed that will allow her to use her listen-ing gear. She will direct her 'oppos' while they tear in with their depth charges. The whole set up looks too damned efficient for my liking.

My heart sinks with the periscope as it returns to the well. With batteries draining away and several hours of bad air already making things stuffy in the boat we are not in any position to play silly buggers. All we can do is creep along as we are, like a flaming ostrich with its head buried in the sand, hoping the danger will go away.

'One hundred and fifty feet!'

Down we go again, into the realms of cod and whiting and now I know how they feel when those trawlers come blundering along above their heads. Like them we have no friends here in the cold sea, with its deep valleys and frozen shores. There seems little point in altering course before they have located us.

'Slow HE approaching — dead ahead.'

'Another?'

'Yes — I reckon so.' Formby's voice is certain. 'Must be at least four of the bastards up there.'

It's obvious that they have tumbled to my brilliant strategy now and are coming in with determination and method. For a moment I consider turning south and trying for one of those channels — better to risk the rocks than the oncoming devastation that seems almost certain to arrive within a few moments. For one thing we haven't the speed to break away, and for another I have no confidence in my ability to negotiate the passage.

'All HE slow now, Swain. They have spread out across our bow to listen for us.'

It is as though the bastards have us on the end of a long string and are just playing with us for the sport of the thing. I go and look at the chart — the gap between the lighthouse and the mainland is roughly thirteen miles; rough is the word, for the Norwegian coast looks as though it has been chewed by a mad dog with dental problems. Halten Lighthouse is the name on the chart and if I stick to this course we will clear it by about three miles, and, in doing so, move inside the one hundred fathom line where there are soundings shown of twenty-two fathoms. In such places we could sit on the bottom, especially as the little notations on the chart show the bottom to be shingle. It restricts our diving capabilities of course, but first things first.

My optimism doesn't last very long though, for when I take the deviders and measure the distance we have to go before we reach that point they take four three mile strides and I reckon that to mean four hours at this speed. With those jokers up top it might as well be four thousand.

I toy with the idea of running for cover amongst the rocks and islands, then wonder if I have gone stark, staring mad to even contemplate such a suicidal move. It would be like tiptoeing across a hundred yards of barbed wire in stockinged feet. No, there is no point in deviating from our course yet a while; let us just continue slowly, with as little noise as possible and hope the Germans are hard of hearing.

'Swain!' It's Morgan's rough voice from the fore'planes. My eyes automatically look into the face of the depth-gauge and find the needle resting nicely on one, fifty feet — but he using 'dive' on his hydroplanes.

'What's wrong?'

'Don't know. Suddenly she wants to come up.'

'Easy enough.' My fingers move to the panel.

'No — hang on, Swain — I'm not sure — wait a second.' His worried tone arrests me before I begin pumping water all over the boat.

My eyes dart from his indicators to those of Guns on the after 'planes. On the face of it all seems to be going on as it should.

'What then?'

'Just a moment — there — see?'

See I do as the bubble on the spirit-level moves aft and the depth-gauge needle wavers before swinging clockwise. Now there is full 'rise' on the 'planes, and it is some time before the boat responds and begins to rise to her correct depth. Within seconds she is back to full 'dive' and struggling to reach the surface.

'Do your best,' I tell him, 'it's our slow speed and the fact that we are going through different densities of water. Try to keep her under control if you can; I don't want to use pumps or increase the speed for fear of waking up our friends up there. The important thing is to keep her down.'

This worry has been with me ever since we left the fjord. It requires a perfect trim to keep the boat under full control at this speed, when the hydroplanes have little effect. I hadn't done too badly, under the circumstances, but I had not counted on the outpourings of thousands of mountain streams and rivers to decrease the density of the sea in patches so that we get light and heavy as we move from one to another. To try to compensate with every alteration will result in chaos, even if I ignore the amount of noise involved when I use the ballast pump. No — my best plan is to try and maintain an average and hope the 'planesmen will cope by using their controls intelligently.

With that decision made we are soon porpoising between ninety and one hundred and ninety feet. I take a philosophical view of the situation and hope that our antics will confuse the enemy if they detect us — perhaps they'll take us for a pair of fornicating whales.

'I think they have found us, Swain.'

Formby's voice falls like a hammer to crush my optimism in one go. This is it then, if they have our number we are due for a determined and well formulated attack, with us as a sitting target, with no means of wriggling clear or of trying any fancy changes of course and speed to baffle the Germans. It's like setting the local hunt on the trail of a tortoise.

'Fast HE closing — red one five and green three oh.'

Here they come, the bastards. Plough on little submarine and try to stay in one piece when all hell breaks loose in a moment or two. Everyone is listening for the first sounds of those charging destroyers, tensed up to breaking point as fear grips our insides and turns our guts to water.

'Two hundred feet!' I order, more to have something to say than with any real plan in mind. Perhaps a few more feet will make it more difficult for them, at least our see-sawing antics might make them misjudge our depth — I've a feeling that we'll be performing even more impossible gyrations any minute now.

'Here they come,' says Formby and snatches the earphones away in anticipation of the first shattering explosions we all feel must come.

Now we can all hear them as the two destroyers come in together. God! if they plaster the area together how can we hope to survive? In the past we have always been attacked by one ship at a time, while her mate stood by listening and guiding her runs — this is something entirely new in our experience, and particularly nasty.

Thrush thrush thrush, here come the swine, right over the top, just as though we were on exercise and trailing the 'buffs' (floats which stay on the surface and mark our progress for training ships). In those halcyon days all they ever dropped was clangers. The whole boat seems to be holding its breath as the sound moves right overhead. I grip hard at the back of Morgan's seat, waiting for the earthquake that must follow, and praying that when it comes, let it come quick. I don't want to know anything about it. Let's not have a maniacal mêlée of flailing arms and legs, screams and panic, while icy water bursts in and hurls itself through the boat to smash and tear at us as we become like animals. If we have to die, then let us do it with dignity, and a little peace.

Nothing happens! The propeller sounds fade and die away while we sail on smoothly and reaction drains what remains of our resistance. I feel like screaming at the bastards for playing this cat and mouse game with us. What have they in mind? For Christ's sake!

'HE coming in from astern,' says Formby steadily. I must have missed some of his reports as the two destroyers charged on to make a wide sweep, but here they come again.

'What are they up to?' I murmur, half to myself, but Formby hears me, because he has snatched off his earphones again.

'It's a copy book attack, Swain. I don't see how they can miss.'

'Port twenty!' I order, and even remember to check that Bunts is making a note on the chart. The order is no more than a gesture, anyway, for the sounds of those propellers are already clearly audible to everyone.

'HE moving to starboard,' announces Formby. 'They seem to be trying to get at us from the starboard quarter, Swain.'

My port turn was fortuitous then. Accidentally we have presented our stern to them. I realise that we are no longer hearing them and move over to Formby while I try to puzzle out what the hell they are up to.

'HE moving across our stern — port to starboard.' His voice is puzzled now, matching my feelings exactly. 'They seem to be keeping their distance, Swain.'

Sadistic sods! I think to myself. I try to get a picture in my mind of what is happening up top. The formation of four destroyers as they came down from the north, all nicely spread across our intended course, followed by a classic attack, with everything pointing to complete success. Now they are moving about up there as though they have lost us, but I can't really believe that for their last run was smack on target and their diverging courses have left no doubt in my mind that they are fully aware of our position for they crossed over us with a precision that would have earned them accolades at any fleet revue.

Now they are moving together across our stern and keeping at a distance in the process, with their two companions standing off with their hydrophones trained in our direction, listening to the steady beat of our one propeller. They have us cold and yet they are reluctant to complete the job — why? It is almost as though they are waiting for us to make the first move, and perhaps I've obliged them by turning to port for it seemed to have the effect of getting them off our backs for a few moments.

This thought leads me back to the chart again and I study the course we are on and where it leads. An extension of the line takes it right into the mass of islands and rocks; at our speed the pattern changes very slowly, but if we stay on this course it won't be long before we are running into all kinds of navigational hazards. I don't think I've ever seen such a mess of natural hazards in one small area before. We have been running blind for some time now and I'm tempted to risk a look through the periscope.

'Can you give me a position for each of the ships, Formby?'

'Do me best, Swain.'

I wait for him to train his gear round in a full circle, listening with those precious, highly skilled ears of his for every slight clue that will provide a picture of the enemy's movements. Finally he straightens up and takes one earphone away.

'The two destroyers that attacked us are slowed down and on our starboard quarter — I'm not certain what they are up to — they seem to be just buggering about in a tight circle. The one that was on our port bow has moved almost dead astern and there isn't much noise coming from her at the moment, so I presume she is almost stopped. The last one is on her way to take up position to starboard – it's an assumption on my part, but the whole picture seems to show them trying to string out in some sort of line to starboard, as though to ensure that we don't break out that way.'

That's the picture I get too. They seem to be obsessed with the idea of keeping us turned towards that potential ship's grave-yard. Well, let's put it to the test and see what happens when I do a one eighty degree turn and try pushing through to the east.

With the helm over to port and our one screw adding its thrust we are soon facing back the way we came and I wait to see what effect it has on our persecutors. I haven't long to wait before Formby warns that the two nearest destroyers are work-ing up to full speed and swinging round to come for another attack. Further reports suggest that they have misjudged our position slightly and are heading to pass across our bow. I have a nasty feeling that even this is no accidental move on their part and only serves to confirm my suspicions that we are being herded towards those rocks by those well trained sheep-dogs up there.

This time the charges do come, two of them, as though to let us know that they will stand no bloody nonsense and we are firmly tabbed by their listening gear. I don't argue, and in a few minutes we are back on a westerly course and they are suitably placated; lying off contentedly while we plough on towards that jagged line of broken teeth. I can almost hear them purring as they sit there like cats with a mouse trapped in a corner.

Having confirmed our suspicions does little to solve the prob-lem of what it all means, however. I have never heard of a situ-ation like this before. Finding a submarine is hard enough, and holding on to her is no easy task when ships have to increase speed to carry out attacks, so when anti-submarine forces latch on to a target they don't hang about. Kill the submarine is the order of the day in such circumstances. Pound the area to hell with as many depth-charges as possible and don't let up until you see the blood and guts on the surface. To allow one to crawl along like this, albeit in a predestined direction, is to offer a chance of escape and no navy in its right mind gives even half a chance to a submarine – the whole idea of doing so is crazy – yet here are four front line destroyers of the most ruthless navy in the world doing just that.

I get a cold, nervous feeling down my back as I realise that I am being made to do exactly what they want. I can find little comfort in the fact that they haven't put paid to us in one or two substantial attacks, for it seems to me they are only prolonging the agony. If the boat was fully operational and we could use full power to dodge and weave our way out of a situation their action would have been a God-given opportunity, but now it is only torture.

I study the chart even more closely and decide that there isn't really a lot of choice between the menace astern and the one ahead, in fact the destroyers will most likely complete the job with a lot less agony than the rocks ahead. It's a long time since I looked through the periscope. Formby's reports are okay up to a point, but when it comes to working out a position with any real accuracy they leave much to be desired. The enemy seems to have settled in a semi-circle stretching from far north to just-off our port quarter and a little south of our position. They are close in too, pressing us further towards those waiting teeth. I wonder what would happen if we really had a go at breaking out. The whole thing is daft really, it seems neither side can win.

'HE closing, red one seven five — sounds like two ships.'

'More destroyers?'

'Don't think so, Swain. Sounds more like submarine chasers, smaller and slower than the destroyers.' He listens carefully. 'They are coming up from the south and I'd say they are those special little bastards specially designed for the job, with a big capacity for carrying depth-charges and all the latest detection gear.'

We exchange glances as the same thought comes to us both and we know the reason for the strange behaviour of our enemies. I kick myself for being so bloody stupid not to have realised it before. No hunter would or could have resisted the urge to complete the attack on a helpless quarry if he had the means of doing the job. The only possible reason they would have had for holding back and waiting would be for lack of depth-charges. They have most likely been carrying out runs on real or imaginary targets all over the place and are down to their final reserves — by chasing us into this trap they have laid it on for their mates coming up for the final coup-de-grâce. If I had chanced my arm it is possible that we could have sneaked away. Not now though. The real experts have arrived, all ready to show their mates how a submarine should be killed.

As though to confirm our thoughts Formby reports that the destroyers are building up speed and coming in for a final fling before these intruders take away the glory altogether. I think there is no doubt we are in for at least a token attack from them before they reluctantly hand us over to the tender mercies of their oppos.

There's no future in what we are doing and I feel I have to make some sort of gesture to show I'm still in command of my faculties; even if it is only to surface and run up the white flag; which seems the only real solution on the face of it. The boat is porpoising along, barely under control, and we are running blind towards an area of ocean that any sensible mariner would avoid like the plague. The hounds are after us with their engines pounding away and their depth-charges primed. It doesn't seem right to just plod along and wait for it all to happen.

'In port tail-clutch. Group up — full ahead together!'

There is a moment's hesitation while the helmsman looks at me to check that he has heard correctly, then the telegraphs ring, and almost immediately Welks is bursting into the control-room with a wild expression on his fat face.

'What the bloody hell are you doing?' he yells, as though I'm standing on the mainland. 'You'll rip all the packing out of that thrust block.'

'Yeah, I know,' I answer calmly, 'and the water will come pissing in again. Maybe you would like to go on creeping along like this while they plaster us with everything they've got?'

I unhitch the tannoy, now is time to let the crew in on what is going on, 'This is the Coxswain. I don't have to tell you that we are in all kinds of trouble and the Germans have brought up two more ships to pound hell out of us. Not too far ahead is a group of islands and rocks, and I think if we can get in amongst them they will be unable to carry their attacks without risking being wrecked, so I'm going to take a chance and run in there. I don't mind admitting that we are just as likely to hit one of those rocks as they are, but there is no future in plodding along out here with six ships on our tail. It means the engine-room will prob-- ably flood again, but there is a chance we can escape them and surface to pump it out again. There is one other advantage; that is we will be in shallow water and able to bottom if things get really out of hand — it's all I can think of in the circumstances, so bear with me and pray for a miracle. In the meantime, good luck and thanks for your efforts.'

The click as I switch off is like the final punctuation of all time. Welks steps back with a look of utter disbelief on his face as Formby calmly goes on with his reports, showing that on the surface things are livening up and the destroyers are shaping up for their runs. Our own speed moves up from that of a tired ped-estrian to that of a marathon runner, but at least the 'planes-men find it easier to control the boat and keep depth.

'I want some soundings, George,' I tell Formby. 'As soon as you can start giving me the depth under the keel. I don't think there is anything to gain by listening to those ships any more, there's nothing we can do even if we know where they are. I want to try and get a picture of the sea bed to tie up with the sound-ings on the chart.'

Those ships are not to be ignored now, though, and the first one comes ploughing in over us with the sound of an express train. Sweat breaks out on my forehead and there seems to be a chunk of iron wedged somewhere inside my stomach. I glance at the faces about me and see that they are not the faces of men I know, but of frightened strangers with the stench of death about them; eyes hollowed and glazed with fear, mouths that sag open and fingers that twitch and clutch nervously. Gone are the jocular, quietly efficient shipmates, to be replaced by anxious, frightened men, desperately wishing they could be anywhere but here.

I think some of us scream when the first charge thunders alongside us. The boat heaves over on her beam-ends, com-pletely out of control, and things are breaking loose to fall about as she staggers upright again and the crew scratch and claw their way back to their positions. We have a sharp bow-down angle, but the depth-gauges stay at roughly the same depth. It is the depth-charges controlling the boat now, heaving her bodily about like a toy in a bath. We poor humans are thrown about like so much garbage inside the bucking submarine, while the sounds of hell come from outside. Yet, even through it all, with my brain crying for sanity, I can think enough to realise that our sudden burst of speed has caused them to misjudge that first attack, and they seem to have got the depth wrong again — haven't we all?

The next attack comes — further away this time. They would do better to wait until the disturbance caused by the first attack has died down to get a better idea of where we are.

'Two-forty feet,' says a voice.

'Eh?'

'Two hundred and forty feet, Swain,' repeats Formby, frowning at my unprofessional acknowledgement of his first report.

I slump visibly, for a moment I had thought that it was a report from the 'planesmen. I move to the chart — two-forty divided by six is roughly forty fathoms; we are over the one hundred fathom line and, running my finger down the chart there is only one place I can see where the water shallows to that depth within the range our slow speed allows — south of a marker called 'Gimsan' on the chart. If that is the case, we are headed right in to an area of shoals, with depths marked as shallow as thirteen fathoms — seventy-eight feet.

'Bring her up quickly — fifty feet!' To hell with caution, we are running in to an area that looks like a disease on the chart, just waiting to rip the guts out of us if we plough on like this. It's all we have though, and if I'm right those German ships won't be able to follow us in for too far, let alone make attacking runs. Strange that the prospect of becoming wrecked on pinnacles of scraggy rocks doesn't seem as bad as being crushed by depth-charges — the result is the same and we will be just as dead at the end of it all.

'Five hundred feet!'

Bloody hell! I look closely at the chart and take back my outburst. The report is right on the nail when I compare it with what shows on the chart and I hardly dare to hope that I have made the correct assumption on this occasion. The depths hereabouts alternate from this depth to nought with gay abandon.

'Fast HE approaching from starboard.'

'Stand by for depth charges,' I order unnecessarily, and listen for the sound coming in from astern like the hoarse whisper of death.

Here it comes, that steady, even beat, menacing in its consistency as it grows in volume to fill the boat with sound and we can visualise the black hulls gliding over the top of us; the sharp keels not very far above the tops of our periscope standards.

A giant fist hits the boat amidships and our legs are pushed up into our bodies as the charges go off beneath us. Our climb towards fifty feet has saved us this time and the charges help us on our way at a mad rate. A jet of water, like a solid bar spurts out across the control-room and the lights die for a few seconds before recovering again.

'Keep her down!' I scream at the fore'planesman.

'I'm bloody trying, ain't I?' blurts out the poor bloke in his frustration as he tries to force his hydroplanes past maximum dive. The needle moves swiftly up to zero feet and she heaves and wallows as we broach to display ourselves for all the world to see.

The Germans must be having the time of their lives up there, as they watch our crazy antics. There's a crash overhead as a shell smashes into a chunk of superstructure. Madness, that's what it is, pure unadulterated madness — the stupid things we bloody humans get up to!

We force ourselves under again and the needle creeps round to thirty feet. 'Hold her there!' I yell. 'Up 'scope!'

They know exactly where we are now so I say to hell with the consequences and try to get a bearing — it's important I find out exactly where we are.

'Stand by to write down these bearings, Bunts.'

The periscope breaks surface and I am looking into a brilliantly clear sky, with watery sunshine gleaming on the surface and sparkling like strings of gems only a few inches from my eyes. I swing round to starboard and almost immediately focus

on a black and white tower, sitting square on a rock. I shout the
description and Bunts reads off the bearing from the back of the
'scope. I swing to port and find another to repeat the process.
It's as much as I can hope for, but I must take one more full
sweep before we go blind once more.

It's like the Spithead revue up there, with ships everywhere,
all chasing round while our last attacker is heeling over as she
tries to haul round in a tight circle. She's the eager-beaver it
seems, for the others are laying off, seemingly reluctant to risk
running on to one of the jagged rocks that pockmark the area. A
flash catches my eye and I am puzzled for a second or two before
the scene is obliterated by an explosion of white and orange and
the periscope dies on me.

'Down 'scope — fifty feet!'

Marvellous! Now I've lost the best of our two periscopes by
holding it up too long and allowing everyone up there to get a
range and bearing on us. I must be going out of my tiny mind.

'Fast HE approaching, red one four zero!'

That must be our persistent friend again; belting in to give us
another dose. Once again we brace ourselves and listen for the
beat of his props.

'HE moving right, across our stern — he's sheering off!'

'I've got to see — I've got to see! Up 'scope.' The attack periscope this time with its smaller lens and restricted view.

This time I'm focused on the last reported position of the
attacking ship, and there she is, swinging away in a wide circle,
spray flying from her plunging bow and glinting in the morning
sunlight. 'Now what?' I wonder as the periscope lowers into the
well.

'Fifty feet!'

Down we glide as I move to the chart with the slip of paper
that Bunts hands to me with the bearings on. I'm doing well
with my estimations it seems, for when I plot the bearings on to
the chart I can see that we are almost spot on where I thought we
were, and I can also see why that submarine-chaser didn't
pursue his attack. The whole area is a nightmare of broken
rocks and reefs, with the odd small island thrown in for good
measure. My guess is that the feeling on those German ships is

that anyone who can get through this lot and survive, deserves to.

Welks comes into the control-room wearing a scared, wild look on his face. He ignores the jet of water that is beginning to build up pressure again as we descend and plants himself squarely in front of me.

'We're flooding up aft and you've used nearly all the battery — we've had it, mate. For all our sakes; call it a day, and let's get up top. There is nothing more you can do.'

For once he is right. The boat has had it and time is slipping away. If I hesitate much longer it will be too late to do anything.

'Surface!' I order and the ERA's fingers move swiftly down the panel, admitting high pressure air into the ballast tanks. The hydroplanes go to full 'rise' and I station myself under the conning-tower hatch.

'Pass the word — everyone up top as soon as we are on the surface.' I turn to Welks, 'You must set the scuttling charges, chief; we are not going to give her to those bastards.'

'We are not going up!' says the fore'planesman. 'I can't get the bow up — she isn't responding, Swain.'

Helpless we watch as the needle on the depth gauge sweeps round the wrong way, steadily through forty, fifty, sixty feet, moving on, despite full 'rise' on both hydroplanes and a slight bow-up angle. We are sinking like a chunk of rotten wood.

'What's the depth?'

'Ninety feet under the keel,' answers Formby smartly.

Ninety feet! That bloody sunshine is only ninety feet away if we hit bottom here.

'Hold on everybody — we're gonna hit the bottom!' I brace myself for the impact. 'Stop both!'

The motors stop and we sink slowly, powerless, with just the slowing impetus of the dead screws. The Germans are completely forgotten now as all eyes focus on the depth gauge and its swinging needle.

XII

We hit the rock while still moving at something like six knots, and it is like slamming in to the side of a mountain. Everyone is thrown off his feet and the yells that come aft from the forward compartments tell me that there is something close to panic-stations up there, in the fore-ends. I pick my bruised body up and hurtle forward; passing several inert bodies on my way, while others are picking themselves up from the deck, or just sitting there, shaking their heads in bewilderment.

I can hear urgent cries and the ominous sound of water coming in under pressure. An acrid, nasty smell permeates the atmosphere and I am conscious of the angle of the boat becoming more acute as our bow sinks down, and we have a slight list to port. I have to fight my way past two soaking wet sailors as I go through the bulkhead door into the fore-ends.

In the forward part of the compartment men are struggling to shut the tube-space door, while a solid mass of water bursts in over them; threatening to sweep them off their feet. One look tells me that they are fighting a losing battle.

'Leave it!' I yell, 'leave it! For Christ's sake leave it! Get aft — through the bulkhead — it's our only chance — seal off the fore-ends.'

They don't seem to hear me, and I have to take hold of some-one's shoulders to heave him clear, away from the struggling mass of men. I have never known anything like the biting cold of that water as it sluices over me, freezing my genitals with an aching grip that makes me gasp with its intensity.

They don't seem to hear me above the roar of the water and already the fore-ends are filling. We have a few seconds only in which to get the hell out of here and shut the after bulkhead door. I scream at them the urgency of the situation.

'Get aft! Get aft! It's no good, I tell you!'

The angle of the boat steepens and we are pushed up against the bulkhead as we fight against the sloping deck. What's the matter with these stupid sods? Can't they see it is useless?

'Come on!' I snarl at them. 'If you don't come aft now, I'll bloody well leave you all here and save the rest of the crew.'

'Scouse and Smithy are in there!' yells a gaping mouth, inches from my ear, and I vaguely recognise PO Dickens, Soleway's second-in-command. 'We can't leave them there, Swain.'

The noise is overpowering. I can hear the fore-ends flooding up behind me. 'Where are they?' I scream.

He lurches aside and allows me to move into the gap. A struggling mass of humanity is undulating somewhere in that cauldron of swirling water, like clothing in a washing machine, and it is difficult to see if they are still alive or dead, but one thing is sure — it's them or us and the rest of the crew.

'Leave them!'

'Fuck off!' yells Wally Barnes, and I realise who the other struggling man is. 'You go if you want — we're gonna save our mates.'

'They're dead, you bloody idiot! Can't you see that? It's only the water that is moving them about like that.'

Dickens seems to get the message, and his white face swings on me, haggard and grief-stricken, pausing for a moment as he looks deep into my eyes, as though to see if I am lying — decides that I'm not and yells at Wally, 'Come on, there's nothing more we can do for them.'

Barnes might have heard him, but makes no move to obey. He is up to his shoulders in the icy water, reaching down into the deluge to reach the bodies below.

'I've got one! — I've got one! — Help me!'

Automatically we bend and shoulder our way in beside him, to reach down with him. I grab some clothing and heave. For a moment it's useless, then all at once, it breaks free from whatever it was caught on and a solid, slumped body comes surging up with the water and we fall back into the fore-ends as the weight is taken by the water pressure. We fight together, the three of us, dragging the limp form up the slope of the deck

towards the bulkhead door. The water is waist deep even midway across the compartment and threatens to tear us away from
foot and hand holds.

We reach for each projection to find something to haul our
bodies aft with and the door seems miles away, above our heads.
I pray that someone doesn't shut it before we get there, because
I can see water washing over its sill already.

'Move!' I urge. 'We have got to shut that door before the sea
reaches the batteries.'

In one way the water is our saviour, for it lifts the dead weight
of our burden and helps us to struggle aft and upwards, towards
that gaping door. Gasping and groaning, we heave and haul the
body through the door, into the compartment beyond, out of
reach of the rising water — for the moment. There is no time to
spare though, for a small cataract is pouring over on to the deck
already.

'Help me to shut the door,' I breathe to Dickens, and together
we move forward. There is a hinged clip hanging down on the side
to hold the door open and I reach in to lift it clear. I can get at it all
right, but I can't lift it clear from this compartment, because of
the pressure holding it firmly in place. There is nothing for it but
to clamber through into the fore-ends again and use both hands.

'Hang on to me when I go through,' I shout to Dickens, only
to find that he has anticipated me and is already climbing
through, himself. Grimly I cling to him as he battles against the
water to struggle with the clip.

'Here, let me go through as well,' says another voice in my
ear, and I swing to see the gun-layer at my side, with Formby
close behind him, adding their weight to the situation. It's all up
to Dickens though. He has to push that door back a fraction
before he can release that clip, and that small fraction is a
massive obstacle as his feet slide on the deck and he tries to
balance in the swirling water, against the slope of the deck.

We try to help him as much as possible, but it'll do no good if
we all go bunching through the door. The baleful glow of a light
in the fore-ends shows the black water rising and rising. Already
it reaches the deckhead at the forward end. Soon even this door
will be useless if we don't get it shut.

Suddenly the clip flies off and Dickens is thrown backwards into the fore-ends and the door swings heavily into the opening. In desperation we strive to push it open again and I can see him wallowing in the water as he struggles to find his feet and crawl back to us. We heave and fight against the mounting pressure, but, despite our combined efforts the door pushes against us, closing the gap until it is much too small for a man to get through. A clutching arm comes through, fingers flexing and grasping at life, as though it can be clutched from thin air. The door clamps on that arm and a frightful scream is wrenched from its invisible owner.

No efforts of ours will ever shift that door — the screams come persistently as the edge of metal bites into the flesh, gnawing at it until only the thickness of the bone keeps it ajar. The water is thrusting through the gap and this time it is Formby who states the obvious.

'Leave him, Swain. Come on, it's time we were out of here; I can smell gas already.'

The two of them grab my arms and drag me aft with them. I can smell the sickly, sweet smell of chlorine gas as the sea water reaches the batteries. Back through the passage we go, into the control-room where other shapes are waiting.

'The engine-room!' yells Formby. 'It's the only chance we have now, don't hang about — get aft, into the engine-room.'

Dumbly we follow him up the sloping deck, shadowy figures moving in the baleful glow of the emergency lighting. The cold is shattering, penetrating into our bones and sapping away our energy. Breathing is an effort and I know only too well how soon the will to struggle for survival will diminish as the air gets foul and lassitude takes over. It'll seem easier to die then, than face an impossible future and the need to force a reluctant body to make an effort.

Guns and Formby are still with me, and for some reason I am still dragging that soggy body along with me, even though it is quite obvious to anyone with half an eye to see that it is dead. I glance back once more to see the water still flooding in through that distant door with the pathetic arm still waving at me. The sight chokes me for a moment, and, despite the madness of it all I can feel the overpowering grief press down on me.

I am being bundled through into the engine-room now, amidst a mass of labouring men, into a stagnant, metallic cavern where the inert heart of the monster sleeps in cold ignorance of all the catastrophe its ineptitude has caused. All about me shapes move like ghosts, unrecognisable as humans and hiding their fears beneath a facade of industry.

The door clunks shut behind me and for the first time there is a substantial barrier between me and that wild, black, invading water that contaminates and defiles the place where we ate, slept and laughed. It has turned the boat from a living thing with warmth and light into a dank sewer; more suited to the twitterings of rats than the talk of men.

The engine-room seems choked with men, mostly crowded in the centre passageway, hemmed in each side by the diesels and the electric motors. There is the sound of water here too, and I have no doubt that the leaking gland has been wrenched open again to add its menace to everything else. As yet the water is well below deck level and confined to the bilges, but soon it will come seeping up through the plates, bringing with it the scum and filth that will coat our bodies and all else that it comes into contact with as it grows up insidiously to equalise the pressure inside the boat with that of the water outside. At this point it will stop rising, lapping against our chests and undulating along the compartment with every move we make, freezing the marrow in our bones and choking our lungs if we slip and swallow it.

In general service ships it would all be over now. The sea would have finished it all, once and for all, and men would no longer need to struggle on for survival, but would have succumbed to the merciful oblivion of death. Submarines don't allow that, for even when the sea has won the battle, and buoyancy is destroyed men can still crawl into corners and hope for life. They can become like animals with only the one selfish desire to reach fresh air and safety — no matter who they tread on in the process. Better to die quickly and quietly, I think, for even if we reach the surface we will die in the icy sea, away from the sight of men and in the middle of a cruel ocean that holds no mercy for frail creatures like us who dare to invade her realms to fight our wars.

It is while my mind is plunged into these sombre depths of depression that a memory comes struggling through. A vision of watery sunshine gleaming on a sparkling surface of a brilliant sea. That last glimpse through the periscope of a glorious morning with its promise of warmth and comfort and a future for all of us. I'm the only man in the boat who saw it — all the others can remember is the drab, grey world of the fjord. If anyone in the boat has the reason to push on for life it is I, and it is up to me to convince them that it is worth trying. Ninety feet — that's the depth — nearly, but not quite the three-figured depth where people talk of no hope for escape. Ninety to the sun — it's well worth fighting for.

There is a more insidious enemy now, more intractable and uncertain with its unknown quantities of claustrophobia, coldness and the weakness of the human body when asked to function in conditions it was never meant to cope with. We have been dived a long time and the air is bad. There is no heating, so the cold clamps down on our bodies with a relentless grip, squeezing the strength and will-power out of us. We are all different in temperament, stamina and mental capacity, so each man will be affected in a different way by a situation they have no conception of. The strong can dissolve into shattered weaklings who have to be helped by their comrades, who have their work cut out looking after themselves. A well-organised crew of co-ordinated, functional seamen are suddenly a mixture of individuals unless there is a nucleus of strong minded men to keep them working together — I have to find that strength and sort out others who will be able to back my efforts to bring order to chaos and hope to despair.

These thoughts come as I struggle through the mass of bodies engaged in various self-imposed pursuits, the aims of which are known only to themselves. Two or three are trying to rig the twill trunk (a canvas cylinder that frames the escape hatch and can be brought down and fastened to the deck with four lines, so that the lower rim hangs about three feet off the deck. When this is done the whole compartment can be flooded up until the pressure equalises and leaves an airlock in the top of the compartment where men can stand with their heads and shoulders above waterlevel. The trunk can then be flooded right up to the hatch, allowing it to be opened by some brave soul who climbs up the inside and back again to report his success. All pretty marvellous — in theory.

My eyes are getting used to the emergency lighting now and shapes are beginning to take recognisable form. Sounds are starting to make sense and sort themselves out so that I am able to take stock of what is going on about me, to some small degree.

'What the 'ell are you doin', Dinger?' says a voice from the shadows.

''Avin' a piss.'

'Eh, you dirty bastard!, we'll all be standin' in that lot soon.'

'Well I'm warming it up, ain't I!'

Further aft, where the motors leave a lot more space in the passageway and there are fewer hard projections to knock against, I stop and try to look about me to get an idea of what is going on and who has reached this sanctuary with me. Despite my fears and the general chaos that seems to exist there appears to be some sort of order starting to show through. At last I see someone who will help me to build to some real co-ordination.

'Sparks!' I croak hoarsely, for my throat is choked and tight.

He stares at me for a long moment in bewilderment, and I realise that there are two types in the engine-room — those who had been in the two after compartments when the boat hits the rocks and have stayed dry and reasonably clean — and others, like me, who have fought a hard, scrambling battle, half drowned in the oily, freezing water and are covered in filth from head to foot. I am about to tell him who I am when he suddenly recognises who this blackfaced, white-eyed minstrel is and his mouth grins widely as he claps me on the shoulders with a hearty hand that almost floors me.

'Swain! Thank the Lord for that! I thought you had had it.'

'Not yet I haven't. We are gonna have to organise this lot somehow and try to get them out.'

'Who's that?' asks another voice, and Bunts comes into view from somewhere, 'Bloody hell, is that you, Swain?'

Self-consciously I wipe a hand across my oily features, making things even worse in the process. 'Yes, it's me. What have you got there?'

The signalman holds up a mess kettle and places it beneath my nostrils. 'That'll bring the colour back into your cheeks.'

'Rum!' I blurt out. 'Whose idea was that?'

'Guns thought of it,' says Kirby, 'and I went round the control-room with him and Morgan — we've collected all the spare emergency lights and DSEA sets. They are all piled up in the strokers' mess.'

It's my turn to grin widely. 'Thank God for blokes like you. I hope you haven't dished out too much of the bubbly.'

'Give us credit, Swain.'

'Yeah, okay, I should have known — thanks, lads.' I accept the offered cup and drink deeply of the fiery spirit. I know the experts say that this is exactly what I shouldn't do, but the warmth spreads through me to take away the worst of the numbness so it can't be all bad; maybe later I'll regret it, but I have only enough will to think of the moment now.

It's all very 'stiff upper lip' stuff and I'm going to have to bring them back to reality in a minute or so, but for the moment I savour the liquid and look about me. It's not what I see that stops me in mid-gulp, it's what I hear above my head. Some-where up there water is surging through the casing and the significance of that sound seeps in to my addled brain. I've been a submariner long enough to know that there should not be noises like that at ninety feet. A glow of cautious optimism spreads through me, and it's not just the influence of the rum.

'What sort of angle would you say the boat is lying at, Sparks?'

The inflection in my voice causes him to exchange glances with Bunts and their eyes light up with interest as he looks at the way our bodies lean back to compensate for the sloping deck and the way a piece of rag some stoker has hung on a wheel hangs clear at something like twenty-five degrees.

I try to visualise the shape of the boat and its length overall, something over a hundred feet from the bridge to the stern and the same forward. Two hundred feet — at this angle there must be a section of the stern sticking out of the water. We must be sitting on a rock amidships, with all the weight of the flooded forward compartments holding her nose-down, like a bloody see-saw.

'The stern's awash,' says Firth. 'At this angle there must be a few feet showing above the surface.'

The excitement in his voice warns me that it is all too easy to expect too much from the situation. Before the war *Thetis* had her stern stuck out of the water after she hit the bottom and only four men out of a hundred or more got out alive. Already the air in the engine-room is rank as we crowd together in less than one-third of the normal living space.

There is no time to stand about and ponder and I take a deep breath in preparation for bellowing out orders as loudly as I can — the result is pretty pathetic — for one thing, people don't normally bellow orders on submarines and, for another, my throat has contracted to about half its normal size.

'Everyone stop what you are doing,' I croak, and no one takes a blind bit of notice. I'm about to try again when a hand lands on my shoulder and almost sends me sliding down the sloping deck.

'Allow me,' says the deep, resonant voice of Stoker PO Finney, carefully lifting me back to my feet again, by the simple process of grabbing two ham-fisted handfuls of my clothing and hoisting me upright and to one side.

For once in his life he is no more scruffy than those about him, and his deep, gravelly voice overpowers all else. The nearest equivalent I know is the deep-throated blare of the *Queen Mary*'s siren.

I can see the immediate effect of his bark as he moves aft, half sliding — half scrambling down the incline. Men move back to squeeze their bodies into any corner that will allow them to lean or sit against the slant of the boat. Some climb on to the diesels and sit on the cold metal, like owls in a tree. In a moment the centre passage is clear — except for one crouching shape near to the twill-trunk, straightening up slowly, to stand, leaning against the slope — glaring aft at me with baleful eyes.

Welks' hair hangs over his face and his shoulders hunch, making him look more ape than man. Facing aft against the slope he has to stoop and the effect is to make him appear even more monkey-like. All along the compartment men have settled into silence; watching and waiting expectantly. The only other moving person is Finney, who, having reached the bulkhead, turns to begin making his way up the slope towards us — coming up behind the Chief ERA's back.

I feel a sinking despair as I realise that even in these circumstances my old enemy is not going to relent. It is written in his face as he lunges towards me; full of menace. Now is no time for personal clashes, for time is of the essence, and unless we keep going with our attempts to escape everyone will lose out. I decide to take the bull by the horns.

'If you're going to co-operate, Chief — okay — if not, get out of the way and let me get cracking.'

'We were bloody cracking until you came into it. We have already rigged the twill-trunk, and even you must see that the quicker we are out of here the better.'

'We won't need the trunk,' I say steadily. 'If you listen you can hear the waves up top and at this angle and depth my guess is that the hatch is above water.'

I'm chancing my arm now, basing my assumption on a mental picture built up from pure speculation. If the depth is more than ninety feet the hatch will still be under water and I will be able to open it, because it is only a few inches below the surface. Once the sea starts coming in there will be no stopping it as it fills the compartment, and if the boat is resting on a precarious ledge or merely holding this position because of the displacement of water inside her, the added weight will sink her completely. Nonetheless, logic is on my side; because the twill-trunk will not work at this angle.

Welks throws his arms up in disbelief, 'You're mad!' he splutters, turning to the others for support as he rants on. 'You'll drown the lot of us with your stupid ideas. We've gone along with you up to now, and look where it has got us. For Christ's sake let's do it by the book!'

'Belt up!' rasps that deep-throated roar from behind him, and he turns to find Stoker Petty Officer Finney looming over him. There is no doubting the threat in his voice and a shadow of anxiety clouds the belligerent features of the ERA.

Welks came into the service as an artificer and was promoted automatically, as is the way with artificers. Finney on the other hand has had to crawl up through stoker, to stoker first class, to stoker petty officer over a long period and in slow, difficult stages, and it shows in his blunt features and tough exterior. He spends little time in the mess — much preferring to hob-nob with his stokers, aft in their tiny little quarters or in the engine-room. His past is marred by several demotions, following all manner of misdemeanours. I have only known him as a PO, but no-one — least of all myself — ever doubts his overall competence.

On one occasion I overheard the First Lieutenant talking to him like a father, following an episode that almost had him demoted again. Why was he so irresponsible? Jimmy had wanted to know, and Finney had shrugged his shoulders and offered no reply. Later I overheard him repeating it all to some of his stokers.

'Irresponsible!' he was saying derisively. 'I could teach him somethin' abaht irresponsibility — I'm an expert at it. Believe me, lads, if you're on the bottom rung of the ladder there's nowhere to fall. If I go rahnd guts achin' abaht promotion I'd be grey by now. Remember one thing though; never let them think you're an idiot. Slope along easy most of the time, but be there in the right place, at the right time, and they'll all say, "Old Finney might be a skate, but 'e knows his bloody job."'

Right now is one of those times, I hope; for I need his gruff voice and the loyalty of his stokers. Looking at him now as he shapes up to Welks I know I'm home and dry where he is concerned. The ERA has no doubt either, for, after a moment of hesitation he backs down and steps back against the engine, allowing Finney to come through.

'What's the drill then?' asks the stoker PO.

'I reckon the hatch is above water,' I say, with a query in my tone.

He squints up at the hatch with his fishlike eyes wavering about like jellied eels, as though gauging the slope of the boat, before shaking his head, 'Hard to tell for sure.'

'I reckon it is,' says Bunts.

'So do I,' I agree, 'but I'd like to be a bit more certain before we open it up and chance letting half the North Sea in.'

'Hang on,' says that hard, gruff voice, and Finney shuffles past me in the direction of the stokers' mess. A moment and he is sliding back towards us, holding a small brass brooch – a replica of *Scavenger*. 'I made this for one of the lads; it only needs the chrome finish now, but I made it to scale, so we can use it for a model.'

I latch on to it like a leech. It is a perfect model, with a fantastic amount of detail etched into it.

'Where do you reckon the hatch to be?' I ask.

He points to a position roughly midway between the bridge and the stern. 'There to within an inch or two.'

Eagerly we seek out a flat piece of shelf on the side of the motor and place the model nose down, at the angle of the boat. Finney measures roughly half the boat's length with a pencil and marks it on a piece of wood batten. He places the mark upright against the model, 'I reckon that to be about one hundred feet.'

The mark comes to a point just aft of the bridge and seems to leave the hatch barely above water level, with the tail sticking out to expose the hydroplanes. The position of that hatch is very doubtful, and depends largely on my assessment of the depth being correct at ninety feet. Even so, we are going to ship water with every wave if there is a swell up top.

'Not much to play with,' I grunt. 'No time to ponder though, the cold is getting worse and so is the air. I want everyone wearing a DSEA set, or at least a life-belt, and line them up aft, towards the stern. When the hatch is open you and I, Finney, will see them out one at a time. We will try to sit on the stern for as long as we can, so that we stand a chance of keeping together; the air-bags on the escape sets will keep us afloat when we do have to get off.'

Like a lot of bloody lemmings they shuffle aft to line up, ready to follow each other out into the icy North Sea. I move to the hatch and watch them settle with their eyes focused on me.

'All right, stand by, I'm going to open it up. Go out quickly and quietly, and climb aft on to the stern, if you can.'

It's all in the lap of the gods now, and I reach up for the hatch with one last prayer on my breath.

XIII

Thanks to the effort of Firth and Bunts everyone is fitted with a DSEA set, and as I make ready to open the escape hatch, I check that the crew are in position before I start taking the turns off one of the wheel-clamps.

'When it's open, you and I will take up position, one each side and push them up through, Finney.'

'Ar — okay, Swain.' The deep voice is comforting as he stands close behind me, while I work, standing on the second rung of the ladder.

The wheel seems to take an age to come right off, and then I begin to unwind the other one. In the centre of the hatch is a small lever which controls an air vent; for a moment I am tempted to use it to establish whether it is in fact under water. Common sense stops me, for I realise that the pressure inside the boat is enough to prevent water from coming through such a small orifice. Any thought of waiting for the pressures to equalise is unavailing when I consider how long it would take to do so. It is one thing to vent air out of the small area remaining when the twill-trunk is rigged, but quite another to cope with the whole compartment. The only way to do the job is to open the hatch in one go, and use that pressure to force the hatch open. It should fly open when the clips are released.

The second wheel is off now and I freeze for a few seconds, at a loss to understand why it remains shut. I look down into the upturned features of Finney who shrugs his shoulders as if to say, 'Don't look at me, mate. I don't understand it either.'

On the face of it there is nothing holding that hatch shut against the pressure inside the boat, unless there is water lying heavy on top of it; but that doesn't make sense, for even if I have misjudged the depth it must still be shallow up there. I decide it is a case of brute force and ignorance and climb up two more rungs so that I can place my shoulder under the hatch and straighten up, using all my strength. Finney has climbed up behind me to place his hands on my rump, ready to add his ten-pennyworth.

I brace up hard against the cold metal, take a deep breath and heave. For a second nothing happens, then all hell breaks loose. The hatch leaps open as though it had waited purposely for me to get into this position. Like someone charging a locked door that suddenly springs open my whole body shoots out through the opening into brilliant sunlight.

Desperately I try to stop myself and drag my body back into the boat again, but I am already three-quarters of the way out and another man is pushing up behind me. I scramble clear, clinging to the holes in the casing as a huge wave bursts over me and threatens to tear me away from my hand-holds.

I fight my way back to the hatch where the black shape of someone is climbing out, and I try to help him. It is not much help though, for I am finding it difficult to hold on myself as a series of waves come leaping in at me, blinding me and beating against me with devilish persistence. Gradually I work myself around until my back is towards the weather and my vision clears a little.

What I see almost makes me wish I had not succeeded, for water is pouring over the lower rim of the hatch and struggling, gasping men are fighting their way through one after another — the top half of a man emerging before the legs of the preceding one have got clear. Now I can work at them and grab handfuls of clothing to heave them clear. The wind howls and the stern is pathetically small amid all that white water. There is hardly any casing to hold on to.

'Keep together — your sets will keep you afloat — try to stay still!'

A shuddering jar almost shakes me free and to my horror I feel the boat move. There is no doubt, the boat is slipping away and the hatch is already half under. The men are having to fight more desperately to get out against the solid mass of water pouring in on them. The murderous bloody sea is determined to finish her before everyone can get out.

'Come on! Come on!' I'm yelling at them, up to my waist in water, with waves smashing over my shoulders and icy wind knifing through my wet clothing.

Agonisingly slowly they struggle out; a man is crying great sobs as he strives against the water, one shoulder clear, but caught up somewhere below. The more he struggles the worse it gets.

'Go back a bit,' I yell at him.

'I can't! I can't!' he screams at me. 'There's someone pushing up behind me.'

With a gigantic effort I heave my body upright, until I'm sitting on the casing and able to place my feet on him to push him back down again. He is spitting filth at me as I force him down, tearing his fingers away as he fights against me — terror and hatred on his face.

At last he wrenches free and falls into the boat; for a moment the hatch gapes empty and I start to go down into it. Before my feet reach the top rung of the ladder they are pushed roughly aside, and the wild, twisted features of Welks come bursting through. Nothing will stop him as he comes heaving through, with no other idea in mind, other than to get out of that hole. He rips and tears his way out, panting and grunting like a wild boar — oblivious to all else, until he is on the casing and clinging like a huge, wet seal, wide-eyed and shuddering.

The submarine lurches violently as another head comes through the hole. I feel myself being dragged away from the deck as the hatch slips lower and lower into the sea. I try to grab the outstretched arm of the next man, but already the boat is slipping away. Pleading eyes stare up at me through the water as the boat gives a final lurch and sinks.

We are left struggling on the surface, like garbage in our yellow DSEA sets and black clothing. Hoarse shouts and coughs are the only signs that men are alive in this desolate waste. Overhead shrieking seagulls yell their derision at us. There isn't much struggle left in me now, and the cold clamps on my body with a relentless grip; willing me to submit and allow myself the luxury of giving up the fight and find the peace and tranquillity of death.

Close by someone is coughing, harsh, racking barks, and instinctively I swim in the direction of the sound. Waves burst over my head, choking me and tumbling me about like a bag of washing. The world is narrowed down to an area no bigger than the reach of a man's arm and the only distance is upwards into that pale sky that shows through the curtains of spray whenever I am heaved over on to my back.

I bump into something and reach out desperately. Fingers intertwine with mine before gripping hard. Gasping and spitting I fight my way round to see who I have lurched into and come face to face with Welks. For a second or two fury overcomes all else and I almost scream my rage at him, but the sea is contemptuous of the petty differences of men and hurls us together into an embrace from which there is no escape. Locked together we are whirled round and round by the sea. If he is alive there must be others.

The next time my mouth is clear I yell; a pitiful, plaintive sound that is lost in the scream of the wind and the roar of the sea. Only the seabirds have voices to carry above those wasted surfaces, and they seem to pick up my cry and mock it with their cruel chatter.

I shout again and again, searching with stinging eyes across the tops of foaming waves in an attempt to see beyond the few yards that is the limit of my visibility. Welks makes no effort to help and seems content to remain passive in my arms, moving his own in a slow swimming motion, as though unconscious of what he is doing. It doesn't bother me at all. I don't want to share anything with this man. My only hope is to find that someone else has survived.

Soon there is no strength left for shouting and I lapse into a silent struggle, my arms automatically pulling at the sea in a vain effort to swim nowhere — just to keep moving is all I must do to stay alive. Stop moving and the end will come quickly.

My eyes are useless now, closed for much of the time, and stinging pools of agony when I force them open. The DSEA sets are all that keep us from drowning, I no longer have the will to control my breathing and I swallow sea water over and over again. Bumping and tumbling together we allow the sea to drive us along in any direction, alone and lost in the sadistic surf.

Hope fades and it seems that to struggle on is to prolong the agony, for the sea has us both as surely as if we were ten fathoms down. There is nowhere to swim to, no one to find us and no other human left in the limits of our pitiless world. Far, far away people are warm and comfortable, oblivious of these two discarded shreds of humanity, and it matters to no one that we will drift in these alien seas until our bodies bloat and decompose, and those shrieking birds feed on our eyes and shout their superiority to the north wind.

All the strength is gone from me now and I roll over on to my back like a dying fish. My arms move only with the motion of the water, without any will of their own. The dead weight of Welks hangs on me like an encumbrance willed on me by years of selfish living — atonement for my inadequacies. A strange peace is coming over me, as though there is nothing left in the world for me to bother about and the whole burden of living has been lifted from me.

'Argh!'

The sound comes close to my ear, an urgent, grunting noise; not really human at all, although I know it comes from Welks. I ignore it, for the sound of his voice is offensive to me and nothing he can do or say holds any interest for me.

'There — look!' the voice persists and the arms tighten desperately about me, tugging at my clothing.

'Shove off!' I rasp.

'Look, Swain!' His voice is stronger now, and filled with anxiety. I can feel him struggling with renewed vigour, pulling at me while his feet pump at the water. His face is close up against mine, pleading for me to take notice. Reluctantly I force my eyes to focus and find myself staring up at a solid chunk of rock, not ten feet away. Together we struggle towards it, and almost without any real effort on our part the tide washes us up on to a scraggy chunk of flint-like granite. Separately now we clamber up on to a ledge, away from the clutching fingers of the sea, to stretch out on the frozen snow.

It would be easy to just lie there and rest, free from the

choking sea and blustering waves. From somewhere inside me a spark of optimism flickers and forces a will to fight back into my protesting brain. Even to get into the lee of this rock would be something. Stiffly I clamber up to half stand with my shoulder against the rock, straightening slowly until I am standing more or less upright.

I completely ignore the slumped figure of Welks as he lies there, motionless. I can do without that bastard now, and forever more. Taking stock of my position an extreme effort to sidle along to a jagged corner that seems to offer some kind of shelter if I can get around it.

Ice is freezing white on my eyebrows and beard, my teeth chatter and my face aches with the cold. The wind groans like a sick organ through the crevasses and pinnacles somewhere above my head. The clothing on my body is stiffening up as it freezes along with everything else. Each step is a tortuous movement as my joints ache protestingly for not being allowed to seize up quietly. There is no feeling in my hands or feet and I shuffle along like a zombie until I reach the corner.

There is no describing the glory of the moment I step out of the wind. Just to stand there in the peace and quiet of that sheltered place is beyond belief. It seems that biting wind has gnawed into my bones for an eternity and turned them to ice. Here, out of its cruel blast a man can breathe, think and see again.

There is a large plateau too with pieces of scrub clinging to it in a desperate fight for survival. It represents some sort of life and gives hope to one who had been ready to submit so recently. This barren, lost outpost of uncompromising rock may never have felt a human foot before, but it is home to me now. Amazing what frail life-lines a man will hang on to in circumstances like these.

Movement is easier now. I can step away from the wall of rock, to angle out towards a bluff that hides another part of this small island. Something drives me towards it with a determination to find out what is on the other side. The land slopes down gently to the sea on this side and the ocean looks calm and innocent on this side of the rock, a pale green with hardly a ruffle to mar its surface.

Now the rock wall slopes down to a low profile of jagged toothlike hillocks, and as I come towards them I can see a shelf opening out on the other side. I see something too; a sight that makes me gasp. A group of small black shapes are there, tiny moving figures that look like seals, but the yellow patches tell me that these are no seals; these are the living members of *Scavenger*'s crew with their DSEA sets still strapped on.

As I go through one of the gaps in the teeth someone sees me and arms begin to wave. The tiredness and pain are remote now as I stagger towards them. Someone has left the group and he takes shape as we get closer, until there is no mistaking the squat figure of Bunts. We need no words as we meet and clasp each other. Others are coming up now, and I count five in all; so with Welks and myself that makes seven survivors out of a crew of forty odd.

'Bloody hell!' croaks Bunts, staring over my shoulder.

I swivel to follow his gaze. A grotesque, half crawling, half staggering figure is coming through the same gap, arms out-stretched as he falls, pick himself up again and stumbles on. Silently we watch him stagger blindly on in a pathetic zig-zag. His mouth sags open and his head hangs back as though he is looking at the sky. He has no notion of where he is or where he is bound — a dead man walking with a crablike, shambling gait.

Near to we can hear him gabbling incoherently, lips quiver-ing as the senseless noises come from his gaping mouth, then he realises he is amongst us and stands, tottering with his legs splayed wide apart and his head held back, squinting through red-rimmed eyes into the glare of the setting sun, bathed in its yellow light as it sinks below the western horizon. At last he falls to the ground and for the first time someone moves to help him.

We are dead now — I am convinced of that as I watch the poor bedraggled figures shamble about, dirty, cold and totally exhausted. We have used up more than our fair share of ex-tended life and there is no way we can survive a whole night in the open. I haven't even got the energy to search for shelter and my body shakes uncontrollably as the clammy wet clothing begins to freeze on my body.

Instinct draws us together and we settle in a small group of dejected humanity, working our quaking frames into the shapes of our companions to gain shelter and warmth. The wind moans mournfully and high above us the moon drifts through a break in the clouds and disappears once more, leaving us in the total blackness of night. Nothing can save us now and I am convinced that few of us will see daylight again; one by one we will go through the door of eternity with no more effort than is required to stop breathing. Perhaps I will finally find the peace that my whole being yearns for, to sleep and forget the tragedy and turmoil that has weighed so heavily on my shoulders for as long as I can remember. I draw the collar of my jacket up round my ears and snuggle into the back of a companion in preparation to die quietly, with the least amount of inconvenience to anyone else.

As I wait for sleep to come I am aware of the slow thump of my heart pumping on manfully. The beat is unbelievably slow and heavy with a rhythmic double thump every now and again. It becomes hypnotic and overpowers all other sensations. I try to shut out the sound but it persists louder and louder, growing in intensity until the ground seems to shudder with each pulse. It is obsessive, pounding into my brain with relentless persistence until I can stand it no longer and am forced to cry out loud and sit up.

There are others sitting upright too; staring about them in bewilderment as the sound beats into the night. No heartbeat this — somewhere deep underground a machine is working. Thump Thump Thump Thump-thump; steady, perfectly regulated beats easily heard above the whine of the wind as when I raise my head I can detect the direction from which the sound comes. My memory reminds me of a long ridge visible close by that hid the far side of the island. Distance is hard to judge in the void of that empty world but I can remember large boulders and sharp crags showing up quite plainly, which probably means that the crest of the ridge was quite close. What lies beyond that ridge?

'I can see a light.'

The voice is unrecognisable but in the darkness I can make out the shape of an extended arm and follow the line indicated to peer through narrowed eyes into the blackness. At first there is nothing to relieve the darkness but then when I am about to shrug it off I become aware of a dim glow that brushes the heavy cloud with just the faintest of light as though an artist has breathed colour unto a black canvas. Almost reluctantly I realise that there is need for further effort and it is up to me to seek out the cause of that light.

Every tortured muscle protests as I force my body up to stand swaying in the biting wind. My mouth hangs open and my eyes are blinking stupidly as I drag each foot into a more acceptable position — someone, I can't tell who is rising up beside me and I can hear his grunts and groans as I help him to steady himself against me.

'Who's that?' I croak.

'Morgan.'

Beggars can't be choosers. 'Come on — we'll see what's making that row.'

That row is almost undetectable now we are standing up but the glow is there all right like the dawn of new hope and shows the heavy clouds moving slowly across the top of the ridge.

'What about the others?'

'Leave them lie,' I counsel. 'No good all of us shambling out into the night. Just make sure we can find them when we return.'

With no further words we set off through the scrub and broken rock. Every third step is a stumble and it seems an age before there is any perceptible change in the light ahead. Eventually other features begin to show up, the uneven rim of the ridge and even the ghostly shape of a conifer, while all the time the glow beckons us on and we force our legs to comply. One more supreme effort and perhaps we gain a new lease of life. I urge my legs to take a few more shuffling strides.

The light is dimmer now and there are no features to be recognised, just a moving swirl of greyness with no up nor down, no left nor right. There is grit between my groping fingers and I know I am on my knees, clawing at the ground. A great sense of well-being sweeps over me as I realise that there is no living nor dying anymore. The pain is gone and there is need for no further effort as I sink into utter peacefulness and even breathing is no longer necessary. I sink easily into a black void that holds no fear, no cold, no agony — just sheer, blissful oblivion.

I struggle against a new invader now — a pale-grey intruder that threatens to bring more pain and suffering. Sound and light seeps into the void that was once a brain and despite my protesting mind it begins to register and my eyelids unstick to allow vague shadow penetrate the narrow slits. I hear a gutteral croak and realise that it comes from my own swollen lips. I am conscious now of a soft warmth that is comforting my body.

'He's coming to.'

Phantoms flit and waver in the mists that surround me. Noises lift and fall in a whispering world of strange sensations.

'Swain!'

Pale shadows move in across me like grey clouds and a weight presses down on my side. I am floating in a viscous liquid that allows my body to sway and undulate.

'Swain! Are you okay?'

My eyes blink open and the shadows are still now. Heads, bearded, grey, deep socketed fill the sky. I focus on them and they resolve gradually to take shape. They are familiar, old faces from long ago; from the time before I died. They would revive me if I let them: bring back all the effort and responsibility I have to so recently got rid of. They won't allow me to die; they want me to share their hopelessness and futile existence, but I'll have none of it. I shut my mind to them.

I am wrenched harshly back to life as an arm circles my shoulders and I am levered upright. Hot metal presses on my lips and a warm fluid floods my mouth. Oh the sublime taste of it as it rolls back across my tongue and searches into the extremities and channels of my gullet. I choke and splutter but more soup is injected. There never was a taste like this and the newly awakened craving sets my jaws to work and loosens my tongue. My eyes blink open and I find that it is Morgan who feeds me. He is wearing an evil grin as always and seems surprisingly cheerful for one so close to death.

My senses tell me that there is no wind biting into my bones anymore and I am not looking at the sky but at a timbered roof. Above all I am wrapped in dry clothing and in a warm, cosy atmosphere. I am truly alive with a sense of well-being buoying up my spirits. It's not heaven I'm in — that's for sure — but I'll settle for it as I gulp down more of that delicious liquid. I am conscious of men's voices and flickering lights that dance in time to the crackle of burning wood. The smell of a log fire is in the air and the mellow glow of returning life surges through me. Living is good I decide — not to be given up lightly and well worth fighting for. I close my eyes tightly and am grateful.

Real sleep comes now, relaxing, revitalising sleep that regenerates the body and dispels the aches and pains of an exhausted body. To waken from such a total rest, warm and cosseted, is to come out of a bad dream into a bright world filled with hope. The brain accepts new ideas and is willing to probe into problems and investigate sounds and shadows which take form to be analysed clearly with awakening interest. I can inspect my environment and take stock of my situation.

Heavy timbers span the area above my head to support a pine roof. A large stove vibrates with the energies of a lively fire and the long stove-pipe shimmers in the gleam of errant fingers of flame that lick mischievously from the edges of the round lid. Fuel is stacked alongside and the scent of pine mingles with the delicious aroma of coffee. A small, square window frames a landscape of scraggy hill and scrub. It is a scene created by the constant battering of a relentless wind.

There are other people in the cabin, seated at a heavy table and talking in subdued tones. They are muffled in heavy garb with shoulder crouched behind nodding head. I strain to hear the words and realise that the conversation is a mixture of American and good English. Someone glances over his shoulder and sees me awake.

'Heh! Look who's come to, you guys!'

Grinning faces round on me and they are all heaving their bodies upright to cross over and loom over me, staring down with open amusement.

'How goes it, son?' drawls a rich brown voice. 'Welcome back to civilisation.'

I cannot find any sort of reply as I search for a familiar face. Finding none I refocus on the speaker. The grin has stiffened a little and a serious look takes the sparkle from his crinkled eyes.

I am being studied intently by someone who is obviously trying to weigh me up.

'That's some ordeal you have been through, son! Near to death as is possible without going for good, I'd say.'

Still I don't answer. I know that I should find comfort in the warm American accent but deep inside a nagging doubt niggles at me and I am on guard against something that I cannot fully understand. Reason tells me my fears are unfounded but suspicion keeps me quiet while my brain turns over the events cautiously as they exchange glances with each other and shrug bewildered shoulders.

'You're amongst allies now, son.' The generous lips smile mirthlessly at me but I am not convinced.

'Where are my mates?' I ask at last, peering anxiously from face to face.

'Don't worry about them. Right now they're tucking into big plates of stew in the big cabin; soon as you're ready we'll take you to them.'

I rise up on to my elbows, 'What is this place — who are you?'

'Us; we're just a bunch of Yanks delving into the caves and crevasses of this God-forsaken place. We're looking for bits and pieces left by your ancestors; the Vikings. Until a month ago we were peacefully going about our own affairs and then we got caught up in your war. So far we've been left pretty much to our devices by your opponents because they've been too busy getting themselves established: now you've turned up I guess they'll come nosing round.'

'You mean the Germans are not here yet?'

'Not yet; the weather is breaking now though so I reckon it's just a matter of time.'

'Haven't had the time to bother with the likes of us up to now,' pipes up another, thinner voice. 'This ain't an easy place to get to — if you hadn't turned up I would have thought they would have left us alone for some time.' The tone is accusing.

The first speaker notices my aggrieved look and pats my arms condescendingly. 'Not much war left now, son. Brave effort you limeys have put up but you're out on a limb, all your buddies have let you down — there's no way you can carry on by yourselves. Trouble is you guys don't know when to give up and a lot of folks are gonna die before you get the message. The Germans outgun you in every department, your equipment is ancient and for the most part obsolete. Man, they will starve you out within six months. Best thing you guys can do is to wait here with us and then spend the rest of the war in concentration camps. We will look after you in the meantime.'

I sit up abruptly. Cold anger wells up inside me and I choke back angry words that threaten to explode from my protesting mouth. Sod them! Sod the lot of them! These condescending bastards with their platitudes and overbearing superiority. What the hell do they know about anything? Who are they to tell me what I can and cannot do? I want to shout my defiance at them as their easy logic undermines my world. In the past few days I have seen my mates die and I have dragged the crew through the depths of hell. We have died and lived again in the face of a grey machine that moves across the Continent of Europe, crushing all in its path. A faceless monster that has no time for people and wishes to change the future of millions like me. Some day intruders could be battering at my door and forcing their way into my home where my own fireside will no longer be my own and even my thoughts may not be expressed with the freedom earned by generations of my forebears. I'll die before I'll submit to that — I've never been a patriotic bastard but Christ! my home is my home and no Yank is going to tell me to give that up.

'Get stuffed!' I growl. 'Give in to those morons! I should say so — I'd rather be castrated.' I am panting with the exertion and shaking with rage in the short silence that follows.

'What you gonna do then, Limey?' sneers the thin, reedy voice, filled with contempt, 'Wait for us to pull you out of the shit like last time?'

'Shut your mouth, Brad,' snarls the first man, 'The man's got guts, I'll say that for him.'

'Yeah, pity he ain't got the brains to match!'

'That ain't for you to say. Fact is, son,' he says to me in little more than a confidential whisper, 'you haven't got much choice — like the girl said when she was getting raped — you might as well relax and enjoy it.'

'Where are my mates?'

He sighs heavily, 'Can you get up?'

I swing my legs over the side of the bunk and find that I am strong again. With growing confidence I stand up and someone catches me as my legs give way; my body is made of rubber.

'See what I mean?' says the first Yank. 'You ain't fit to take on any more. This is why we wanted to talk to you alone: your companions are talking like crazy men. You will have to stop their crazy schemes before they get themselves and us into a mess.'

'What crazy schemes?' I collapse back on to the pillow again and regain some composure.

'They want to sail an old broken down tub back to England. They won't listen to your engineer; even though he is the only one talking sense at the moment.'

Welks! That whining, cringing bastard is still undermining every initiative. Just for the pleasure of seeing his miserable face ground into the soft dirt of English soil I'd like to take them back home. Not the most honourable of motives, but it does to strengthen my resolve as my own words come echoing back to me — those ill-founded promises I made so long ago, before I knew what I was getting them all into.

'What sort of a boat?'

'It ain't a boat: it's a wreck — a heap of corroding rust aground on its own garbage,' chirps Brad; he must be the American equivalent of Welks. 'It's bin abandoned for years and its engine is a load of crap.'

'I'd like to see it.'

'Even if you could get that far there isn't any point,' soothes the first man. 'Believe me, there's nothing left in that boat.'

I look away. 'Can I see my mates?'

'Sure.' Sighs of resignation all round: there is nothing to be done with idiots like me, 'I'll go and get them.'

Bart is not so easily won over; he waves an aggressive finger at me, 'We ain't sticking our God-damned necks out for you. You want to play your half-arsed games, okay; but don't drag us into it.'

I don't need to answer him and he withdraws like the others to wait until the door opens and familiar figures enter with big embarrassed grins on their homely features. 'How goes it,

Swain?' says Dinger Bell. His face has lost its boyishness; the eighteen-year-old is an old man and a century of tragedy shows in his eyes. I look from face to face and find them all aged and haggard. Bunts, Morgan, Finney and Bell. I look past them at the closed door. 'Is that all! Are you all here?'

Their faces harden and Bunts becomes spokesman. 'Welks is pretty bad, we left him in his bunk.'

Even so, I realise there are only five of them. Out of a crew of forty-two only six of us survive and they have been through so much there cannot be much left for them to give. Yet that Yank said they were still talking about getting home in some kind of boat. Surely that can't be just blind stupid stubbornness? Is the American right? Is it my duty now to ensure that these few men at least will live out the war?

'I hear you've found a boat?'

'Some bloody boat!' explodes Morgan. 'You aught ter see the fucking thing; even the seagulls don't settle on it in case it caves in.' He nods towards Finney and twirls his finger near his temple in an indication of how crazy he thinks the stoker PO is. 'He thinks it's marvellous!'

As if in reply Finney breaks wind with relish and shows his contempt for the AB. 'That's what I'd expect from a bleedin' dabtoe; I know what 'm talkin' abaht. I could get that engine going — no sweat. If you can keep the boat afloat I can keep the thing moving.'

'Jesus Christ!' blurts Morgan. 'You've never seen anything like it, Swain. It took three of us with crowbars ter open the wheelhouse door and I put me foot through the deck — marvellous says Stokes. Bunts grabs the ladder to climb up to the bridge and it comes away in 'is 'ands and this flipping idiot keeps saying fantastic!'

'What about the engine?' I ask, knowing Morgan's habit of building a story out of nothing.

They collapse with uncontrollable mirth, all except Finney who stands back in all his outraged dignity.

'Engine!' splutters Morgan, doubled up and almost beside himself, 'Engine! Three of us heavin' on a wrench couldn't even turn it over. It is seized up solid.'

'Well?' I ask Finney.

His watery eyes wander vaguely towards the light bulb and swim vacant for a long moment. "E knows nuffin' abaht anyfink. I know and I'm telling yer I could get that engine going and keep it going — you don't have ter believe me.'

'All right, so I'll believe you about the engine — what about the boat itself?'

Bunts comes in quietly, 'When I first saw it I wrote it off straightaway, Swain; and I still have my doubts but the bilges are dry and she might be held together by rust but if Stokes says the engine is okay I reckon there is one trip left in her. She is steel hulled and there is hardly a lick of paint on her,' he shrugs easily. 'I would be willing to gamble on her getting us home if we really gave her the chance and had a bit of real luck for a change.'

'We'd 'ave ter go by night,' says Morgan.

'I thought you were dead against it?'

'I ain't stayin' 'ere on me flamin' own.'

I look from one to another trying to work out the expressions and find it impossible, except for Morgan and Welks who make no bones about their feelings about such a mad-hat scheme. Morgan I know will go along despite his better judgement and be an asset if only because he is not carried along on a wave of enthusiasm. Welks; well, that joker has been a burden on my back for as long as I can recall and there's no cause to expect him to change now.

'Each one of us will need to pull his weight on this one — we can't afford any passengers—' I would have gone on to say that anyone who wanted must back out now; Finney anticipates me and comes in sharply. 'It's all of us or no one, Swain. We agreed on this before you too. Only Welks is capable of running that engine besides me and, in any case I want to see that bastard brought to book in Blockhouse. Sorry, Swain, I'm not tryin' ter run things but you were out a long time and we've had our 'eads together and more or less got it sorted out — you're still boss man of course but we felt we couldn't wait; the Germans will be here soon, I reckon.'

I grin at him, 'You're right, Stokes. Anyhow we are a small group now and there's no need for skippers. Let's have a look at this marvellous boat.'

XIV

It is everything they say and more. A corroded heap of scrap metal fit only for the junkyard, with an engine that looks as though it will never growl again. The wheelhouse is festooned with a drapery of cobwebs which enclose the wheel itself in a cocoon of gossamer and I half expect to see the bony fingers of some ancient mariner clutching the small spokes with skeletal hands. Everything I touch is filthy and the rust comes away in showers when disturbed. The remains of muddy brown paint can be seen in remote corners, but for the most part rust has taken over. Beneath my feet the wooden timber of the deck is rotten and there are gaps here and there where it has disappeared altogether. I am supposed to take this thing out into the wild ocean to cross five hundred miles of some of the most treacherous seas in the world with a bunch of deadbeats for a crew: the prospect is awe-inspiring.

Finney is hanging over my shoulder to make certain that he sees everything that I do as we come to the centre-piece of it all — the engine. It sits there, dusty, oily and greasy; its cold body sleeping away the years in hard-earned retirement and I feel that to disturb it now will cause it to crack and spill out a glutinous mixture of oil and dirt and slowly bleed to death.

'It deserves to die in peace,' I say.

'Don't you believe it; there's life in the old bastard yet. That oil and grease you see there shows that someone cared for it right up to the end,' Finney enthuses with a great deal of confidence. 'I'm telling you that once we start her she'll tick over like a dream. You can't kill these old Britt engines and provided they are oiled and greased they'll go on forever. Nah, those Yanks 'ave got fuel, oil and grease for that pump of theirs, and a battery with enough guts to turn it over. Once she starts she'll not stop until we cut off her fuel supply. I've looked at the prop-shaft too and there's nothin' wrong with that. Nah, Swain; she might have bin sleepin' for a long time but she ain't dead yet — not by a long chalk.'

'My guess is that she'll shake out a rivet for every mile we go and fall apart long before we reach the other side.' I sigh and thump the side of the cabin with the heel of my hand — about ten pounds of rust falls into the cabin. 'Okay; let's give it a whirl.'

The next few hours are filled with activity. Bunts, myself and Dinger clean up the wheelhouse and find the compass missing from the binnacle — so what! the sun goes down in the south-west this time of year and I can take note of the stars, if we see them. With allowance for the turn of the earth we should head in something like the right direction. It should take us towards the Shetlands and they're only two hundred miles away. Who knows? Some sharp-eyed Scottish trawler skipper might see us and change course to see what strange, demented creatures venture out in a rust bucket like this.

Morgan is off on the scrounge and arrives from time to time with all manner of things, ranging from food to ropes and shackles. I ask nothing but my guess is those Yanks are unwittingly aiding our war effort. I ask them for one final concession that won't involve them too much in our affairs. It is obvious that their work here is essential and they do not want to antagonise the Germans who have left them pretty much to themselves up until now, but they agree to keep the cabin lights burning brightly tonight and the atmosphere is clear enough to keep them in sight for some fifty miles or so. By taking a bearing on them and keeping them in line with the cornerpost of the window and what used to be an aerial mast I will start off in the right direction anyhow. Like Mr Micawber I will hope for something to turn up.

As I stroll back to the boat there comes the sound of heavy coughing and wheezing, as though the world's biggest sea elephant is dying of asthma; followed by a rumbling noise with the occasional clank. Looking ahead a dense cloud of black, oily smoke rises skyward while seabirds scream their outrage and scatter in all directions. The rumble continues with occasional explosions and curses, the tone changing constantly as someone makes adjustments. By the time I am standing on the bank peering through the haze a steady, healthy roar is pervading the atmosphere and a solid jet of water is pumping out of a pipe projecting from the stern of the boat. There is no doubt that give or take a hiccup or two the engine is functioning well — better than I could have hoped for. A black-faced Finney is staring up white-eyed at me grinning from ear to ear and I can see the large rump of the ERA filling the hatchway as he bends over the engine.

'Told yer! Didn't I tell yer. Like a fucking Rolls-Royce.' Finney steps back laughing as Welks heaves his body into sight and turns his sour features towards me. The engine falters and Finney places his boot on the ERA's rump to shove him into the engine compartment. 'Get back there, yer swab. I've done the 'ard work nah yer can get it purrin' like my old woman's tom cat.'

Muffled protests come from the engine compartment but I think it best to turn my back on this display of blatant insubordination and proceed to where Bunts and Dinger are wiping rags over the windows. Inside the wheelhouse the cobwebs have gone and the wheel looks as though it has been polished. Things are looking up and I resolve to ensure that the deck party doesn't let down the engine-room when they have done so well.

It is late afternoon and the blackgang do not want to stop the engine now they've got it started so I decided to slip our moorings and proceed down the small channel between this and a neighbouring island that will take us out to sea. When dusk fades to darkness I look back and the light in the cabin ashore burns brightly to stay with us for over an hour. My hope for a star or two fades as heavy clouds begin to come in from the west and our bows start to pound into a hefty sea. Still I assume the wind will stay in one quarter and by keeping it slightly off the starboard bow I feel we are still heading south-west. What the hell! If we miss the Shetlands we'll hit Scotland or Ireland or America eventually.

She's a lively little craft and if we can ignore the increasing streams of water entering through rivet holes and open seams we can feel a certain amount of satisfaction in her performance. I estimate that we are making about eight knots and with the crew bailing out every half hour with buckets and tins we should keep her afloat. The tune of the engine is slightly off-key and a gasp every now and again reminds us that she is an old lady but willing to give her best for our cause. The only villain is the sea which has begun to look a bit nasty now, with white-crested rollers coming in out of the dark to throw big helpings of the North Sea over the bows and swamp the square cockpit aft. The engine grumbles as the propeller ploughs deep and roars in outrage when it lifts clear again to spin madly in thin air. Loose gear clatters all over the place and she rolls her beam-ends over. I'm on the wheel and all except Finney and Welks are with me; staring out into the night and trying to stay upright as she staggers from wave to wave. Low clouds weigh heavily overhead and rainshowers rattle on the deck in frequent squalls that heave the boat over and scream through the tattered rigging. We bail out more frequently now and the bilges are constantly flooded so that floorboards lift and float away.

It must have been about midnight when Bunts and the other two went down aft in response to a plea from Finney to help him fasten the hatch leading into the engine compartment. The existing doors were almost useless but Morgan muttered something about using the old seats and floorboards to batten down and they went off with varying suggestions as to how to cope. Now I'm still alone and the scream of the wind and noise coming from below shuts out all communication with them. I have my work cut out just keeping the boat into the wind now that the storm has reached alarming strength. I would dearly like to know how things are going aft but I'll have to wait and wonder.

What's that? Over to starboard a huge cloud is lowering down on us with a pale edge boiling ahead of it: Or is it? Christ, no! It's not a cloud; it's the crest of a huge sea racing in towards us like the side of a house. I spin the wheel to bring the bows over and yell 'Hold on!' into the wild wind. She doesn't come round, the rudder is out of the water half the time and the extra ballast of encroaching sea makes her unmanageable. The wave hits us in a solid mass and lifts the small boat bodily; throwing her over on her side and hurling tons of water inboard to smash the wheel-house window. I crash against the bulkhead and cut my hands on broken glass. The wind shrieks its hatred and the wheel spins out of control. The world heaves and swirls as the little metal boat tumbles and buckets in the arms of the huge monster. All a man can do is hang on and pray until the madness is over.

It seems a lifetime before that wave passes, but pass it does and I drag myself to my feet with water two feet deep in the wheelhouse and the door swinging uselessly at my side. A pain grips my left arm and I cough brine from my lungs as the next wave hits us and all hell breaks loose again. How we survive I do not know but survive we do and go on to survive a succession of such waves until all strength is gone and the murderous sea has us in its grip. The whole night through the fight continues but we live to see the first pale streaks of a new dawn spread across the tormented ocean. Huge, leaden bodies of water move in ranks across the surface but the wind is easing as we lift to the full-bodied swell and plunge to the bottom of deep valleys. Perhaps the worst is past.

I am not surprised the engine has stopped. I am only amazed that we are still afloat and I am able to get on to my feet and drag myself aft to the cockpit which is totally deserted and a shambles of tangled gear and splintered woodwork. I wade waist deep through the mess and heave aside the makeshift hatch. A heavy body bursts out from below, pushing me aside in its haste to get out of the claustrophobic innards of the boat.

I strive to recover and try for the hatch again. More bodies come hurtling past and I feel these must be the last throes of the stricken boat. I turn to follow them towards the bridge and fall over a body. It is Welks and he blubbers like an idiot when I drag him to his feet and shake his shoulders. His eyes stare wildly at the foaming crests rising into the pale sky to hang as though poised for the final blow.

'We can't last in this!' screams a voice I cannot recognise.

'A sea-anchor — we have to rig a sea-anchor to keep her bow upwind,' I yell at him as other shadows come crouching in on me. I still clutch Welks although he is nothing more than a shuddering lump of useless lard, 'Rope some of this debris together and secure it to the bow, Morgan!'

'Right, Swain.' Hell! he is right at my side.

'You, Bunts and Sparks see what you can rig; scratch round for anything that will lash together into a floating mass. I'll go below and see if we can get the engine started.'

Their pale faces are becoming visible in the growing light and somehow the coming of day brings relief even though it unveils the full extent of the damage and shows the menace of the boisterous seas.

'You can forget the engine.' It seems Welks has come to his senses and regained his usual optimism. 'You can't work down there in that shambles; the water is up to the sump gasket.'

'Rubbish! It's daylight now and I'm sure we'll do okay if we persevere — You underrate yourself, Welks.'

Reluctantly he allows himself to be propelled back into the watery hell that is the engine-room. It is almost pitch black here although there is an oil-lamp swinging in one corner, glowing balefully over a scene that defies description. Finney is in one corner and nursing a leg with both hands as he groans in agony. His face is ghastly and twisted in pain.

'What's wrong?'

He stares vacantly at me for a moment as though trying to fathom out who is speaking to him, 'My leg — my leg — I think it's broken.'

'Christ!' I curse hopelessly. 'There's nothing I can do for a moment, Stokes. Try to hang on till we get this engine started and then I'll make up a splint or something. Sorry, mate.'

'It's — only — the bloody — fuelpipe. It's — oh Jesus! — it's broken.' The boat heaves over to an impossible angle and he screams. Water is everywhere and there seems no chance she will come upright again, but she does and we stagger to our feet.

I unhook the lamp and bring it close to the engine, sure enough the copper pipe is fractured close to its connection to the fuel injectors. I stare hopelessly at it and Welks makes no effort even to look at it. I turn to the tortured Stoker PO. 'How could we fix it?'

He is almost to the point of passing out and stares vaguely at me for long moments trying to remember why I'm there and what I'm asking for. 'In my belt pocket — several french letters

— ohh—' he turns his head towards the bulkhead and groans. I feel he has had enough and there is no more sense to come from him and begin to move away. He clutches at my arm. 'They — will make a temporary joint — try it — it's all you've got.' He nods at me to make me see he is sane and serious. I rummage in his belt pocket and there are three contraceptives. I take them out and hold them in front of his eyes. 'Square up the ends of the pipes — use — this to butt them together.' He turns away to groan in agony.

'Did you hear that?' I ask Welks. 'You are going to repair that pipe and start the engine.'

The boat heels over to lie with her gunw'lls under while water pours in through every opening. I can hear yells from up top and feel the deadweight of the bilges pulling her down. Again and again she is thrown further over to lie on her beam-ends. Gulping masses of ocean, almost as though she wants to end it all and slip down to the peace of the depths. We do nothing but hold on and try to ignore Finney's screams. She struggles hard before staggering upright again with the help of a further wave that comes good for a change. This can't go on for much longer, I'm sure.

In the cramped confines of the compartment it is difficult to get at the broken ends of pipe and when I do I find them jagged. There is a roughened section of decking which can be used as a makeshift file if we can disconnect the pipes without any further damage. A silent Welks gingerly twists the long end of pipe and is rewarded by a responding twist of the nut holding it to the engine block. I take care of the other end and we work in silence to grind the ends square, scrubbing like fury without any obvious results for some time before we achieve reasonable results. With an old-fashioned look he takes the contraceptive from me to begin winding as I hold the ends close together. Carefully he bandages the joint with layer upon layer of the thin rubber until he has built up a solid mass.

'You'll have to hold the ends together,' says Welks. 'Once the engine starts the vibration will wrench them apart otherwise.'

I nod and clasp the cold metal as he moves away to bleed the system through with painstaking care. It is important that there will be no air-locks when he primes it ready for starting. I curse

his slowness and my hands become numbed by the cold before I
realise that what I'm doing is futile before he is actually ready.

'What about a splint?' I yell over the noise of the weather.

He looks at me as though I'm crazy and then glances over at
Finney.

'No, not him — the pipe — what if I bandaged it with a splint?'

'You can try.'

Ungracious bastard! I find two slats of timber and rip away
part of my trousers. In a short time I have bandaged the pipe
and strengthened it so that it will stand up to the vibration — I
hope. Once done I sit back on my heels to watch. He has
finished the bleeding and is slowly turning the big flywheel with
a great deal of effort. I have to admire his deliberation when the
boat is carrying out all manner of maniacal gymnastics. at last
he finds the spot he is looking for and rocks it to and fro, feeling
the compression and balancing it just right. I glance at the big
battery with its base in the water and pray that it has enough life
to turn the monster.

The ERA stares for a moment at the engine as though ensur-
ing that it is prepared for the sudden burst of energy he is about
to thrust into it. He presses the button and without so much as a
preliminary cough it bursts into a full-throated roar. I hear a
distant cheer from the wheelhouse and the motor settles to an
even tune — even steadier than before to my ear. We are under
way, the madness eases and the boat responds to the screw with
a sluggish reluctance. Men come tumbling down and bailers
begin to heave bilge water overside. Hope, like the new dawn
that is spreading across the baleful face of the grey sea warms
me. Surely now we must win through?

We are all grouped tight in the wheelhouse mid-morning
when Bunts sights the first smudge of land far away on the starboard bow. I alter course and we all stare ahead in silence as it
grows slowly out of the west. It is black and craggy, lifting
pinacles of flint-like rock in spires toward the sombre sky. It is as
forbidding a piece of masonry as I have ever seen, with a skirt of
angry surf ruffling the iron rocks at its base. There will be no
landing there and as we come near we find it is an isolated rock;
like a black iceberg swimming in the midst of the ocean; grim

and stark it might be, but it is part of the British Isles and not to be despised, for somewhere just beyond the horizon there are folk who speak our language and offering warmth, comfort and that long sought after sanctuary we yearn for.

All day we plod on onto that sea and pray we will not see another night out here, but already the shadows are spreading over the scene and the leaden hues of evening turn the sea to steel as the first star shows high and clear. It hangs there like a celestial beacon just off the port bow and I offer up a silent prayer of thanks for its guiding light.

'There's a light!'

I round on Morgan angrily to deliver a stinging response for no reason to find him pointing bent-wristed across the bows. We follow his outstretched arm. 'It's there! Look! It's there! It's a bloody lighthouse!'

True enough, there it flashes, steady and true with a rotating beam of white light. At times these northern lights are switched on for passing ships feeling their way round the dangerous reefs and currents of the Firth. It brings more hope, for it means that somewhere in this region there is another vessel and she is one of ours. True it is a big ocean and both of us are blacked out with every chance that we will miss each other completely, but we live on hope and optimism now. With that thought in my mind the light extinguishes itself, leaving the night even blacker than before.

'Not to worry,' I tell myself. We can't have all our own way and with a little imagination things can be seen to be going our way. I am certain in my mind that we are close in to the Scottish coast and the entrance to the Pentland Firth; I can't believe that we are any farther north than the Orkneys, anyway. 'Keep your eyes skinned now for a sight of Bonny Scotland,' I tell them.

It is hard to keep this newfound confidence alive as the night closes about us and the cold comes creeping in while we bucket on through the void with that star still hanging there, unmoving and cold-eyed with its vacant glow.

A soft sound, like that of a popping cork precedes a glare of violent light turning night to day and we look up to see a flare hanging in the sky, to be followed by another and another in the usual starshell pattern — placed so that they blind us but show us naked to the waiting gunners poised with their weapons loaded somewhere out there in the blackness. This time they must be disappointed to find that what promised to be the conning-tower of the surfaced U-boat is just a rusty old bucket that seems to have escaped from a scrapyard. We have no doubts in our minds as to who they are though, and begin to wave and shout until the loom of an approaching ship grows out of the north.

There answering shouts; indistinct, but enough to make us realise that we are seen and about to be rescued. She slows down, rolling in the swell with sparks tumbling out of her funnels amid the scrid smoke that stings our nostrils. I steer the boat toward her in a wide sweep that would do credit to an admiral's cox'n to lay alongside where boarding nets are lowered for us. On her decks seamen are running with large fenders to ward us off her vulnerable flanks and we bump alongside. I'm not doing a bad job, but the time-lag between my shouted instructions to Welks and the response is such that we are carried along towards her bows in a series of abrasive collisions while shouting men chase along above us, desperately trying to drop ropes into the clutching hands of my crew. At last, with a great deal of acrobatics and the belated effects of the reversed propeller the boat is brought under control and hauled back to the nets. All is achieved without any real communication for words are carried away on the wind and it is left to the instincts of the seamen to co-ordinate our efforts.

Everyone is in a desperate hurry and we are deposited roughly into any corner with enough space. Bruised, disorientated and with my head whirling I struggle and protest until I find myself half sitting against the hard heel of a boat davit. Wet faces lean in to me, dripping with rain and spray; eyes screwed up — puzzled.

'*Woher kommen Sie?*'

I groan in anguish, 'Jesus suffering Christ!' I can't believe my ears. Shattered I stare back into those enquiring eyes.

'*Das wiederholen?*'

I slump down and close my eyes. The vague sounds of night close in on me and exhaustion joins hands with utter despair to relieve me of any further effort. The velvet void swirls in front of me for a moment before all turns black.

All too soon I am dragged out of my deep sleep and rough hands are hauling me out of my soft bunk. I have a vague impression of a sick-bay before I am dragged along passages and through small bulkhead doors — much smaller than those on British destroyers and far more numerous — the Germans build their ships with more eye to the unsinkable than the comfortable and this vessel is honeycombed with small compartments and they can soak up quite a lot of punishment. Curious glances are thrown in my direction but I can see that they are stood to, at action stations, and there is a tenseness in the atmosphere that comes only when the prospect of action is imminent. She is vibrating and pitching heavily as she plunges through the water at a speed that is full of urgency and purpose.

I am bundled in through a cabin door to find three officers standing there facing me across a table that still bears the remains of a snatched meal. They wear sea-gear and steam is rising from their shiny oilskins as they drip on to the carpet. The only real sign of rank I can make out is the scrambled eggs on the peak of the cap of the smallest member of the group and I sense he is the destroyer's skipper. He barks an order at one of the others, a lean-featured youngster with hollow eyes and a twitch that drags down the corner of his mouth every now and again. He is the one with the English, and very good English it is too.

For a time we play the usual game — he asks me questions he knows full well I will not answer and I repeat name, rank and number in a monotone that I hope will convince them that I will not break. At last there is an impatient outburst from the captain and he delivers what is obviously a dire threat to the others before going out to attend to the more urgent affairs of his command. The other two study me silently for a moment and then exchange looks before the third member of the group speaks for the first time. My eyes are drawn to him even though his words must be repeated by the younger man. He is square-faced, dark-eyed and has those swarthy good looks that women go for. It is his mouth that spoils it all, for it is set in a thin line that promises a ruthless intolerance of anything that does not fall into line with his way of thinking. There is a cruel, merciless nature built into this one and I know too well that there will be no games played at his expense. A cold shiver goes down my back — I have always thought that this sort of character lived only in the minds of spy-thriller writers. Those walnut eyes of his stare right into your soul and he hates me just for being there and is looking forward to breaking me.

'Your boat is Norwegian — so we know where you have come from. Your uniform — or what is left of it tells us that you are British and naval personnel. We must assume, therefore that you are Naval Commandos. The Führer has ordained that such piratical units are to be treated as spies and saboteurs. Therefore it is greatly in your own interest that you convince us that you are not part of such a group.'

'I am a Chief Petty Officer and not part of any Commando unit. I haven't got the energy for those sorts of exploits. You've got my name rank and number and that is all I am obliged to give under the Geneva Convention.' I'm beginning to sound like a lower-deck lawyer.

'Then what were you doing in Norway?'

I tighten up my mouth and look away to show that as far as I am concerned the conversation is at an end. I'll give Thin-lips his due; he waits a full five seconds before launching into a volley of invective that causes the youngster to draw in his neck like a worried tortoise. His tirade continues for some time before the other summons up enough courage to stutter some sort of response. The voice assumes a low, menacing tone now and the features of the youngster show anxiety as he absorbs the words and contemplates their implications. Being the subject of their discussion my guts are churning somewhat as they transfer their attention from each other and focus in on me.

'We have a radioman, a signalman, an engineer and seamen so it is not hard for us to establish that you are from a ship — the question is what kind of ship. One of your colleagues wears a white sweater that is standard issue to coastal forces — we think it from such a ship you come; a motor torpedo boat perhaps?'

They will have to wait forever for any reaction to that one and I see Thin-lips watching my eyes intently. He's no slouch this one when it comes to interrogation — he is watching my eyelids for he knows full well that I may control my facial expression but, like any custom-man he is aware that a man's eyelids give him away. They have a tendency to flutter when under stress.

'A small ship of some kind which has been sunk off the coast of Norway?'

No response at all and they puzzle for a moment before the tight-lipped one barks a suggestion. The youngster turns on me again. 'Such sweaters are also worn by submariners — are you a submariner?'

My hesitation speaks volumes and they both register it with no difficulty at all. I say nothing and tell them all I am the lousiest liar even when I'm saying nothing.

'I thought so!' He glances at his superior who gestures at him impatiently to continue before I recover my composure. 'What is the name of your submarine and where was it sunk?'

I clam up and look away, but I have a sick feeling now, for I know what their game is. They can now interview another member of our crew and tell them what they know, plus a little guesswork put together from their own intelligence. Each man will either confirm or admit further pieces of the jigsaw until they build up the entire picture. They have no further reason to play games with me, except that it is obvious that Thin-lips is in a hurry and feels that things can be hurried along a bit by more direct methods — or perhaps he is anxious to test out the methods he has been trained to use by the more sinister sections of his background. After all it may be just as valuable to find out how to break a man's resistance as to glean the information itself — so why miss an opportunity?

'The *Leutnant* is tired of your insubordination and reminds you that we are officers and worthy of your respect, such as you would afford your own superiors. The answers to his questions must be accurate and precise; he will know if they are not. He says, your country does not honour conventions so you should not expect us to either. Therefore you will not be surprised that he will use any method in his power to extract the vital truth from you. Remember, no one knows you are here and you are completely expendable.' He nods to the other man to show that

I have received the message. A sharp question comes back like the report of a rifle.

'What is the name of your ship?'

'I do not have to answer other than name, rank and number.'

'Ve shall see!' Thin-lips is goaded into using his limited amount of English to spit this at me and it reflects his annoyance at my persistence. He moves to one side of the cabin where a square, black box sits on the polished shelf of a cabinet. Taking this with hands that seem to caress it with loving care he brings it over to the table and deftly slips the catches that clamp down the lid. The inside is taken up with an electrical unit with dials and leads. He pulls out the leads and tests the crocodile grips on the end of each before laying them on the table top. From another compartment a pair of handcuffs appear and my hands are fastened behind my back and through the spokes of my chair.

The youngster is sweating along with me for he obviously has little stomach for what is about to happen and would rather be miles away. He listens to the level tone of his superior for a moment before coming back to me. 'This machine is capable of delivering a heavy charge of electricity and there are extremely sensitive parts to which the wires can be attached. It is best that you provide us with the simple answers to questions which in time we will find out anyway. Refuse and you will endure much suffering to no avail — no one can withstand this method of persuasion for very long.'

I'm sweating along with him now for there is nothing heroic about me when it comes to enduring pain as my dentist will readily bear out. I wonder for a moment whether to give the bare details of the boat on the assumption that they will already know of it sinking. However my common sense tells me that the main reason for this interview is to assure themselves that there is nothing going on beside what they do already know and I will be taking a load off their minds if they can establish that. Much to my surprise I resolve to clam up and keep them guessing, and I look at the bulkhead intently as I strengthen my nerve to stand up to what is about to take place.

Somewhere up there there is a God looking after me, despite my wayward past and he chooses that moment to produce a miracle in the form of a crackling tannoy that bursts into life and delivers a strident order that even these two cannot ignore. They spring into action, calling in the waiting sentry and giving him instructions as they push past on their way to urgent affairs of far greater import than this much relieved minion.

This time I am led aft to be pushed and prodded through a further series of bulkheads and out onto the steel deck where the wind is in command, wailing through superstructure and knifing through bones as it buffets in from the gloom of a new dawn. The ship is heeling to a skidding turn, smashing her flank into the seas while the acrid tang of burnt engine oil searches the back of my throat. I am hurried past busy men working on torpedo tubes, overlooked by others grouped round gun mountings. I have never been on this end of a depth-charge attack before but I can easily recognise the preparations taking place on her square stern. Already the depth settings are being put on the primers and I know now why that blinking light was displayed from the bleak headland. British submarines travel northward up the east coast in convoy until they reach the Scottish ports and often continue on their own through Pentland Firth to carry out working up trials amongst the Western Isles. At such times a Captain might ask for a light to be shown to take bearings before entering the wild waters of the Firth. It is a calculated risk and today it hasn't come off, for this machine of destruction was waiting in secret and even the starshells have not given her away.

My thoughts are interrupted as we arrive at the hatch leading down into the steering compartment, or tiller flat as we call it. I am pushed unceremoniously down into the smelly, claustrophobic area where massive rams and pistons are pushing the giant tiller to and fro. The vibration of the speeding ship is felt more here than in any other part of the ship and combines with the exaggerated motion of the hull to make things very uncomfortable. One dim lamp casts shadowy light across the scene to turn it into a kind of devil's grotto. On the bulkhead various pieces of equipment are clamped. Blocks and tackles, an extension piece for the tiller, and other items for use if the other main and auxiliary steering positions are out of action. The sentry makes no move to follow me down and the hatch is clamped down over my head.

'Stand by for depth charges!' grunts Morgan's rough voice and I see that, except for Finney, all my crew are here, huddled together in one corner. I settle with them and we wait for the inevitable, feeling sympathy for those colleagues of ours who are about to receive a load of destruction from the stern of this bastard. It is most likely that a big percentage of the crew in that submarine will be having their first experience of such an attack and we have all been through that deadly experience.

'Christ! listen to those revs buildin' up,' says Morgan, and we listen to the increasing sound of the screws and feel the judder of increasing power as she pounds through the sea on a dead straight course now, for the rolling is even and the short tiller stays amidships. It is an exciting sensation and we can sense the thrill of attack flowing through the ship.

No other type of warship reacts like a destroyer, for she is built for speed and punch. Her lean body is packed with machinery and two spinning propellers are connected to engines and boilers that occupy a third of her length to thrust her vibrant body through the oceans at forty miles an hour. Every available space is used and the whole length of her upper deck sprouts the machinery of war, guns, torpedo tubes, depth charges and light weapons while the masts and bridges are festooned with aerials and detection gear, range finders and direction finders, navigational aids and wireless gear. Somehow they manage to find places for men to eat and sleep between magazines and stores — but only just. The result is a fighting unit sleek and lethal and designed for a multitude of fleet duties; but mainly that which her name implies — to seek out and destroy the enemy; above or below the surface. There is no doubt in our minds that this ship is an extremely efficient example of such a unit and somewhere up ahead anxious ears are listening to her approach with nerves tensed and stomachs churning. We can only lie here helplessly with our imaginations painting pictures that defy description.

Helpless? The word burns in my brain like a tumour. To lie here in a group listening to all the sounds that precede the destruction of a boat and the death of our colleagues; it can't be so! In the dim light the heavy steering gear moves in response to the hands of the helmsman as he steadies her up against the pull of wind and sea. Each time he spins the wheel the noise of hydraulic gear comes and the big rams exert their powerful thrust to the tiller. I can see it in the baleful light, gleaming dully in a skin of oil and an idea is forming in my tired brain.

'Welks!'

No response, yet I know that I have yelled loud enough to be heard even above the cacophony of the machinery and the outside noises. He deliberately turns his back to me and settles himself into a position where he can study the bulkhead and withdraw into himself. He is determined to ignore me and as I stare at the back of his bullet head I feel a burning anger welling up inside me once more. Even now he is the bane of my existence.

'Chief!' I shout, and dig a boot into his rump to emphasise the word.

'Yeah?'

'That steering; what do you know about it?'

He lifts his head sullenly and studies the machinery for a moment, watching the elephantine limbs of the monster operating with the soft slither of oiled joints. 'I've seen it before.'

The others are stirring now, aware that something is going on and that we two opponents are at it again. They realise that I have an idea forming and are eager to see what it can be − not him − he stares blank-eyed into a corner, determined that he will never become involved with any of my mad schemes.

'Can we sabotage it?' I insist.

He looks up with hate-filled eyes. 'Not another piece of bloody heroics. Haven't you done enough already? You've lost nearly all the crew; are you gonna slaughter the rest of us too?' He turns to the others for support and finding none, turns back to me. 'I'll not be part of any more of your mad-brained schemes: earn your own medals.'

I look at the others in disgust. 'I'll not waste any more time on this bastard. Give us a hand to wreck this bloody steering gear. Maybe we can wedge something big enough into the works that'll lock the rudder hard over, or at least cripple it. Anything we can do to mess up their approach will give that boat out there another chance to get away − we can't let our oppo's die.'

They are all on their feet now, searching round for anything that looks hefty enough to do damage to the metallic monster that guides this potential killer.

'If I 'ad a spanner I could do something,' says Welks suddenly, as if he is trying to redeem himself.

'Well you ain't got a fuckin' spanner, yer silly old sod!' yells Morgan, 'this ain't Pompey dockyard.' He reaches up for the extension piece that fits on the end of the short tiller when emergency gear is in use and wrenches it free from its stowage. Using all his strength he hoists it high above his head before bringing it crashing down on copper pipes. They break away and spurt a black gout of thick oil across the compartment. At once the tiller swings over to smash against the stops to lock the rudder hard over — further than it is meant to go. The full force of the huge propellers are hammering on the flat surface and all hell breaks loose as the juddering grows to a degree that sets our teeth rattling. No ship is built to stand up to these extreme pressures and the strain places impossible stress on her frames as she leans into an impossible turn with the added sound of gear breaking loose and yells from on deck.

Beneath my feet the deck itself seems to twist and we hold on grimly as our feet actually leave the iron deck in the violent shaking. Paint shakes loose from the deckhead and there is a loud crack as one of the big rams leaves its socket before smashing into the intricate mass of the steering-gear. The tortured scream of metal on metal drives through my brain and still the mighty engines are going flat out. More shouting from up top and we have all noted the bangs of the depth-charge throwers as they hurl their deadly cylinders in lofty arcs away from the vulnerable hull. It seems we are immaculate in our timing for the destroyer is swinging in a turn that takes her right back over her own depth-charges. She will rip her own guts out and there is nothing she can do about it for to stop now will only tighten the turn and leave her helpless in the centre of the pattern, and as though to emphasise the calamity we hear cannisters rolling off the stern.

A gigantic fist smashes into the deck beneath my feet and I am thrown into a corner. One after another five charges explode and a seam splits open across the stern to admit light and water. The hatch bursts open above my head and an

ear-piercing scream of tortured steel comes from below as a propeller shaft twists out of shape. With one accord we scramble up
through the hatchway into the vicious wind. Men are struggling
to set things in order and we are completely ignored as we find
shelter beneath the overhang of the after gun-deck.

The engines have stopped now and we are wallowing in the
deep swell. A dripping, anxious figure arrives to wave an auto-
matic weapon under our noses and we recognise our sentry, his
young features screwed up into an anxious mask. We raise our
hands to show we are impotent and go out of our way to reassure
him, for he is a bundle of nerves and none of his mates have time
to reassure him. The last thing we want is a nervous youth
waving a gun barrel at us with itchy fingers. He may not have
the imagination I have but he knows things are not as they
should be and he is living through a nightmare of indecision.

Somewhere out there is a submarine that has been let off the
hook in a way that must have left her bewildered and if she
hasn't sneaked away gratefully she is even at this moment stalking us with her periscope trained on our peculiar antics, trying
to reason the cause of the mad capers we are engaged upon. It
won't take her long and a sitting target is not to be ignored even
by an inexperienced crew.

Even as the thoughts flood my mind the first torpedo explodes
under the engine-room and splits the keel asunder and the
whistle shrieks in torment as the destroyer lists over violently
with superheated steam bursting from her innards in a great
gout. As though to hurry things along another torpedo hits the
bows. She is finished and sliding fast into the churning mass of
tormented water. Our sentry panics, staring wildly about him
with mouth opening and closing. I snatch his weapon from him
and he follows us like a faithful puppy as we make for a liferaft
that hangs by one shackle on a frame nearby. Others are moving
in that direction too but they are not prepared for a concerted
attack from an enemy that is supposed to be locked away in the
depths of the ship, out of harm's way. They fall back from us
and spill over into the sea in many cases as we sweep through
them like a scythe. The deck is almost level with the sea now and
it is simplicity itself to board the raft and shove away from the

sinking ship. Paddles appear like magic in the hands of Morgan and Bunts and we push ourselves away from the ship.

Only minutes have passed since the depth charges exploded yet three-quarters of her length is beneath the surface and her stern rises into the sky at a sharp angle in preparation for the final plunge. Men are dying in steam filled boiler-rooms, in water-filled compartments, in claustrophobic magazines and in the cruel grip of the icy sea. The air is filled with the obscene bedlam of dying men and it matters not what language is used to make those hopeless cries they fill a sailor's heart with grief.

In the gloom of that grey morning small lamps flicker on the life jackets of floating bodies and pale faces stare empty-eyed at the lowering clouds as the submarine moves in through the midst of all this flotsam to search out the living. We take a long time to convince them that we are who we are and the bluff lieutenant who skippers this boat is not really convinced until we are taken aboard the depot ship at Rothsay.

Long after the long interviews and post-mortem I stand at the guardrails with Bunts, Sparks and Morgan looking out across a peaceful Scottish loch where the glazed water is disturbed only by the wake of seabirds and the world takes a breather from the torment of war. The Navy has decided that we have performed well and we will receive token of their appreciation in the form of medals at some future date. The memory of dead shipmates will ghost through my life until I join them and there is no feeling of achievement for me and my future approach to the trade I have chosen will not be coloured with highlights of patriotic fervour. Experts will invent new machines of destruction and I will take my part in learning and using such engines of war but I will do it coldly and without feeling, for I have not seen difference in the shape of death whether he lays his hand on friend or foe. I'm part of a grey, cold world and will become grey and cold in accordance until the sun pokes through again at the end of it all.

'Swain!' Morgan's gruff voice disturbs my contemplation.

'Yeah?'

'Seems appropriate, don't it?'

'What?'

'That we were saved by a flipping french letter.'